To Judy

Peace & Harmony

Gayle.

ANCIENT WISDOMS

Exploring the Mysteries and Connections

By

Gayle Redfern

authorHOUSE®

AuthorHouse™
1663 Liberty Drive
Bloomington, IN 47403
www.authorhouse.com
Phone: 1-800-839-8640

First published by AuthorHouse 12/28/2009

ISBN: 978-1-4490-5760-2 (sc)

Library of Congress Control Number: 2009913160

Printed in the United States of America
Bloomington, Indiana

This book is printed on acid-free paper.

Ancient Wisdoms: Exploring the Mysteries and Connections Returning to Balance

Part I --Introduction

PREFACE

A few years ago, my spirit friends told me it was time for the world to revisit the teachings and guidelines of the indigenous of the world and the cultures of long ago. Indigenous means *living naturally in a particular region, the innate. Innate* means *belonging to the essential nature of something.* The indigenous people know how to live in the present by accepting the lessons of the past and accepting it as gone. They learn from the past and move on -- *life is.* One way of teaching our young is taking the gentleness and humor of the world's past and assimilating them into the daily life of our time. Once we understand that when *life is,* the gentleness and humor of our ancestors carries no fear, AND THEN we move into the future in peace.

These spirit friends gently remind me that modern society, particularly Caucasian, forget these teachings, trying to create a blend that *in their opinion* excels the wisdom of ancient ancestors and the indigenous of their lands.

After the magnitude of this task sunk in, I began analyzing how to include ALL cultures, soon realizing this is nigh impossible. My next step became looking for cultures around the world that honor their ancestors, bringing their teachings and lessons into their daily life over time. Many global cultures follow this guideline with integrity. Consequently, I had to arbitrarily make choices. This does not mean my choice of cultures makes them superior to other societies. It means instead, there are cultures where I had personal contact or where friends or authorities put me into contact with in depth books or information pertinent to the mission. Exploring data going back four or five millennium instead of a few hundred years helps narrow the decision. The reader will find technical data mixed with a plea for human integrity. It is becoming imperative that we return to ancient teachings and learn how to blend them with modern technology. Some cultures honored the evolution of social rules and guidelines. We need to capture this evolution.

After studying with Solar Brother Hunbatz Men, I found out that they received a similar message from spirit guides. The indigenous Maya people of Mesoamerica have a way of teaching us how to acknowledge the *Ancient*

Wisdoms of our world. In a recent note, Mayan Elder Hunbatz Men reminds us that by bringing this awareness to our modern world are keys to peace. He states:

"It is very important for the general public to know about the way our ancestors used to think. You know, we will be able to understand our future only if we understand our past first."

Solar Brother Hunbatz

It becomes difficult to change current lifestyles *after* closing their door on past and ancient wisdom. Following the lessons of the Ancients helps us understand the present. Our ancestors knew many of the secrets that we share today.

As I began studying literature and social structures in preparation for this book, I discovered how my previous writing contributes to understanding the basis of this book. Part of the understanding of our past includes learning how the people view the elements of life, one of which is the dimension of living. In my previous book -- *Within & Beyond, the Connection,* I introduced concepts understood millennia ago and still applicable today. The exciting aspect here is the animal world knows these concepts and accepts them as truths, without titles or labels. Our forefathers did not require the specific labels that we do today. *Within & Beyond* explains the concepts in detail, providing visual examples. For an overview of the principles of *Within & Beyond,* refer to the Appendix.

The three principles, (1) CLP, (2) Planes of Reference and (3) Manu Nymba, illustrate the focal points of a culture, demonstrating which one was the strength of a region, what is present today and what skills and knowledge needs to be brought forward into current time creating a composite blend of all three.

My spirit friends showed me how a universal *Philosophy of life* applies to all humanity, regardless of location or time. They pertain to people whether they live in 3000 BCE or in the 21st century, or in Asia or North America. Time and location is irrelevant. What we need to do is:

- re-examine the history of ancient lands
- explore the travels and explorations of our ancestors and then
- look closely at each one

3

The planet's Ancient Wisdoms may not appear logical to the reader, but I encourage you to draw your own conclusion as to how practical and applicable they are in the 21st century.

As you think about the ancient indigenous people with their wisdom, pride and joy, ask yourself six questions:

1. Why is it important to explore the Ancient Wisdoms at this time in our history?
2. How much intelligence do they hold that applies today, in our present time?
3. How much of our current life and beliefs do we still hold that reach back to ancient times before the Common Era?
4. Is there a link between these cultures and if so, what is it?
5. What communication styles link cultures and eras?
6. Do we still carry the gifts of the White Wings, peace, knowledge and transformation?

Many of you ask the first question -- "Why now?" The primary answer is that we are entering an astrological time known as the Photon Band.

I must thank my husband, Bill for his support, his editing and patience, all given to me with humor and patience. I thank the indigenous leaders who gave their support, commitment and verified the accuracy of the information. Unfortunately, there are too many Nations and Leaders to mention. Each one gives support, energy and integrity. They all know it is time to awaken the knowledge of the planet.

The sixth question above refers to the *White Wing* visually shown to me to demonstrate the peace, knowledge and transformation. While you may NOT see the visual, the principles are there for you to review.

VISUALS

Early in my writing, a beautiful image of *white wings* emerged; representing the **Dove,** the **Snowy Owl** and the **Butterfly.** The wings utilize gifts and skills, teaching us how to incorporate them into our current living without judgment or hate. They embody the *Light of our Spirit.* They teach us the secrets of living in the present. These images appear throughout time and history. Sometimes all three emerged, other times only one materialized. I tried to include an overview applicable to each culture.

Artist -- Todd Jason Baker
Permission granted by Marlene Baker, mother of the artist.

The Dove, a white winged bird, is the symbol of Peace and Prophecy. When Ted Andrews summarizes this imagery in his book, *"Animal Speaks,*[1]*"* he tells us to mourn what has passed and awaken to the promise of the future. Nations such as the Hopi of North America or the Kogi of South America recognize this, move forward, blending the past with the future. Their history shows how they use their knowledge peacefully in communal life, willingly sharing it with neighbors without violence. Today, they ask other modern societies to observe the condition of our planet and act responsibly. Whenever the dove or a white wing comes into our mind's eye, remember we have a choice of taking the best of our past into our present and future world peacefully, or acting violently, grabbing more possessions and protecting these possessions. Our goal is living peacefully, not violently.

The dove reminds the Hopi of the need for peace and prophecy, and works with other Indian tribes living on the North American prairies. According to the Lakota Sioux legends, the dove, watches over buffalo herds ready to protect the white Buffalo Calf Woman when she returns; Buffalo Calf Woman teaches humility. The Pueblo Indians turn to the dove to guide them to the nearest watering hole. Peace, prophecy and water are the keys of successful living. The dove helps us reclaim the missing serenity.

Just as the dove guides us to watering holes, it also becomes vital that we recapture the importance of water to our being. It has and always will be a key component of our environment and living. Left undisturbed, the fresh waters on the earth are alkaline, a requirement for optimum health. Unfortunately, the chemicals and pollutions in modern society increase the acidity of our fresh water. When acidic water becomes the major fluid intake, the body no longer heals itself and we face more illness and death. Our ancestors knew how to protect the water and our environment. Once more, the dove sits silently reminding us to honor and protect our water sources.

The snowy or Arctic owl also has white wings. Owls have remarkable wisdom and ability to see in the dark. They search out the sacred hidden truth, teaching us to be silent. Ted Andrews honors this animal with the native characteristics of magic, omens, silent wisdom and night vision.[2] As well, they carry prophetic vision and healing powers. Although snowy owls are residents of northern lands, the Mayans name the fourth moon in their calendar after the owl, including them in statuesque images.

Ancient Greeks honor the owl and thank them for the connection with the goddess Athena, the Goddess of Wisdom. This culture acknowledges owls' wisdom extending around the clock. . However, they worship at night when protection of secrets and knowledge is paramount, calling upon the wisdom of the white wing of the owl.

The final white wing image is the white butterfly, the Pieridae, also known as the cabbage or stocking butterfly. Butterflies begin life as a caterpillar. When a creature begins life on our planet Earth, they have no idea who they might be or what the future brings. An embryonic caterpillar does not fear the unknown world as humans do. Their cocoon wrapped them in a world of peace, respect and safety; this secure tranquility carries them into their next life stage. Regardless of the phase, butterflies do not worry about their past or future, they live in serenity. The caterpillar does not know it transforms into a beautiful white butterfly fighting for its life in a world of hate and anger. A butterfly does not know it may die because of pesticides or pollution.

Members of butterfly families migrate over vast regions. This annual trip includes several generations but they begin and end at the expected, traditional locations.

The Monarch butterfly begins their journey on the north side of the Great Lakes and the Eastern edge of the prairies, flying down to the Sierra Madre Occidental Mountains in Mexico. Each Fall as the air begins cooling; the butterflies begin their horrific six weeks journey from Canada down to Mexico. How they succeed flying across a large lake mass such as the great lakes, or vast desert is a mystery. Through this vast voyage, they rely upon wind patterns, sun patterns and earth's magnetic field. During this trip, they go through four generations, laying eggs, and changing from caterpillars to butterflies in different states. They then settle in the same place on the northern edge that their parents or grandparents left.

On these trips, they leave behind segments of the knowledge they learn and pick up new knowledge, or wisdom, from each region, ready to pass on to residents in other areas. Extensive scientific research on the Monarch Butterflies confirms this. While this species is not completely white as is the Pieridae, their white spots and white wing tips contribute to its dazzling beauty.

The knowledge imparted by each generation of butterflies reminds us that as we travel around the globe, both regional residences and travelers learn. When a butterfly or cocoon appears to us, it is an opportunity to pause, pick up the wisdom of the region or territory and carefully note what knowledge we can leave for the present and future generations of the region. Butterflies evolve from egg to caterpillar to cocoon to the beautify butterfly, that we love and admire. At each phase, the butterfly lives in peace and the immediate present. The difference between butterflies and humans is we have choices as to how we live. Butterflies have one, living in peace and harmony. For humans, choice one is initiating global changes that damage the Earth. Choice two leaves the planet just as we find it with no improvement or developments, all lessons are lost. Or, the preferable choice, involves revisiting primordial cultures, selecting the best characteristics from each era and blending them into our modern technological world. Each era and each society leaves a legacy of good and bad.

I feel if we pause, learn lessons from each generation and then integrate the good qualities with each generation's technological advances we transform life on this planet into the civilization envisioned so long ago by the indigenous people.

The caterpillar/butterfly move through life in harmony, incorporating environment, life changes when needed. There are civilizations such as the Hunza of Pakistan who live long lives, use the knowledge of their ancestors, yet adapt to the modern climate and geographical changes. It seems to me that travelers exploring other countries such as this home focus only on the aggression and anger of present time. These people are only one segment of a society of this region who integrates the best of the cultural changes and advances. Too often travelers become blasé and oblivious to positive opportunities appropriate for their homeland. This image represents an opportunity to alter who we are today. If we draw upon the emblematic butterfly, we have the opportunity to pull cultural renovations into our society.

Reviewing cultures or leaders of long ago, we find teachings of the three white winged teachers are ever-present. We have knowledge and wisdom – from the owl. We have peace, protection and natural health – from the dove. We have metamorphic transition – from the white butterfly.

All three gently remind us to reclaim control of our lives.

PHILOSOPHICAL GUIDELINES

Today, we carry a philosophy paralleling the *Philosophy of Life* of each culture. Every society carries commandments similar to those of the Mohawk nation of North America. These are:

- Treat the Earth and all that dwell thereon with respect.
- Remain close to the Great Spirit.
- Show great respect for fellow beings.
- Work together for the benefit of all Mankind.
- Give assistance and kindness wherever needed.
- Do what you know to be right.
- Look after the well-being of Mind and Body.
- Dedicate a share of your efforts to the greater good.
- Be truthful and honest at all times.
- Take full responsibility for your actions.

These instructions are pertinent to life whether it is in 3000 BCE or in the 21st century; whether it is in Asia or North America. Time and location is irrelevant. What we need to do is:

- Re-examine the history of ancient lands
- Explore the travels and explorations of our ancestors and then
- Look closely at each one

The planet's Ancient Wisdoms may not appear logical to the reader, but I encourage you to draw your own conclusion as to how practical and applicable they are in the 21st century.

As you think about the ancient indigenous people with their wisdom, pride and joy, ask yourself six questions:

1. Why is it important to explore the Ancient Wisdoms at this time in our history?
2. How much intelligence do they hold that applies today, in our present time?

3. How much of our current life and beliefs do we still hold that reach back to ancient times before the Common Era?
4. Is there a link between these cultures and if so, what is it?
5. What communication styles link cultures and eras?
6. Do we carry the gifts of the *White Wings,* peace, knowledge and transformation today?

The primary answer to "*Why now*" is that we are entering an astrological time known as the Photon Band.

THE PHOTON BAND

The concept of a photon has been around since the 1920s. **Photon** is another name for a *unit of intense light*. Today, we call them x-rays, lasers or gamma rays. Photons emit highly energetic light, one photon at a time.

Consequently, thousands of photons release energy, producing a beam of light such as a laser beam. Scientists first discovered the photon band, or belt, in the early 1960s when they began sending exploratory satellites into space. They identified this band as containing *many* particles of electromagnetic energy and having an indefinitely long lifetime.

Inside the book, *Within & Beyond*, a MANU NYMBA refers to the smallest component, or nucleus, of life. A photon, therefore, is a cluster of many **MANU NYMBA**.

Each MANU NYMBA is the cosmic blend of electric and magnetic energy storing all galactic wisdom. When we travel through the photon band, this knowledge becomes available to all species. The popular titles Galactic Light or Galactic Day make sense when we understand the quantity of photons in this belt.

My spirit friends expanded on this information by saying:

"Knowing we are entering the photon band reminds us of the unification of all beings and a reminder of the original residents of the planet. All events lead forward so that we understand how to return to the love and cooperation that is so much a part of the universe. It is back to the beginning, back to basics and back to the light."

With this information, the photon band now is an - *unvarying band of intense light flowing through the universe.*

The astrological timing of the earth's movement in and out of the photon band correlates with the estimated dates of cultural disappearances as estimated by the Maya calendar. Barbara Hand Clow's book, *The Pleiadian Agenda* provides a comprehensive explanation of the photon band.[3]

Since the width of this band is stable, the time in the photon band is constant for all suns, and stars. The variable key is how long a planet stays in the Galactic Night. This depends upon the position in the galaxy. If we use Alcyone, the farthest star of the Pleiades as an orientation point, then the farther the sun or planet is away from Alcyone; the longer the planet stays in the galactic night.

For example, Maya, one of the Pleiadian seven sisters is in the Galactic night (dark) for approximately 1200 years and in the photon band (galactic light) for 2000 years. Earth, much farther away, is 11,000 years in the dark and 2000 years in the light. While this phase is a consistent length of time, we still pass through the band at the end or beginning of various ages.

A zodiac map shows this band running between the Age of Aquarius and the Age of Leo. Whenever we are in any of the other ten ages, we are in the dark for *most of the time*. It is important to remember that Earth rotates around the sun and the photon band passes over the rotational elliptical path regularly.

The figure below demonstrates the planets of the galaxy moving along the elliptical circles. At various times, each planet passes through the band between the parallel lines.

Planetary elliptical path with intersecting photon band

During this period, the Galactic Light shines on the planet for varying lengths of time. This is in addition to the standard Galactic Light of 2000 years. For the remainder of the period between 8600BCE and 2100CE, the Earth was in the "dark". Each astrological period embodies a polarity pair such as Care of Self versus Care of Others, or Emotional vs. Power. While every era exhibits a dominant trait, there are brief periods or pockets of light, carrying the complimentary non-dominant trait.

We are leaving the Age of Pisces, *the Age of Christianity*. Prior to this, we were in the Age of Aries or *the Age of Judaism*. Other names include the Age of Blind Faith or Compassion instead of the Age of Pisces or Age of Aggression or Enterprise instead of Age of Aries. The point here is while the name, *Manu Nymba,* may not specifically appear in each culture and time, their Elders who knew of the concepts and applied it to their specific communities.

The advantage of being in the Galactic Day, absorbing the intense light, is that we are able to learn about all dimensional levels or planes of reference and move freely from one to another.

The label, "dimension" implies stepping progressively from one to another without being able to jump back and forth. For this reason, the term *dimension* became *Planes of Reference* in *Within & Beyond.* It is a powerful phase of our evolution, learning to move freely from one dimension to another, back and forth. Unfortunately, there are points of our history where our ancestors did not learn to move and remained *stuck* in one level. When humans are only aware of one or two dimensions, they cannot comprehend anything else, including the feasibility of people moving in and out of them. Dimensions were a nonexistent theory. To them, people disappeared; hence the notion of the world ending.

If we look at the 2,000 year span at the opposite end of our current Photon Band, we discover a time when the speculated disappearance of Atlantis occurred. Plato estimated the destruction of Atlantis occurred at approximately 9000BCE. The estimated time period of the Age of Leo was between, 10,800 BCE and 8640BCE.[4]

Although the actual existence of Lemuria is still speculative, scholars and spiritualists believe it existed in the Pacific around the same time, beginning approximately 25,000 years ago[5] overlapping into the Atlantis era. This puts it in the middle of the last Age of Aquarius, which lasted from 23,700 BCE to 21,600 BCE. With this data, we have the mythical disappearance of two highly evolved cultures that apparently lived on earth at ends of a Photon Band, in Galactic Light.

Various writers do not refer to dimensions specifically, rather talking about telepathic abilities, invisible to a human's average senses. These are key elements of different dimensional levels or planes. It seems therefore, that these cultures did not disappear as archeologists and anthropologists suggest but are simply using a dimensional level or reference plane, unachievable by humans today.

Since the Photon Band engulfed our planet when vital cultures disappeared, we can only contemplate the history. However, looking at a current astrological map, we see that we will be completely into the Photon Band by the year 2012. Returning to the *White Wing* triad imagery, the Owl appropriately defines the knowledge. The Dove shows us the peace of the living in the Photon Band. The Butterfly teaches us how to include ancient knowledge and ancient peace into modern society.

When our recent planetary movement began at the harmonic convergence in 1987, José Arguelles published a Mayan prophecy. Our Sun enters into the Band in 1998 and we move into the Band in 2012. This is the Mayan prophesied end of the earth. While researchers cannot agree on the specific date, I consider it irrelevant. The important point is that we are coming close to a time of transition.

There are phases of history when ancient societies were concerned only about themselves, very self-centered. Then, as the planet's elliptical path moves through the photon band, a growing concern for others develops. Sometimes, a society might be possessive and controlling and then for a short time in their past became giving and sharing.

It becomes important we recognize the ebb and flow of universal energy and know we have a choice. Throughout every complete life, each entity has a choice. People do not have to understand the technicalities of Photon Band or where a specific civilization sits. It is vital we know we have a choice.

First, during the shorter, occasional trips through the Photon Band, individuals could cling to the dark.

The second option is developing the necessary skills when they have a chance. This promotes movement up through the photon band. As people develop these abilities, they also discover they can eventually return to the comfortable blanket of Galactic Dark.

A third choice is an important one for humans, something to consider seriously today. Knowing how to pull in personal Galactic Light permits people to step into the light at any time, allowing them to alter their genetic code for future citizens. The key skills involve stepping, that is moving, in and out of the basic dimensions or the *Planes of Reference.*

Shamans and Elders of ages past knew this and knew it was not the time to teach others in their tribes. Today, people are independently discovering this knowledge; it is time to teach them in detail.

Photon Summary

Churches and meditation groups will always chant. Chanting does nothing more than open up the body's energy centers and take the individual to a specific plane.

Many argue that the purpose of chanting is opening up the chakras and nothing else. If that is the only conscious objective, then that is fine. However, people get a side benefit. Their chanting introduces awareness to surrounding sounds and as a result, the planes.

The Dimensions or *Planes of Reference* give people a new viewpoint for understanding. Up until now, our ancestors had to *sense* the levels; while the shamans *saw* the multiple planes. The remainder of the population stayed in one level at a time.

Since science likes proof; our scientists conducted experiments and mathematical analysis to prove there were different planes. *Within and Beyond* contains a new set of definitions. This allows people to understand the planes either as a technical scientist or someone expanding their perspective of living.

As we approach, and live in the Photon Band, each person must understand the principles and learn how to move freely from one plane, or dimension, to another. This is why I compared it earlier to driving a car and being completely aware of your surroundings, lights, pedestrians and cars.

Our ancestors did not need labels for the energy levels; they were not necessary. Spiritual leaders in the indigenous communities knew how to transcend planes and levels. When it was necessary, they taught their people or gave them their prophetic warnings. They did not give us solutions, we search for the option. Now we have to learn how to honor the planet.

Warnings speak of caring for the planet Earth. When we care for a planet, we care for all life upon it. The MANU NYMBA's Cosmic Life Pattern includes all seven planes. One reference plane is telluric or caring for the planet. The next two tell us who we are and how to survive. The fourth and fifth are the compassion and caring for yourself and others. The last two include individual psychic wisdom and, of course, the ultimate connection. The ultimate connection allows us to send healing without being aware of the need, or how we send it.

Since primeval times, it seems we get information only in images, circles, statues and ruins but not in written text. Our ancestors of the past five millennia translated the messages and details into their language. Since then scholars translated them into pertinent languages. Unfortunately, it seems people ignore this knowledge.

However, before we can do this we need to review the great philosophers and thinkers of the past three thousand years. Both the traditional and the interpretative data helps us understand how we digressed from the straight evolutionary path. The core knowledge is not wrong, it is simply limiting.

It seems that philosophers and intellects focused only on the physical component of life, a logical phase through the transitional evolution of academic thinking. Those who did study the soul had a different interpretation and did not consider the complete cosmos as relevant for human study. The cosmos may have been a tool for clocking or mapping out a life cycle, such as astrology, but it lacks features that may have been of pertinent value. There was no contemplation about the possibility of universal life for all living. Although the scholars develop personal perspectives, there were still common threads.

Part II -Orthodox Beliefs

Many individuals and schools of thinking contribute to present-day societies. Some schools such as Buddhism survive from one era to another. As we study cultures worldwide, we discover international schools with emphasis in particular regions. Since it is impossible to include every logic school or alternative thinking, I arbitrarily include samples from disciplines either clearly following the *Rules of Life* or introducing innovative ideas for the time. The Rules of Life include compassion, honor, humility and equality. An innovative idea linking two worlds is the word -- *K'U*. Tibetans, not necessarily Buddhists, define K'U as essence. In Central American cultures, K'U is the generator of thought.

All schools of thinking in this book originate in what we call *Before Common Era - BCE*. First, we have three religions -- Islam, Christianity and Judaism connecting through Abraham. Next, we have four Eastern faiths, Buddhism, Confucianism, Daoism, and Hinduism connecting through the *Rules of Life*.

Although Islam, Christianity and Judaism share a similar concept base, they evolve into different schools. The *Rules of Life* are inherent parts of the other schools' teachings.

Islam

Their leader, Mohammed, lived in the Middle East between 570-632CE. He is the restorer of the original monotheistic faith of Abraham, Moses, Jesus and other prophets from the BCE. Islamic tradition holds that Christianity and Judaism distort the texts given by God to these prophets by either altering the text, using a false interpretation, or both. The word *Islam* means "submission", or the total surrender of oneself to God. The faith is based upon five pillars, or duties.

These are:

1. Shahadah – profession of faith ,
2. Salah – ritual prayer,

3. Zakah – alms tax,
4. Sawm – fasting during Ramadan and
5. Hajj – pilgrimage to Mecca

Christianity

Christianity is a monotheistic and evangelistic faith centering on the life and teachings of Jesus. Like Judaism and Islam, Christianity is an Abrahamic religion. There are numerous schools based upon the lessons of Jesus.

Judaism

Judaism is the religion of the Jewish people, based on principles and ethics embodied in the Hebrew Bible and the Talmud. According to Jewish tradition, the history of Judaism begins with the Covenant between God and Abraham (2000 BCE), the patriarch and progenitor of the Jewish people. Judaism is among the oldest religious traditions still in practice. Jewish history and doctrines have influenced other religions such as Christianity, Islam and Baha'i.

Daoism

Philosophical Daoism, also known as Taoism, traces its origin to Lao Zi, 607-520 BCE. Tao or Dao means the *path* or *way*. Daoism emphasizes compassion, moderation, and humility. The thought focus is on non-action - spontaneity, transformation and emptiness/omnipotence. These thought patterns stress the serenity of life. To achieve this, Lao Zi encourages individuals to *withdraw* from society or empty their mind during meditation. There are approximately between two and three million followers in the world who understand and follow the Yin/Yang.

Confucianism

There are more than six million Confucius followers around the world. Confucius lived between 551 – 479 BCE. The hub of these teachings is Morality and is about *involvement in* society.

Even though their thinking travels a long way from their origin, these leaders succeed in maintaining a link with their beginning on Earth. Leaders modify the original knowledge to suit the lifestyle in their current world without sacrificing the key values of equality and cooperation.

Hinduism

Hinduism is the third leading religion in the world today, following Christianity and Islam. It is also the oldest continuous religion, beginning sometime between 5500 – 2600 BCE. Throughout this time, it connects to other cultures of the world.

There are four goals in the life of a Hindu:

1. Dharma: correct action according to duty and scriptural laws
2. Kāma; sensual actions and beliefs
3. Artha: material possessions
4. Moksha: liberation from Samsara (reincarnation or rebirth)

The first two goals are usually part of the early adulthood whereas the third and fourth are after age 60. The early adult ages are the procreation years, thus the goals correspond. Someone pursuing Dharma and Moksha is a *wise* person. This means that everyone, regardless of training or caste is wise and formal education is not always necessary.

A Hindu soul moves up and down an infinite hierarchy of rebirth, depending on their behaviors in a particular physical life. They base their justification of the caste system on this belief which explains why the caste system survives. Westerners look upon the caste system with pity and scorn, and overlook the pride carried by the individuals regardless of caste. We call this *job art*. *Job Art* is the pride and skill a person displays as they perform their chosen work. Even begging has a "job art". Long ago, people in Western society were proud of the work they did whether it was farming, factory work or running a large corporation. Gradually the reaction of tourists and children caused their elders to feel guilty and discontent.

The Hindu beliefs carry forward the ancient truth molding the following paths to salvation:

- The Way of Works (rituals)
- Take pride in the work of whatever your caste life fulfills
- The Way of Knowledge (realization of reality and self-reflection)
- Reflect upon yourselves and your role in this life
- The Way of Devotion (devotion to the God you choose to follow)[6]
- Spend time on personal devotion

Throughout our past, academic thinkers study religion, and society's *Rules of Life*. Analysis of these thinkers' and philosophers' findings is vast, worthy of study and comparison.

Part III - Mysterious Connections

GLOBAL RULES OF LIFE

Mysterious connections exist between the cultures of the world. First, is the consistent set of *Rules of Life*. Many societies follow similar *rules* regardless of an immediate and common need. The second possibility is genetic connections. Numerous links exist through evolution and DNA. Yet, it is often unclear as to how people from one culture manage to travel from one part of the globe to another.

In this situation, they do not necessarily follow *life rules*. Their guidelines evolve to meet the needs of the time. It becomes interesting and mysterious how two distant groups develop corresponding requirements regardless of where they live. Either way, we find the earth flooded with common rules or values.

For thousands of years, communities and societies develop guidelines and health practices according to the requirements and supplies of the time. Ecological evolution often initiates these changing needs. Many consider this information irrelevant to current life. However, since ecological changes on the planet are cyclical, it seems appropriate that when we return to a phase of the world cycle we should be able to pull in the knowledge and practices from our past journey through that phase to help us for the future. Doesn't it make sense that if guidelines apply to a specific era, why we should not put their learning to use when we re-enter a similar phase again? We refer here to droughts, ice ages and health concerns.

Regardless of the era, there is one consistency spanning the ages. Whenever people leave a community, they take a simple set of *Rules of Life* with them, reflecting peace, support and communal integrity:

> Do no harm
> Honor Life
> Respect the dead and ancestors
> Honor all cultures

The Hopi people of the present Four Corners in the United States, regardless of where they live or the ecological circumstances, they show us how we can apply these values to a modern society. Their name – Hopi -- is a shortened form of what these people call themselves, *Hopituh Shi-nu-mu*, "The Peaceful People" or "Peaceful Little Ones." Like other cultures, they chose the white-winged Dove as a symbol of peace. This peace symbol carries prophecies to the Hopi, telling the importance of truth. *Truth does not happen, it just is.* This comes from their True White Brother, Pahana. The dove symbolizes peace and prophecy for the Hopi as well as other Indian tribes living in North American.

According to the Lakota Sioux legends, the dove protects the white Buffalo Calf Woman when she returns to teach humility. These sacred instructions bring humanity into an oneness of heart, mind, and spirit, applying them to all cultures. We summarize these in ten guidelines:

1. Take care of Mother Earth and the other colors of man.
2. Respect Mother Earth and creation.
3. Honor all life, and support that honor.
4. Be grateful from the heart for all life. It is through life that there is survival.
5. Thank the Creator at all times for all life.
6. Love, and express that love.
7. Be humble. Humility is the gift of wisdom and understanding.
8. Be kind with one's self and with others.
9. Share feelings and personal concerns and commitments.
10. Be honest with one's self and with others. Be responsible for these sacred instructions and share them with other nations.[7]

Two authors summarize these. Bette Stockbauer, a freelance writer, writes about principles similar to these Rules of Life on her *Ancient Prophecies* website.[8] The book, *Sourcebook of the World's Religion*,[9] by Joel Beverslius demonstrates how modern society still refers to principles comparable to time gone by.

Cultures around the world appear to have similar ways of handling the cyclical changes whether they pass through the phase at the same time or not. Ancient societies such as the Hunza of the Himalays, Hopi societies or other very old or extinct indigenous cultures have creative ways to handle these changes. What worked once might work again. First, ask ourselves a few questions. "How old is the planet?" "Where did humanity begin?" "Why did they settle where they did?" "What is the bond?"

Scientists report the Earth is at least 3.75 billion years old. Carbon dating takes the Earth back 4.5 billion years. Life forms, such as bacteria, are 3.8 billion years old.[10] Therefore, we can confidently state the planet is approximately four-and-one-half billion years old. The questions to ask are: What was in the environment that encouraged inhabitation? Where did humanity begin?

Four billion years ago, there was no oxygen in our atmosphere. This planet's composition was carbon dioxide (CO_2), steam, ammonia (NH_3), and methane. Today, the planet has both gaseous and liquid states. Now the composition of the planet is 21% oxygen, 78% nitrogen, .04% carbon dioxide and approximately1% argon.[11] Of the original liquid core, only 1% was hydrogen. This may seem a small amount but it equals just over 70% of the observed mass of the universe.[12] Hydrogen is volatile and accounts for pressure building within a rock formation. Even if 1% hydrogen accumulates inside this boulder planet, the pressure builds, searching for a way to escape - volcanos and hot springs being the most common routes. Instead of thinking of *pressure building* within a volcano, think of a volcano *oozing*.

Ancient volcanos did not always erupt. Instead, the excess gases oozed out, balancing the surrounding gaseous and energy state. This balance is crucial. If the universe's plan is harmonious, then everything happens in a gentle, fluid motion. There is never a need to discharge large quantities of these excesses. Earth energy ebbs and flows continually in balance

Living beings settling on this planet naturally look for locations that would maintain the balance of their being. Volcanoes and hot springs meet this requirement. The MANU NYMBA, the *Nucleus of Life*, combines the magnetic Earth energy and the electrical Universal energy maintaining the equilibrium. A major concept is: "*Volcanoes build bridges.*" This metaphorical bridge combines the magnetic and electrical energy of the planet, carrying the resulting force into pools and lakes. When this energy tips out of balance, local volcanoes ooze or explode. At this time, the residents discover wonderful new rocks and minerals coming from the Earth's interior. As the population learns about these minerals, they also learn about the necessities of life on this planet. One key lesson is learning the importance of alkaline versus acidity.

The greatest concentration of hydrogen is directly around natural springs and volcanos, making this the ideal location for creating pools and lakes. The hydrogen and oxygen combination produces the necessary alkaline water for the *bed of life*. This alkalinity or *pH* balance of life is crucial. *PH* means *power of hydrogen*. For optimum health, the pH needs to be within a narrow pH band of 7.35 and 7.45. Consuming water in this band is an uncomplicated basic step of maintaining the body balance. When nature creates balanced spring-water, it invites life of many kinds. Microscopic organisms create small colonies around pristine lakes and ponds where they can absorb the necessary nutrients.

The mystery of volcanic eruptions has been with us for millennia. Scientists and philosophers give us provable facts about most eruptions but we still have unanswered questions. In the 1960s and 1970s, satellite monitoring drew our attention to the magnitude of sub oceanic impact. Archaeologists now realize there are more damage sites, potentially caused by dormant volcanos, than previously perceived. If the oceans came into existence long after spring water lake formation, perhaps billions of years later, then it seems that there must also be dormant volcanos and dry lakes on the dry land masses. These dry water beds were potential settlement sites for our ancestors who established the important *Rules of Life*.

At Mount St. Helens National Volcanic Monument, in Washington State, USA, a Spirit Friend gave us a message. The main spirit speaker, a loving Ancient One, living in the caves outside the volcano said:

"Volcanos build bridges. Humans tend to stay in what they call the Now, forgetting that all time is occurring simultaneously. A volcanic eruption builds a bridge and makes changes that are for the betterment of all life. They are a way of bringing peace and harmony to a planet. They create new springs, better (purer) water that pulls in new life from beyond your small narrow plane. In the beginning, all life realized this and they understood.

Today, there is arrogance amongst humans because they believe that only they can build something. They do not understand or accept the principle that there are other ways to create.

A volcano brings new forms of mineral deposits to the surface, which will allow humans to use and see a new potential. We (from other worlds) do not see why all the work of digging or mining, as you call it, is encouraged. When you look at your past, you possibly will see when cultures used what was on the surface or perhaps in a cave and did not need to dig. This was very long ago. This is when the Zimbabwe bird symbolized a sense of freedom. We encourage all who read this to look into their neighbourhood and identify a region that had a disaster early in your lifetime. What did it look like then and what does it look like now. What is the difference?"

Throughout history, natural occurrences met human requirements. Environmental events such as volcanic eruptions or shifts in water supply force residents to move or migrate to another location. We know natural springs dry up, shrink in size or volcanoes die. Thanks to anthropologists, we found locations where small volcanic-shaped mounds of land are barely detectable and unexpected water sources are home to ancient societies. This describes the Yucatan Peninsula of Mexico. There are no lakes or springs at ground level. This prompted ancient Maya people to climb down into deep caverns to retrieve their water. There may be no shortage of water but an individual spring might shrink causing people to move to neighboring geyser or lake. Attentive indigenous people watch for indications of upcoming changes and make necessary adjustments to their lifestyles, perhaps even move.

When we ask aboriginal societies about their history, surprisingly, we get similar responses. The Australian Aborigines insist *"they have always been here"*. The Cowichan band from Vancouver Island believes *"they came from above"*. The Hopi relate tales of *"coming from the North"*. They are from different parts of the planet and have different explanations of their origin, yet they all carry goals of unity and peace. If nations around the globe carry common goals, then perhaps we need to continue passing on this legacy.

Skeptics want scientific evidence affirming whether populations migrated, or evolved independently. Graham Hancock shows computer images of the planet as it evolved through the ice ages, shrinking and expanding the oceans. This shows how land bridges can be formed allowing people to travel from one continent to another.[13] This evidence may support potential migration from the one African origin-source but it does not verify the DNA evidence as provided by our scientific experts. We still need to ask ourselves - How did we share the information between societies?

CENTRAL AMERICA, UNITED STATES, & EGYPT

Several millennia ago, societies in these three regions had comparable *Rules* which honor and respect life. The words may vary but the intent remains constant. We find the "T" design, both natural and man-made, in their rock carvings, stone placements and arrangements of buildings. They are important to look at and it becomes important to understand why so many cultures share the same design. We may not worship the same Gods today but for approximately 5,000 years, humans used the "T" to determine season, energy, sun cycle; all needed for agriculture. It seems humans turned to the Gods with this symbol for nurturing their farming.

We find three meanings for the "T" and *Tau, - hidden wisdom, rejuvenation,* and *immortality.* In his classic book *Atlantis: the Antediluvian World*, Ignatius Donnelly claims *Tau* is an important icon signifying "hidden wisdom" for Mexicans as well as the Peruvians, Egyptians, Phoenicians, and Chaldeans.[14] It is emblematic of rejuvenation, freedom from physical suffering, hope, immortality, and divine unity

The next meaning passed down to us is: *divine breath.* Elders explain the "T" designs of many of Central America's ancient Mayan ruins in this way. The Mayan daykeeper, artist, and historian, Hunbatz Men, explains one of the meanings of this motif:

"A transcendental synthesis of human religious experience is inherent in the word "te", Sacred Tree, which emerged from the word "teol" and teotl, the names of God the Creator in Mayan and Nahuatl. These most revered and sacred words of the ancient people, symbolized by the Sacred Tree, were represented in the Mayan hieroglyphs as the symbol 'T.' In addition, this symbol represented the air, the wind, the divine breath of God."

In the Maya tradition, whenever it appears either as a T-shaped doorway or window, it symbolizes the Sacred Tree at the Center of the World (*Axis Mundi*). The Maya believe this is what the shaman's spirit climbs upon. This portal leads to the Great Spirit, through which the Breath of Life may pass. It became a common architectural shape in stone masonry.

In Palenque and Chiapas, Mexico, we find T-shaped windows in the building called "The Palace". Here you see a continuous flow of Ts gliding into the abyss. Note in this picture you seem to see a T within a T.

The next picture depicts a portion of Chaco Canyon. If you look carefully, you see the steps within the "T". These steps lead through a T-shaped doorway down into Casa Rinconada, the Great Kiva at Chaco Canyon. Naturally, speculation for a practical meaning abounds. The best option comes from Alex Patterson. In the ROCK ART SYMBOLS[15] Patterson quotes Catherine Viele's book, Voices in the Canyon "...the purpose may have been to enter a room with heavy loads on their back or closing off the bottom for warmth leaving the top open for ventilation".

The following photo was taken by the same photographer, Geore deLange. but it is of Walnut Canyon near Flagstaff. For details and aditional photographs, go to his website. He comments on the similarity and importance of the T. His website is http:// www.delange.org/WalnutCanyon/WalnutCanyon.htm

The T-shape in the Greek alphabet, originates around 800 BCE. The Greek letter "T" comes from T known as the Tau Cross. Tau is one of the oldest letters known, originating in Sumeria. This Cross takes the shape of the first letter of the name, Tammuz, the Sumerian Solar God and consort of the Goddess Ishtar. Since he is a Solar God, his death and resurrection are celebrated every spring. Tau echoes the name of the Hopi sun god Tawa. Here Tau links Greece, Sumeria and Hopi.

A key feature of how the T Tau Cross is constructed and built helps our understanding. This feature states:

Every day the sun emerges from the Underworld through a T-shaped doorway, the horizontal bar serving as the horizon.

In North America, the Hopi and Anasazi (ancient Hopi) from Southwest region of the United States frequently used T-shaped doorways and windows in their structural design. At some point in the past, the form of the Hopi kiva (subterranean prayer chamber) changed from round, to rectangular, located on an east-west axis, utilizing the T formation. The floor plan widens at one end reflecting the T-shape?

Next, our traveling takes us to Egypt where we find the "T" icon occurring throughout the Egyptian pyramids. What better place to find a single symbol for *divine breath, hidden wisdom, rejuvenation,* and *immortality.* Pharaohs are divine, immortal and wise.

After extensive study of Egypt, Farouk El-Baz of Boston University introduces the possibility that builders of the three major pyramids of the Giza Plateau modeled them after the naturally occurring, conical hills found west of Luxor, Egypt.[16] The Luxor hills and pyramids in Egypt match the connection between the San Francisco Peaks with the Hopi Mesas.

The Luxor hills correspond to the San Francisco Peaks in California, Humphreys, Agassiz and Fremont. The Egyptian pyramids are places for the revered as are the Hopi Mesas. Thus, we have four locations, two natural and two human created or selected.

The San Francisco Peaks are the winter home of the Hopi kachinas. For the rest of the year, Hopi Elders and legendary Divine Beings move to the three Hopi Mesas, returning the next winter.

In numerous cultures, *tau* refers to abundant water or rain-deities. For instance, Augustus Le Plongeon, one of the first archaeologists of the Maya, writes that the T-shape corresponds to Crux, or the Southern Cross. This constellation appears shortly before the beginning of the rainy season in southern Mexico.

"The ancient Maya astronomers had observed that at a certain period of the year, at the beginning of our month of May, that owes its name to the goddess MAYA, the good dame, mother of the gods, the "Southern Cross," appears perfectly perpendicular above the line of the horizon. This is why the Catholic church

celebrates the feast of the exaltation of the holy cross on the third day of that month, which it has consecrated particularly to the Mother of God, the Good Lady, the virgin Ma-R-ia, or the goddess Isis anthropomorphized by Bishop Cyril of Alexandria."

Once more, we return to the Naga tribe of India. Why else would India and Mesoamerica be associated if the Naga and Maya were not linked in some way?

Is it more than a coincidence that the name of this Mesoamerican tribe, the Maya, should be the same as the Sanskrit word for the Veil of Illusion? The Mother Goddess, Shakti, otherwise known as the Divine Mother Devi, gives birth to all phenomenal forms that we mistakenly perceive as being real. A white elephant impregnated Queen Maya by entering her side and subsequently gave birth to Siddhartha Gautama the Buddha.

Furthermore, Maia was the Greek goddess of spring and the Roman goddess of the Earth or growth. Tau refers to abundant water, or the rain god. Her fertility celebration is either the 1st or 15th of May. She was also the eldest sister and the brightest star of the Pleiades. In the land of the Maya tribe, the sun in conjunction with the Pleiades passes through the zenith during the month of May.

We need to remember, fertility gods, solar and lunar gods and related rituals link *many* ancient cultures. One example is the Egyptian-Maya connection.

The Egyptian carving on temple walls shows an *Ankh* between a pair of scepters. This displays a symbol matching the human shape, arms extended showing a head representation. The "T" indicates the importance of balance in our lives.

I have only included a few features from historical cultures who utilized the T-shape. As you pursue your preferred sections, I encourage you to keep the

Hopi Guidelines in mind. They teach us so much and blend in with so many other teachings.

The Egyptian cross or the *ankh*, without the handle is a "T". The Ankh was the *key to the Nile*, the symbol of fertility. The ancient image carved on an Egyptian wall displays two "T"s with the Ankh between. Thus, the "T" gives sun and rain, and the Ankh gives life, and we see *three* versions of the "T".

Unfortunately, why we find the T-shape images in North America, Central America and the Mediterranean lands remains a mystery. It takes human form but the meanings and needs vary.

Even though a culture does not define the *tau* in a manner of other cultures, the T-shape images carry meanings transcending oceans and land that apply regardless of where humans live.

COLOMBIA, FRANCE, & CANADA

Channeled information received in Canada several years ago corresponds to signs carved on rocks found in Bogotá, Colombia and Glozel France. When we compare these three pieces of information, we gain an understanding of signs from three continents more than 5,000 years ago.

My book, *Within and Beyond,* includes information about the beginning of the channeled triangle of knowledge, description of the signs and the meanings given to me at the time. With the exception of these two phrases, all the signs appeared individually.

The two channelled sentences translate into

#1:   PEACE is WITHIN

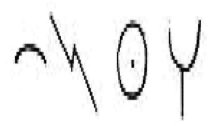

#2:   PEACE and LOVE from BEYOND

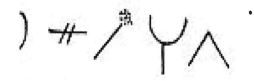

After these sentences appeared, the following sign emerged:

#3:   TOGETHER

In other words, *"We cannot go WITHIN without going BEYOND and we cannot go BEYOND without going WITHIN. They go TOGETHER."* It does not matter whether we write them from left to right, top to bottom or in reverse, the meanings apply. Our Ancient ancestors knew this in their time, we are just rediscovering the wisdom again.

Initially Sumerian cuneiform writing flowed from top to bottom. About the third millennium BCE, the direction changed from up-down to left-right. Researchers find that as the direction of writing shifts over time, the important information for the era also shifts. At this time, working together becomes a significant point for these cultures. It teaches people the importance of living in unison, working toward a common goal.

Erich Von Däniken's book, *The Gods and their Grand Design* includes two important locations for these artifacts. The first was the outskirts of Bogotá Colombia. The other was Glozel, France. The Bogotá carving directions do not appear as directional as the French stones. But this does not mean the writing did not have significance.

While in Colombia, Däniken met Professor Jaime Gutierrez, a university professor in Colombia who showed him several ancient objects from Bogotá. One object that particularly interested Däniken was named a genetic disc.

The genetic disc is a small disc with a center hole, possibly designed for a neck chain or leather chord, with a series of ornate carvings around the outer edge. The etched images are similar to, but not identical to the Middle East carving. The Sumerian culture goes back to 4,000 BCE. While Däniken simply states that the Bogotá discs are thousands of years old,[17] Sam Enslow confirms that ancestors in the Bogotá vicinity go back as far as 12,000BCE. [18] This makes the discs older than the Sumerian era.

If there is any connection between these two locations, then how did people transfer the details? First, we need to look for a water pathway between the two regions of the Middle East and Colombia? The Magdalena River flows approximately 100 km from San Agustin past Bogotá on down into the region surrounding the Sierra Nevada, home of the Kogi. Thousands of years ago, assuming the river existed; it could possibly have been a navigable route. We know the Kogi along with their predecessors, the Chibcha, lived there. Who were their ancestors? Perhaps these societies taught us our navigation methods and implored humans to respect nature and our water. The Kogi remained secluded in the mountains until 1990 when they came down and filmed their warning with BBC. Since the Kogi were crying out for us to respect land and live in harmony, they had to learn from somewhere, their ancestors. These ancestors then would have carved the images on discs and matching stones in two countries. When Däniken saw the Bogotá artifacts, his thoughts immediately traveled to France where scientists found similar stones.

During the 1920s, in a small French town called Glozel, farmers discovered strange stones and pottery deep in a hole in their field. For several decades, these findings became the subject of controversy. Were they fake, forged by the farmers? Archaeological authorities acknowledged they were extremely old. Academics argued that our ancestors simply could not have etched animals that had been extinct for roughly 10,000 years before the creator's lifetime. Furthermore, although the writing is similar to Phoenician writing, the standard argument was *"How could simple, uneducated people write in a style that had not yet been invented!"*[19]

Nevertheless, authorities generally agree that the Phoenician style writing evolved from approximately 1600 BCE, Sumerian writing dates back to 2360 BCE and the original Glozel writing style go back to 7500-5600 BCE.

The Sumerian writing of 3000 BCE was more pictographic, evolving into a cuneiform style which matched the evolution of the Phoenician writing. Students and professors at Tulane University in New Orleans compiled their research into charts illustrating the evolution of language.[20]

Pictographic writing dates back to 3400 BCE. For approximately a millennium, it was a contemporary of Egyptian hieroglyphs and then two paths diverged. The Egyptians stayed with their hieroglyphs for a while longer and the Sumerian introduced the cuneiform style we associate today with their writing.

During the 1950s, a dating method called *Thermoluminescence* dating was developed and accepted as a reliable dating method. Using this method, authorities confirmed the Glozel artifacts do indeed date back to the Magdalenian period, approximately 17,000 – 11,000 BCE. This means the symbols or signs on the artifacts were created sometime between 18,000 – 10,000 BCE. This is 10,000 years *before* the estimated time of the Sumerian and the Phoenician writing.

With Glozel age verified, it became important to connect the artifacts between the geographical regions, Glozel, France and Bogotá, Colombia. Däniken realized the 15,000 year old markings on the Glozel stones correspond to markings on Bogotá stones, but since the age of the Bogotá stones is undetermined, can we assume they are the same era?

Here we have two societies living on opposite sides of the globe leaving similar artifacts, dating back to more than 10,000 BCE. Now we add channeled signs from current time matching both of them.

In the channeled images, most of the sign sequence appears individually. A few do appear in meaningful sentences, but only once, and the signs in these sentences match signs from all locations.

The 15,000 year old artifacts from France and Colombia show analogous carvings. Then when you compare the channeled phrases to these artifacts, you will see their modified individual signs.

All three carry signs similar to a "Y". The Colombian stone shows a "Y" with the upper arms curved and a downward curve at the base. The French stone's variation of this sign displays it as either a reverse peace symbol or human with arms stretched upward. This human-shaped image has arms open wide ready to receive, without the head.

Both stones have a sign matching the channeled one for - *together* – with one difference. The Colombia image added a small curve to the left end, extending the wave. The French stone shows this particular sign on the top row near the center while the Colombian shows it in the upper right corner, beside a circle. Another difference is the Bogotá signs display more curves than the Glozel stone. To my knowledge, none of either stone's markings have been deciphered. Since the age is unknown, it is unclear about the potential language and writing sources. Archaeologists are confident of the connection, though.

Here are the three images: the channeled information, the Colombian - Bogotá stone and the French stone from Glozel.

#1 – Channelled

*Sentence One – Peace is **Within***

*Sentence Two – Love & Peace from **Beyond***

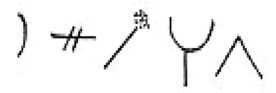

*Sentence Three – What is **within** & from **beyond** is **Together***

*#2 – Symbols from a Stone found in **Bogotá**, Colombia*

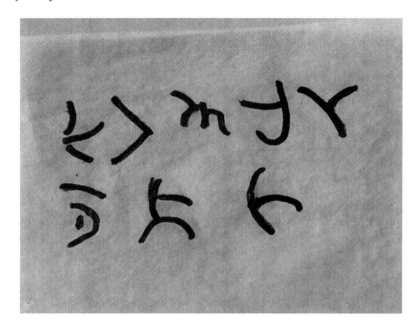

*#3 - Symbols from a Stone found in **Glozel**, France*

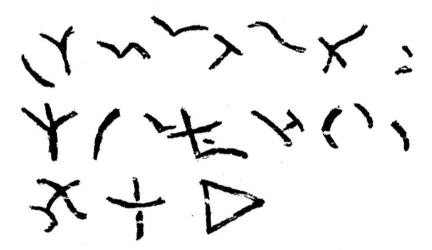

When we compare **Phoenician** writing sample from the Phoenician era from 1000 BCE, we note correlations between the three, channeled symbols, our modern alphabet *and* Phoenician. This is a small segment of their ancient alphabet.

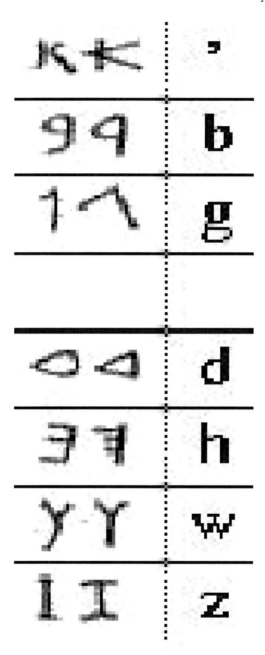

Sumerian *Script dates back even further, providing evidence from approximately 3000 BCE.*

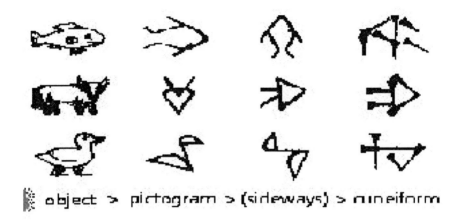

object > pictogram > (sideways) > cuneiform

Five thousand years ago, the Sumerian people drew objects, later moving to pictograms and then cuneiforms. First, they drew them in columns, and then they put them in horizontal lines, and finally the Sumerian developed the cuneiform style of images. The key here is the comparison between all regions, not just a specific time. Some regions progressed quickly, others more slowly. This transition took humans from approximately between 5000 years ago to 3000 years ago -- 3400BCE to 75AD. This clearly illustrates how change occurs in a single culture's written communication. Everywhere on the planet, similar shifts take place, some faster, some slower.

Another consideration is their location on the planet. Both Glozel and Bogotá are located in a volcanic mountain range and natural springs. Glozel is only 20 km. away from Vichy, one of the world's renowned springs. South of Vichy in the Auvergne mountain region, where hundreds of dormant volcanos exist. For example, the extinct volcanic mountain Chaine des Puys in the Bourbonnais Mountains erupted in 4,040 BCE.

Volcanos and hot springs also surround Bogotá. The most notorious volcano is less than 200 kilometres west of the country's capital. Nevado Del Ruiz is in the Cordillera *Central,* almost directly west of Bogotá. It erupted in 1985 and volcanologists consider this eruption as one of the worst in the century, worse than Mt. St. Helens in Washington, USA. In addition to volcanoes, north of Bogotá in the Cordillera Oriental are some of the country's luxurious hot springs. Descriptions of Bogota include "Home of volcanoes" and "Home of Hot Springs".

Key geographical points of this region are:

Firstly, Nevado Del Ruiz is in Cordillera *Central* west of Bogotá. Secondly, hot springs are north of Bogotá in the Eastern mountain range, Cordillera *Oriental*. Bogotá is on the western bank of this range, overlooking the valley dividing the two.

The beautiful river, Rio Magdalena runs through this valley where at the source of this river, we find San Agustin Colombia, home of more mystery. This region contains artifacts similar to those from the Glozel and Bogotá.

Peter Lancaster Brown cites a Journalist, Alexander Marshak, who identified a series of bones marked with scratches correlating with the phases of the moon. These bones go back to approximately 6500 BCE[21]

Unfortunately, many geological experts remain skeptical and might refuse to acknowledge any correlation between this information. If we look at the connection between the Inca, Kogi and the Mayan cultures, then the interconnectedness becomes feasible. They cover northern South America and span a long era. Matching the carvings on the stones of Bogota and Glozel and messages I receive are not complete. Regardless, I believe this tells us it is imperative that we combine all *the love and peace together.*

Part IV --North America

CANADIAN INDIGENOUS

Enormous change and disruption accompanied the European invasion of North America in the fifteenth century. As Europeans arrived and travelled west across the continent, they either slaughtered indigenous Nations, moved them to isolated land called reservations or forced them to adapt to the new ways. Most Indigenous people adapted to the oppressed rulings and systems, becoming quite demoralized. Factions of some nations, usually the Shamans and Elders, preserve their teaching and heritage in isolation. Today, we see a confident sharing of this wisdom emerging. Through the teaching of the Shamans and Elders, these cultures acknowledge their ancient ancestry with pride.

North America is an excellent example of how the Ancient Wisdoms of *many* nations blend. People refer to North America as a melting pot. To many though, this phrase carries a different meaning. It refers to immigration from many countries, bringing together different nationalities and cultures. As newcomers arrive, they ignore blending or merging with the Ancient Wisdoms of the indigenous. They do not consider the merging of Ancient Wisdom and values as important or part of the immigration process.

Each person from every country stores information from their land within themselves. All this knowledge intertwines over time, becoming impossible to separate because our planet and our history are interconnected. There are Ancient Wisdoms scattered around the globe that are integral parts of our life and they all contribute something. Once we recognize and accept this, we begin learning, exploring the mysteries and connections. We may live in only one location, but the wisdom learned by people we never met and from places we never visit is still applicable because we all carry the identical earth energy. As people immigrate into North American society, they begin sharing the learning they receive from the people of different lands and cultures, whom they had never met.

We now have the opportunity to learn from our neighbors. Anthropologists, authors and scientists use the terms *band, tribe* and *nation* interchangeably and inconsistently. There are no constant definitions for all three. However, these meanings appear most frequently: *Tribe* refers to a common ancestry or social group. *Nation* refers to organized groups usually recognized by government, including more than one tribe. *Band*, according to anthropologists, is a social group based on kinship. In anthropological literature, *Band* and *Nation* are usually synonymous. Consequently, I will use "tribe" and "nation" and with no intent of disrespect, I will avoid the use of "band".

Each Indigenous society in North America contributes something to our future. Since there are so many nations, it is impossible to include them all. Therefore, we arbitrarily include a select familiar few.

INUIT

We frequently see societies trying to squeeze a cultural group into one region when it actually spans numerous countries. The Inuit are an example of this. Also known as "The Arctic People", they live in the North American Arctic covering Canadian Arctic, Greenland and Alaska State of the United States with the major homeland being in the Eastern Northwest Territories. In April 1, 1999 a Land Claim Agreement was signed, creating a new territory called **Nunavut**, meaning "our land".

Nunavut includes land north and west of Hudson Bay, approximately one fifth the size of Canada. The formation of Nunavut Territory certainly does not eliminate the Inuit people living elsewhere but it defines their home. These people and this territory exemplify what we need to achieve, progressing through time. This territory is defined as

… a growing society that blends the strength of its deep Inuit roots and traditions with a new spirit of diversity [22]

Tourism Greenland describes the Inuit living in Greenland as:

… a peaceable people that have never waged war with anyone, and people generally show great openness to visitors.

In the far north, human evidence dates back into the Paleolithic times, approximately 10,000 years ago. Authorities confirm the archaeological sites in Alaska and the Aleutian Islands are Inuit, dating back to about 2000 BCE. The Inuit settlements in Eastern Canada, while similar, differ from Inuit settlements of Alaska. The Eastern Canadian settlements became known as the Old Dorset culture dating back to approximately 500 BCE. The Alaskan Inuit developed the technology to build snowhouses, known today as igloos.[23] In spite of minor differences in cultural ancestry, they all respond to the name *Inuit*.

Archeologists connect the Inuit with Siberian cultures since they believe the Inuit ancestors crossed the Bering Strait over the infamous Land Bridge. Others believe they came from Europe as there is still a cultural bond between Greenland, parts of Labrador and Europe. It seems to remain a mystery.

The Inuit demonstrate how a culture adapts to the environment where they live. Their diet does not include vegetation because of cold and aridity. After they adapted to the environment, sea life filled all their dietary needs.

We know members of many tribes living along coastlines utilize the properties of nature. The Unalaska Aleut[24] people are no different. Because these people were very friendly to strangers, there was little need to build walls or use defensive tools again humans. They need weapons only for gaining food and clothing. The Unalaska Aleut built their homes underground with a ladder leading up to the smoke hole and the entrance. In the frigid north, visitors expect this style of house. Unlike Igloo dwellers, many people living in the Siberian, Alaskan and northern Canadian regions built their homes underground.

Literature, both electronic and paper, confirms the Inuit loyalty to their oral traditions. Unfortunately, this is slowly disappearing. Perhaps as loyalty strengthens in small communities this might change. In the meantime, each community has a storyteller who repeats tales of their past. The stories validate legends and repeat stories telling why their values and beliefs are important. Several of their traditional values match those of ancient cultures from other parts of the world:

1. Respect for life and wisdom
2. Lack of individual ownership and greed
3. Sense of destiny, place and freedom of choice
4. Commitment to live in nature's cycles.

For centuries, the Inuit people knew the importance of preserving their lifestyles and values. People who gain their independence today strive to separate their lifestyle from the modern western rush of Southern communities. They recognize and value their simple heritage, carrying forward the basic values they own. All humanity possesses equivalent ethical codes. In many respects, these are the values and actions of all indigenous groups.

After exposure to the modern rush, leaders may not pull in traditional spiritual energy. However, they carry the memory and will set up markers such obelisks. The obelisk shape draws in universal energy and gradually expands into surrounding lands. The Inuit build what they call an inukshuk. These markings increase the speed of the energy flow in the regions. Anyone sensitive to this energy feels the quantity and quality of this energy.

An *inukshuk* means *"something which acts for or performs the function of a person."* These stone landmarks used by the Inuit of the Canadian Arctic equate to cairns used in other parts of the world.

The creativity of the inukshuk is wonderful. The people need landmarks and directional signs guiding people to food sources and settlements. Stones are the only communication resource on a flat, frozen landscape.

Just like so many nations, the Inuit strive to protect and recapture their simple heritage and basic values.

HAIDA

The second North American nation we acknowledge for their heritage are the Haida people. People around the world honor the Haida artists and archaeologists for their creativity ability. The Haida Gwaii, as we know them, insist *they live in the place where time began.* Following this belief, they call their homeland, Xhaaidlagha Gwaayaai meaning *Islands at the Boundary of the World.*

While they carve many sacred animals, they include the sacred images, owl, dove and butterfly and hummingbird images in their creativity. Just as other cultures do, they call upon the owl for knowledge - *Wisdom of Life*, the dove for peace - *Love & Peace* and the butterfly for metamorphous - *Self Transformation, Balance & Joy.*

The Hummingbird reminds us to enjoy what we do, we heal and become happy. Throughout time, people learned to heal and be happy. This is a message we lose over time

Although, the Europeans banned the Haida custom, potlatches, several centuries ago, they continued using these images in secrecy as a means of preserving the integrity of this a religious ceremony. The potlatch main purpose was the re-distribution and reciprocity of wealth. Fortunately, this ritual is returning to their culture.

On the Civilization website[25], Dr. George F. MacDonald, describes the Haida people:

The Haida of the Queen Charlotte Islands (Haida Gwaii) have fascinated all who have visited them, from the first travellers and explorers of the late eighteenth century to the anthropologists of the present. To early visitors the Haida presented a culture, complex in social organization and rich in artistic expression, which displayed a fine and fulfilling balance between man and the natural and supernatural worlds. With continued exposure to the pressures, both spiritual and material, of European culture this balance was disrupted, and the traditional Haida way of life came close to extinction. Today, however, the Haida regard their future with hope, bolstered by recent developments that hold great potential for reinforcing their cultural revival.

Literature report atrocities and slavery done *by* them; yet we hear little about the atrocities, slavery and violations *done to* them. The Haida nation exemplifies great mysticism, pride and gentleness of this tribe. Author George McDonald describes the renewal of pride very well. In present times, we discover other tribes reclaiming their pride, values and honesty. The following description from the Haida people matches these tribes:

"Our culture is born of respect, and intimacy with the land and sea and the air around us. Like the forests, the roots of our people are intertwined such that the greatest troubles cannot overcome us. We owe our existence to Haida Gwaii. The living generation accepts the responsibility to ensure that our heritage is passed on to following generations. "[26]

This portrayal does not sound like a violent, warring culture; rather, they carry the pride, understanding and closeness to nature that all indigenous people of the world carry. The greed and ego of the modern world passes them by.

Their traditional territory encompasses parts of southern Alaska, the archipelago of Haida Gwaii and its surrounding waters. Much of the water is stormy and turbulent. Their territory protects them from these waters, providing safe alternatives. The Haida Nation constitution describes their territory:

The territory of the Haida Nation includes the entire land of Haida Gwaii, surrounding waters, sub-surface and the air space recognizing the independent jurisdiction of the Kaiganii (southern Alaska). The waters include the entire Dixon Entrance, half of the Hecate Strait, halfway to Vancouver Island and westward into the abyssal ocean depths.

Traces of Haida ancestry takes them back approximately 9000 years ago. The carved totem poles awed early explorers which led modern artists to duplicate this art. Today, they ask permission of the tree to cut it down, move it from its original location and carve images upon it. In addition, there are other rituals for basket weaving and canoe creating. Since there are scanty historical Haida records, we do not know whether the rituals continue through generations or are a modern adaptation. Regardless, they do ceremonially asked permission of the tree reminding us that artists respect nature life.

Archeological evidence suggests they traded with the neighbouring communities, Tlingit and the Tsimishian. If the Haida were warring and violent, why would they care about native life? Their boats and spears were for food, not war. Their art tells of the Raven, a powerful trickster, and the Eagle, ruler of the sky.

Their documentations, like other Native teachings remind us:

"Their words are simple and their voices are soft. We have not heard them, because we have not taken the time to listen."

Perhaps now is the time to open our ears and our hearts to the words of wisdom they have to say.

THE COWICHAN PEOPLE

Five years ago, the elders of the Cowichan nation on Vancouver Island, also known as the *Hul'qumi'num* people, began sharing their historical woes. Their horror is not isolated; other native nations in North America suffered similar abuse. For several centuries, their children went away to residential schools and the adults lived upon reservations. Fortunately, this finally stopped and these people began reclaiming their heritage. In spite of their horrendous history, these people today display pride and honor about their world. There is little bitterness. On their website, they say:

"While we are now a modern society, our rich traditions and culture remain woven throughout our culture. Some of our traditional customs and practices have changed – historically imposed but now increasingly by choice.

We are adapting to new realities, and attitudes towards our traditions and teachings vary among our members. Some have maintained our customs throughout their lives, others are coming back to it, and still others say 'no thanks'. However, most of us do not want to stop being Cowichan.

We still engage in many of our traditional rites and ceremonies. We still have a strong tradition of community. We have many artists who have carried on the tradition of carving, canoe building, singing, and dancing. Other Cowichan artists capture our history and traditions in their artwork. Our Elders are actively involved in passing on the teachings of our ancestors through telling stories. We still fish by spear, although we also employ modern equipment as well. We still harvest traditional foods and plants for food and ceremonial purposes. We smoke or cure salmon and prepare other foods in the traditional way.

Language is the cornerstone of our culture. Hul'qumi'num, as with any language, embodies all our thoughts, beliefs, myths and institutions. Within it is reflected everything we have produced and contributed to the world. It is of paramount concern that we preserve our language.

Overcoming the legacy of colonialism, residential schools, and other oppressive measures is a long and challenging process. There was a lot of damage done to our mental and emotional well-being, and that is the biggest challenge we have to overcome.

But in the 25 years or so that we have been allowed some degree of self-determination, we have come a long way. We now provide a myriad of member services, we have an economic development company that provides job and training opportunities and gradually adds to our own-source revenue. More of our young people are staying in school and getting jobs. Healthy lifestyles are gradually being adopted.

Nevertheless, huge challenges remain. Many of our members are still unemployed, there is inadequate housing for our members, funding is an eternal struggle, racism and discrimination still exists. Recognition and more importantly, respect for our culture and sovereignty remains a significant barrier to being accepted by society at large. Self-government and the right to determine what is best for our members still elude us." [27]

Their book, *Those who Fell from the Sky*, documents their archeological and verbal history. They depict their archaeological age as:

"...far older than Egyptian Pyramids of the Giza Plateau, the ancient Peruvian ruins of Machu Pichu, the Cowichan people extends to the very beginning of time, embodying thousands upon thousands of years of continuous habitation along the east coast of Vancouver Island and the larger world of the Strait of Georgia." [28]

The historical region of these people extends into Puget Sound, lower Fraser River and the Gulf and San Juan Islands and the rivers of Vancouver Island. Archaeological evidence dates back approximately 10,000 years. We know they live in harmony with a natural world of land, sky and sea and trade with mainland nations. Archaeologists found Mexican pottery on Vancouver Island, but how the pottery reached this territory remains a mystery. This leads to two possible associations. First, was there a trade link between Mexico and Vancouver Island? Or, second did their ancestors originate in Mexico? Regardless of the explanation you choose, there is a similarity between the totem carving faces of the North American tribes and the Maya stone images.

Throughout their verbal sagas, the Cowichan people repeatedly state their ancestors "Fell from the Sky." This is comparable to the many nations who state "They came from above." The Hopi of the United States, Maya of Central America, Inca of Peru, Dogon of Africa and the Kogi of Colombia are a few of the other nations who believe they *fell from the sky*. They simply word their origin differently.

According to the *Hul'qumi'num* beliefs, twelve men came to populate this region. Their names were Syalutsa, Stutsun, Suhiltun Switthus Sultimul'thw, Skwi'lum, Hwuneem', Thulpul'thw, Kwukwmutsiin, Hwutumtun, Hunimul'thw, Swutun. The first one, Syalutsa, received teachings and then began teaching his younger brother, Stutsun. Just as in modern holy texts, there are many lessons. The *Hul'qumi'num* guidelines include:

- Give all invited guests a gift. Residents must follow this rule for all time.
- Do not kill for the sake of killing. Kill only for food.
- Drink and eat sparingly.
- Bathe in every clear water you encounter. This makes you strong.
- Listen to all that is said and follow it accordingly.
- Know your place in the world,
- Treat the world with respect,
- Take from the world only what you need.

Note the similarity between these guidelines and the other Rules of Life.

STÓ:LŌ

"This is our land. We have to look after everything that belongs to us."

The phrase is the philosophy of this tribe, *Stó:lō* which is the Halkomelem word for the Fraser River. Thus, the Stó:lō nation are *the river people*.

The first trace found of people living in the Fraser Valley date from 8,000 to 10,000 years ago. When asked, the elders will state *"we have always been here."*

Stó:lo Tribal Council members, directors, managers, and staff practice the fundamental values and beliefs as taught by their ancestors including respect, trust, honesty, integrity, and humility.

Recent development uncovered a *transformer stone* at Hatzic, just east of Mission in the Fraser Valley of British Columbia, Canada. Sto:lo archaeologist Gordon Mohs recognized the importance and arranged for the land transfer to the Sto:lo nation. Since then, they began displaying pride and control of their band's education. One of their objectives is upholding their heritage, merging it with modern living. The goals and lessons elders pass to the young are:

- Revive and maintain Stó:lō cultural values.
- Maintain and enhance our unique Stó:lō identity
- Support the growth of Stó:lō identity in our children
- Assist the general public to better understand and appreciate Stó:lō culture, traditions and spirituality

The focus of the site is a large transformer stone bearing the name Xá:ytem, which is also the name for the ancient village site nearby. Around this sacred stone archaeologists uncover over 350 prehistoric sites and an additional 200 sacred sites, all lying in the traditional Stó:lo territory. Xá:ytem gives us two different archeological human time periods. First, they found evidence from 5000-9000BCE and, more recently, around 3000BCE.

Today, the Stó:lō teach in their own schools and conduct their own tourism seminars. Since it is close to a large city, many are able to visit the Hatzic rock.

MI'KMAQ

While the Mi'kmaq nation is familiar to anyone studying North American Native cultures, it was not until I studied Paul Chiasson's work that I realized how much Mi'kmaq influenced ancestral history on Cape Breton Island.

After discovering artifacts buried on the land surrounding a hiking path on this island, Paul Chiasson, Nova Scotia author and architect, began researching and writing about the Mi'kmaq and ancient explorers. The stones and building remains appear much older than the times of the first visits of Europeans. The estimated age of Mi'kmaq settlements in Eastern Canada is approximately 11,000 years. The more extensively Chaisson researched, the easier he was able to prove some evidence definitely belongs to the Mi'kmaq ancestors while some remains a mystery.

The Mi'kmaq culture is profound, it differs from neighboring tribes, yet segments match societies around the globe. In their own words, the Mi'kmaq people recite the same code as other nations. The teachings of the Mi'kmaq say:

"Stated simply, we take nothing we don't need, we waste nothing, and we offer thanks for everything we do take."[29]

Our Western history is so culture-bound that we reject facts suggesting our ancestors might not be the creators or developers of life as we see it; alternatives are unimaginable. Historians may understand and acknowledge other options but this information stays within their community. From this narrow perspective, our settlers consequently assumed natives in North America had limited knowledge.

This is not always the case. Chaisson learned the Mi'kmaq were extremely knowledgeable. I am sure many other ancient peoples of North America carried similar wisdom. Chaisson knew the Mi'kmaq people lived isolated lives, had minimal communication with other people except with those who became stranded on their island. Yet, these people studied astronomy, intricately knew global maps, built ships and had medical knowledge surpassing European wisdom. Remedies used by the Mi'kmaq correspond with those of Chinese society four thousand years ago. He quotes descriptions from Father Le Clercq and Father Pierre Biard:

"...the Mi'kmaq are a noble race who kept themselves free from all that was bad and who lived peacefully in their 'land of friendship...their nation had a highly organized government, a ritualized family structure and a culture that honoured trust and equality.

...They love justice and hate violence and robbery, a thing really remarkable in men who have neither laws nor magistrates; for, among them, each man is his own master and his own protector.[30]

These quotes are from leaders in the 17th century. This describes a group of peaceful and highly organized people. These unique traits did not always correspond with those of their neighbors. Since the neighboring traits took precedence in history, Chaisson had a dilemma of presenting information that was contrary to what historians and scholars presented.

Chiasson continued exploring their written language, technical knowledge and gathering evidence. The Mi'kmaq's written language, clothing, technical knowledge, religious beliefs and legends, exposes deep cultural roots in China. There are several question asked by scientists and historians.

First, what was the navigational route for the Chinese?

In the literature, we discover an ocean current route from China, around the Cape of Good Hope and up to the Eastern Coast of North America.

Second, what drew Chinese people to Cape Breton Island?

There is evidence and reports of Cape Breton Island's mining. The rocks are rich in minerals, particularly coal and gold, evidence shows mining remnants. This island has good harbors, rivers and forests. The Chinese had developed a harmonious relationship with the indigenous people.

Third, why did the Chinese abandon and forget the colony?

If the original intent was financial, and this profit diminished, the reason for colonization disappeared.

The key message from this is understanding the relationship between the Chinese and the Mi'kmaq. They are both gentle peaceful people. Although they knew how to fight, they chose instead to share their knowledge and ways of living. The Chinese introduced the basis of Confucianism:

"Dwell at home in humility; conduct your business in reverence. In your dealings with others, be faithful."

In return, the Mi'kmaq introduced their knowledge of their land and the seasons.

Once we comprehend the Chinese/Mi'kmaq connection, we realize it is unlike the European Renaissance, the Chinese did not lose their traditions and technology. As the Chinese and Mi'kmaq exchange wisdom, Mi'kmaq learned this fundamental point. As time went on, the Chinese no longer came to North American and the Mi'kmaq preserved their wisdom and harmonious lifestyle in isolation.

Many people are skeptical of Chaisson's research. However, similarities in facial structure suggesting inter breeding, clothing design and artistic pattern-making support his theories. As well, numerous authors and scientists contribute segments of evidence that also backs Chaisson's effort.

AMERICAN INDIGENOUS

SOUTHWEST UNITED STATES – CALIFORNIA, ARIZONA

Vinson Brown's writings refer specifically to North America but they can apply to every nation around the globe. Regardless of where the settlement is, as soon as a tribe recognizes the need for a "keeper of the records," they would create one. It signifies a leadership and social system. Vinson Brown made comments about the Indigenous of California. He said they had a harmonious lifestyle until *"white man arrived"*. There was no need for ego-based organizations prior to that.

In a book covering a 300 years history of the Native Americans of the Pacific Coast, there were several references to this[31]. Vinson Brown states:

"Before the white man came, central California was one of the most peaceful places on earth. War was not glorified and peace was promoted. People lived with very little crime or violence…It is a triumph of human existence we would do well to learn from."[32]

He refers to three tribes of Northern California's Klamath River Valley, the Yurok, Hupa and Karok. In former times although their languages differed the culture, religion and general outlook of the three were close.

"There was no government or leaders as we know of them. The word-of-mouth laws produced people who shamed and stirred others into following and obeying them."

Farther down the coast into southern California, the Yokut, and the Salinan tribes combine adopted traits from other tribes and the tools provided by nature, the long grass and the remains of the shellfish. Other tribes taught them weaving. The women wove grass into homes, baskets and many other utensils. After they ate the shellfish from the ocean, they threw the remains into a large pile, creating a hill. Like other tribes, they used these hills for their homes and storage.

HOPI

Take care of Mother Earth and the other colors of man.

Respect this Mother Earth and creation.

Honor all life, and support that honor.

Be grateful from the heart for all life. It is through life that there is survival. Thank the Creator at all times for all life.

Love, and express that love.

Be humble. Humility is the gift of wisdom and understanding.

Be kind with one's self and with others.

Share feelings and personal concerns and commitments.

Be honest with one's self and with others. Be responsible for these sacred instructions and share them with other nations.[33]

These instructions are a means to "mend the hoop" of all nations, to establish brotherhood within the family of man, and return to a spiritual way of life. The Lakota – Sioux said:

Only after the last tree has been cut down,
Only after the last river has been poisoned,
Only after the last fish has been caught,
Only then will you find
That money cannot be eaten…

The ones that matter most are the children. They are the true human beings.

With all things and in all things, we are relatives

The meaning of the name Hopi or Hopituh Shi-nu-mu, is "Peaceful People" or "Peaceful Little Ones." Their legendary beginning taught them to live humbly and peacefully. If they did not live this way, the Spirit Lords took their name away and they received another name. Today, many people use names interchangeably such as Navajo, Anasazi, or Zuni. The Anasazi existed around two thousand years ago and are supposed to be the ancestors of modern Indian tribes like the Hopi, Zuni and Pueblo. However, the Hopi do not acknowledge this ancestry. Navajo use the word Anasazi for some of their ancestors, meaning "ancient enemies".

The Hopi lived for several thousand years in the same location where today, four states meet - Arizona, Utah, Colorado and New Mexico. According to their legends or teachings, they live spiritually on the planet, setting up communities on three mesas - the First, Second and the Third. One of these Mesa is sacred, with no visitors allowed. Tourists can go on the other two, providing they do not bring cameras or recorders.

The origin tales of the Hopi are similar to many other cultures. If you ask them about it, they will say "White men come, white men go, but we shall always be here." Their creation legend takes people through Four Worlds. The First World of "Endless Space" was a pure and happy universe. It was destroyed by fire. The Second World known as "Dark Midnight" was destroyed by cold and ice (our ice age?) The Third World was destroyed by floods. The Fourth World known as "The World Complete," is harsh with violent weather. The Hopi say this is our present world. The Fifth World is just beginning.

> Roughly, 7 latitudinal lines and 170 longitudinal separate the Hopi settlement in the United States and the Tibetan settlement in China. The Hopi mesas are located approximately at 35° N - 111° W°. The Tibetan locations are around 28° N - 84°E. Both nations honor four rules of life, which are:

- Respect for life and wisdom
- Lack of individual ownership and greed
- Sense of destiny, place and freedom of choice
- Commitment to live in nature's cycles.

Sometimes, we discover the vocabulary is also opposing. Sun and moon are contrast and the words in both languages are opposing. The Tibetan name for *sun* is the same as the Hopi word for *moon*. Hopi *sun* is Tibetan *moon*. Three other global nations give us wisdom and principles similar to the Tibetan and the Hopi. These are – the Dogon people in Mali, Africa - 12° N - 8° W. In Colombia next Santa Marta, the Kogi live at approximately 11° N - 74° W. Lastly, the Waitaha live in New Zealand at approximately 46° S - 170° E.

The point here is the five guardian settlements of vital information are located on opposing sides of the planet. Hopi, Tibetan, Dogon, Kogi and Waitaha share similar wisdom ensuring all inhabitants on the earth receive similar lessons.

The focus of the Hopi religion involves ***Kachinas*** representing the spirit essence of everything in nature. They are multi-tasked ranging from ancestral spirits, deities of the natural world, or intermediaries between man and gods. These Kachina Gods or dolls may bring in rain, punish transgressions or cure disease. The Kachina dolls appear either as a masked or costumed individual or as a small figurine representing spirits.

Kachina spirits live in their own land within the San Francisco Peaks for six months of the year, August through January. At the Winter Solstice, they merge with the Hopi people, remaining there until the following year when it is time to return to the Peaks.

The Hopi creation story takes earth life through a succession of underworlds, each of which is associated with a specific direction, colour, mineral, plant and bird.

The *First World* is of Endless Space. It was a pure and happy universe, destroyed by fire.

The *Second World* is a Dark Midnight. Cold and ice destroyed it.

The *Third World* is the Chosen People who survived in anthills, climbing up a ladder made of cane. Floods destroyed this world.

The *Fourth World* is a harsh environment. The complete world is a harsh environment, filled with deserts, marshes, mountains and violent weather. The Hopi say this world is now ending and the *Fifth World* is beginning. [34]

Masau'u, the Fire God, is the caretaker of the Fourth World. He left our world four guidelines that he calls **The Hopi Way of Life:**

- *Simplicity*
- *Brotherhood*
- *Love*
- *Peace*

These four guidelines come as individual principles but they are sequential, it is difficult to have one unless individuals and communities accomplish the previous guidelines.

(1) Living simple lives, not demanding an excess or luxury, lead to a life of cooperation or brotherhood.

(2) We strive for a common goal.

(3) We accept and display love for and between humanity and all life.

(4) Peace occurs. It is impossible to fight with someone when you truly love them. It may be a cliché but it is so valid. People may fight even if they love one another but is it usually over issues omitted from the basic values of our past. Here, fighting is violent and bitter, not simply a disagreement.

We hear these principles individually and do not worry about applying them. The energy flows from one to the next. It does the modern person well if they pause and remember these steps for a quality life. We find the basis of all religions, old or new, includes these principles. The ancient ones contain them so it is up to us to realign our lifestyle to reap the benefit.

MOHAWK

The Mohawk Nation or the *people of the flint* are one of five founding Nations of the Iroquois League. The Mohawk name initially came from the Algonquin tribe, picked up by the Europeans who had difficulty pronouncing Kanien'kehake. The original five Nations in the Confederacy were the Mohawk, the Cayuga, the Seneca, the Oneida, and the Onondaga.

Known as "keeper of the Eastern door" since the League members were spread out from East to west, they were also identified as "people of the Longhouse". Their communal dwelling was long and low.

There is a Mohawk prophecy known as the Seventh Generation. They warned all future Indian generations. This prophecy foretold ten events would occur after living in close contact to Europeans. These are:

- The trees would die
- Animals would be born deformed.
- Huge monsters would tear open the earth
- Rivers would burn
- Air would burn the eyes of man.
- Birds would fall from the sky
- Fish would die in the water
- Man would be ashamed of his treatment of mother and the Earth
- After rising up and demanding their rights, the Earth would be respected and restored again.
- All Indian nations would turn to the *eastern door* for guidance.

The seventh generation's prophecy is the child of today.[35] A set of commandments from the Mohawk nation of North America are similar to those of many indigenous nations. These are:

- Treat the Earth and all that dwell thereon with respect
- Remain close to the Great Spirit
- Show great respect for fellow beings
- Work together for the benefit of all Mankind

- Give assistance and kindness wherever needed
- Do what you know to be right
- Look after the well-being of Mind and Body
- Dedicate a share of your efforts to the greater good
- Be truthful and honest at all times
- Take full responsibility for your actions

SEMINOLE

Most of this book studies people who either lived before the Common Era or have roots extending into this era. It is important, that we recognize nations existing today who are anxious to preserve their beliefs, and customs just as their elders taught them to the younger generations. Today, Seminole natives have no record, either written or oral, as to when their teachings originated, but they knew their beliefs, customs and values were important and must be retained.

Seminole Indians live in a region of Florida, approximately 100 miles northeast of Miami. They are knowledgeable of the everglades (marshland) ecosystem and the healing properties of its plants. They display pride, knowledge, and gentle spirit.

The Seminole nation came into existence during the 18th century. They are mainly an amalgamation of people of the Creek Nation from what we now call Georgia, Mississippi, Alabama and Florida. In spite of numerous battles, they were never conquered and became known as "The Unconquered People." The new name became *Seminole* from the Mikasuki (linguistic spelling) and the Creek word *semvnole* meaning "undomesticated" or "untamed". Gradually the meaning shifted to the Spanish word *cimarrón* which means "wild" or "runaway."

The Seminole are a federally recognized and economic entity of about 3,000 Native Americans. They live in six locations: Hollywood, Brighton, Big Cypress, Tampa, Immokalee and Fort Pierce locations – all in Southern Florida. Because they were undefeated, they do not come under any political jurisdiction. They are the only American Indian never to have signed a formal peace treaty with the United States. They have sovereignty over their tribal lands and an economy based on tobacco, tourism and gambling. In the mid-50s the tribes established self-reliance with economic and education programs separate from the country's systems.

Unlike other indigenous clans in North America, the Seminole clans are matrilineal. Here, inheritance, land, and affiliation come through the women. They may hold higher status because of land and resources, but the men do hold the political reins. The men consult the women of the community before making a community decision. This situation is in transition, some of the women are gradually losing their status position in the society.

Most tribes in North America are reluctant to share their healing remedies for fear of misuse by uneducated. This was not the philosophy of the Seminole.

One of the elders, Alice Snow,[36] was anxious to share her life teachings. She began as a child learning from her Mother about the wonders of the wild. Later, she became very concerned about her people retaining the wisdom. Susan Enns Stans, a assistant professor of Anthropology at Florida Gulf Coast University in Ft. Myers, helped record her heritage.

Her work and knowledge spread to other experts, including an ethno botanist, Gary J. Martin., who says in his book: "*Ethno* is a popular prefix these days, because it is a short way of saying 'that's the way other people look at the world." [37] And so, preserving indigenous knowledge becomes even more important. The Seminole nation remembers their history with pride; accepting the new and modern world. We may not return to their remedies but I believe they teach us a great deal. We can combine modern remedies with local herbal cures

Alice gives a variety of remedies in her book. They may seem quaint but they are effective, local and readily available. They come from your local woods or your local herb shop. When you purchase and use produce from local regions, they are much more effective, quicker acting and *alive*. The recipes work with body, mind and spirit.

NOTE: Although they are highly effective and available, be sure to contact an herbal store or health practitioner before using any native remedy.

General remedies[38]

This list of plants becomes useful for healing and wherever possible, the English name provides easier understanding.

Ak-tv-pē-hv-rak-ko	For sores use a piece of the root
a-tak-rv lvs-te	Kidney problems
Huckleberry	good for anything

Blind deer plant	Cough medicine
Deep potato	Knots in stomach
Rabbit medicine	Muscle cramps
Pine	For sores: crush and boil
White bud on pine	To clean sores
Hog's plum	For arthritis
Deer ears	For arthritis of bones: use whole plant
Yellow Pine	For arthritis mix with alcohol and apply when it turns black
Sunflower,	For pain and swelling in the breast black-eyed Susan
Es-pas-kv-ha-kv	Kidney problems
Moccasin vine or	For snake bites climbing hemp weed
Sundew	For ringworms
Frost weed	Cold medicine
Quail bean	For high blood pressure
Peppermint	For congestion
Owl threads	For cramps
Owl boots	Will force labour
Long ghost hair	For depression
Pv-he hvt-ke,	For headache pv-he hvt-ku-ce
Red fungus	For ringworm
Buttonbush	For alligator sickness
Beggar's lice	When don't feel like eating
White ash from OK	For aching bones and broken bones
Bay	Main ingredient in medicines
Water hemlock	For arthritis pain or itch.
Lizard's tail	treatments after a death
Cedar	Keeps bad spirits away
Sassafras	For cough or diarrhea
Ya-mē-li-kv	For swelling
Buffalo medicine	Stop heavy menstrual flow

These remedies transcend time. The plants still grow and the solutions are still applicable. They come from the plants and herbs around the community. Each land has similar solutions to share with their friends, clan and families. There are remedies other indigenous nations use for healing. Perhaps someday they will share so that residents living near them will be able to receive folk healing.

Alice Snow also shares her life wisdom. Some of the Rules are mystical while others are more practical.

Alice's Seminole Rules of Life[39]

- "You have to teach your children what the elders taught us' how to get married, how to comb your hair and how to behave when kinfolk die."
- "Your eyes reveal the end of the world. You can see the reading in your eyes, and it will be the end of your culture. "
- "When visitors come to our camp, we show respect. We see them coming from far off and walk to meet them. We would say to the young children, "Go get some cold water, they are going to be thirsty." We give them cold water to drink. We put coffee on the fire. We have no doors, so we could not ask them to come in. We would have food on the table and ask them to eat before they leave. Today, people met you at the door and say, "What do you want?" They should invite them in like we learned."
- "When you go to someone's home, sit down and don't move around or touch anything. When we (the children) stayed at home, the seven brothers and sisters played together, but not in someone else's camp."
- "Whatever someone says to you, don't get mad, just go. It will come back to them later."

As I wrote *Inner Bridges*, I stressed the importance of living according the region where you were born. We see this wisdom with the Inuit, the Haida, the Hopi and the Seminole. The four regions we now know as the Arctic, the Pacific Northwest of North America, the Redlands of Colorado and Arizona and Florida, provide vivid examples. Current records state that the location and age of these tribes does not go back very far. However, their verbal history takes them farther back.

The modern world does not consider three hundred years a long time. *our* modern world extends much farther back. This is where the bulk of damage to our world originates. Yet, for 300 years, the indigenous of the Western World were able to preserve their teachings in spite of a "modern" culture surrounding them. Yet natives developed a lifestyle consisting of living their heritage and simultaneously living a compliant lifestyle. Non-indigenous people seem to spend their time concentrating on increasing their busyness, causing more damage to our society and our planet.

Part V - Mesoamerica

Archeologists recognize the Olmec as the predecessors of the Aztec Zapotec and Maya civilizations. They lived in south-central Mexico from 1500 BCE to about 400 BCE passing social procedures and practices to subsequent societies.

They share common features such as theocratic governments (subject to divine laws) with other regional cultures of the era: the Chupicuaro, the Colimas, the Guerrero, the Mixtec, and the Teotihuacan.[40]. All societies used the symbolic owl, dove and the butterfly illustrative teachings as predictors of how digressing from fundamental laws and values produce the Earth's demise.

Contrary to archeological dating, Zecharia Sitchin takes their world back to 3000 BCE.[41]. In his book, *The Lost Realms,* Sitchin mentions Astronaut Gordon Cooper's, discovery of pyramid-shaped mounds, artifacts and human relics in the Gulf of Mexico that were 5,000 years old, or dating from 3000 BCE.

In Gordon Cooper's publication, *A Leap of Faith,* he corroborates Sitchin's estimate of the age of the Olmec era. Both researchers, Sitchin and Cooper, base the age on an Egyptian-Thoth connection with Mesoamerica. Egyptian documentation tells of the Egyptian banishment of Thoth around 3100 BCE. But where did Thoth go? One theory is he and his African followers travelled to a new land called Mesoamerica and these dark-skinned African followers were the *Olmecs* of Mesoamerica.

Skeptics question this theory as highly improbable. But several details support this association. First, the number 52 is a powerful, secret number of both the Mesoamerican cultures and the Egyptian god, Thoth. Both cultures gave Gods the same name. The Egyptian god of science and the calendar *is* Thoth; the Mayan god of light *is* Quetzalcoatl. Subsequent literature then tells us that Quetzalcoatl and Thoth are the same God.

The second fact supporting this connection comes from the Olmec heads. We find large heads attributed to the Olmec people around San Lorenzo and La Venta, Mexico. Some of the stone heads look oriental, leading to an assumption that these people must have come from China. The similarity of the carving techniques used on these heads and the sculptures on Easter Island and Australia, substantiate this theory. Yet, other heads appear patterned after the leaders of the African migration and look distinctly black African, supporting *that* premise.

Whether the Olmec people came from Asia or Egypt is a mystery. If they were Asian, they could travel across the Bering Land Bridge over the Bering Strait, wandering down through North America, leaving a legacy of indigenous nations scattered across the continent. Alternately, if they were seafarers, they could sail over the Pacific Ocean from Asia, straying off course through the Polynesia islands arriving in Central America.

If the Olmec people came from Africa, traveling across the *Atlantic* Ocean, then how and why did the black looking Olmec heads end up on lands around the Pacific Ocean?

One last possibility is a specific group settled in this region without any connection whatsoever to any other species living on this planet.

These options illustrate a common basis and feasibility. It does not matter whether they moved over the Pacific or Atlantic. What does matter is the connection between cultures.

The Zapotec and the Mixtec people, both residents in the Valley of Oaxaca, believe their ancestors emerged from the Earth after living in caves for centuries. Their leaders claim they came from supernatural beings, first living in the clouds and later entering a human form. The Zapotec people were hunter-gatherers, dependent upon rain and light. They relied upon two principal deities for these elements. Cocijo supplied the Rain, (similar to the Aztec God Tlaloc), and Coquihani supplied the Light. People today may not worship these specific gods but occasionally calling upon two deities from the past, Cocijo and Coquihani encourages the requirements for good living – rain and light.

The cultures of Mesoamerica left us a strong legacy. We credit the Maya with developing astronomy, calendrical systems, hieroglyphic writing, ceremonial architecture, and masonry without metal tools. Perhaps this wisdom originates earlier than Mayan society, perhaps not. However, the conquering Spaniards of the 1500s forbade these people to practice their beliefs. The Spaniard goal was blocking all knowledge. Consequently, the Maya Elders took knowledge and beliefs into seclusion. Because of this action, many historians and researchers thought the culture was extinct. However, during the past 50 years segments of the Maya society re-established contact with the outside world, sharing their wisdom. This reconnection comes about for two reasons.

The first reason is the Maya people no longer feel the same persecution. Initially, when the Spanish arrived in Central America, they met beliefs contrary to their own, causing a sense of vulnerability. In spite of their powerful position, they needed to strengthen their identity. Thus, they did not give the Maya an opportunity to tell their story. Today, while Mesoamerica equality is not optimal, it has improved.

Established indigenous societies around the globe split their communities into two groups, predestined elders and the mass population. The Maya, just as the Hopi, Waitaha and Kogi have a small group of leaders remaining true to their long-established values and knowledge. The remainder of the population blends the beliefs of the past with the new. Many recognize the importance of honoring the teachings passed to them by these shamans or elders, their leaders. They exemplify the truths from the past and illustrate how we can incorporate them into our present living.

In 1998, spiritual leaders from around the world created an *independent nonprofit educational organization for the advancement of Spiritual, Holistic, and Environmental awareness.*[42] A participant in this organization, Hunbatz Men, an Elder of the Mayan people, wrote *The Cosmic Return of Spiritual Education*[43]. Just as elders from other indigenous people of the world, he recognized the need to warn the people of the world. He said:

"The whole of humanity today needs the education coming from the cosmos, because, as it is known, the education of modern civilization is not complying with the universal creator's correct education mandates. …Our obligation is to remember."

This paper shows the significance of bringing knowledge and skills from the past into the present. Mayan Elder Hunbatz Men recognizes the importance of this cosmic knowledge and frequently spoke of capturing our *Ancient Wisdoms*. Traditional religions attempt this but some remain stuck in structure and organization. Elder Hunbatz includes information in this article about Lemuria and Atlantis, the lands beneath the seas. He talks about the Magnetic Poles, their importance and how they exist in different parts of the Earth.

When travelers leave each location, they take the wisdom and power of the location with them.

This excerpt from this *Spiritual Education* shows merging of past and present wisdom and nations of the globe sharing their wisdom. Note also how the knowledge of the Owl and the peace of the Dove blend in this teachings:

" *Before the Maya arrived in the sacred lands where today we trod and live, they were in other lands that today are under the waters of the sea. They immigrated to many places as well long ago, as did a lot of people of different ethnic groups. In very remote times, they lived in places with very high mountains sometimes covered with many trees and other times with a lot of ice; they were in desert lands that sometimes became very fertile lands. Many of those lands arose from the waters, others disappeared with time; some transformed into very big lands, others into small lands.*

"The Maya can remember the last great sacred lands of the continent of Lemuria, or Lemulia in the Mayan language, there where the cosmic religion that came from another continent that today rests under the waters of the sea was understood and practiced.

"…In the times of Lemulia, the symbols represented the summary of wisdom. They also represented religion. They worshipped the symbols, not like some religions that commercialize these sacred symbols nowadays. The true sense of these symbols comes from Lemulia. Still the majority of humanity cannot understand them. In order for the human being to understand these symbols, he has to enter into the land of the cosmic initiation.

"Some indigenous groups, such as the Hopis, were in the sacred lands of Lemulia. They came from the south of the American continent in order to settle down in what today is the United States of North America. When they arrived in these lands, many of the lands were under the sea. The Hopis have in their registered memory the big changes that have occurred to the sacred lands of the north of this continent of America.

"Every several thousands of years, the Magnetic Pole of Religion arises in a different part of the Earth. When this happens, the ancient wise men of knowledge travel, taking with them the previous Magnetic Religious power that they took care of in order to deposit it in the new location. When in Lemulia this great power indicated by the cosmos and Mother Earth arose, people with high degrees of initiation traveled to help ease the activation of this new sacred place where the New Spiritual Education would arise.

"Through the passing of the millennia, Lemulia fulfilled its sacred mission as educator of humanity. From here arose many teachers whose names are not remembered by human beings today. From this continent, we inherited many symbols of cosmic wisdom that are still used today. When the time of Lemulia completed its cycle indicated by the Mayan calendars, Lemulia returned under the waters of the sea.

"The Itzaes can remember when we were in the continent of Atlantis or ATLANTIHA in the Mayan language. For thousands and thousands of years we lived in these sacred lands where we ended up understanding the reason for our existence on these lands created by our supreme HUNAB K'U. In those remote times, our sacred religious symbols were in all the locations of the continent of ATLANTIHA and those that inhabited these lands could understand these symbols that represent all. When ATLANTIHA arose from the waters of the sea, many teachers came to deposit the religious sacred wisdom to this new place; they came following a cosmic order. The LemuliaNS were present in order to deposit the great power to the ATLANTIHANS. With rites and ceremonies, they made the transitions of power. Then Mother Earth was pleased by the great respect that was given, for in that time the human being understood when Mother Earth gave an order to change the Magnetic Pole.

"In lands of the continent of the ATLANTIHA, many communities understood the cosmic spiritual work. Inside these communities, the old Itzaes, for many hundreds of thousands of years, cohabited with this cosmic wisdom in the continent of ATLANTIHA. The cycle indicated cosmically by the calendars also marked that the continent of ATLANTIHA would arrive at its end. When this began to happen, many communities immigrated to other places. In this way, great ATLANTIHA arose from the sea and in this way returned to the sea. The Magnetic Pole of Spiritual Religious Education had already fulfilled its cycle of educating humanity, and cosmically the order had already been given that this great power would have to be in another location on Mother Earth.

"Many teachers of ATLANTIHA immigrated to other lands and took the spiritual and scientific knowledge with them to their new establishments. The ATLANTIHAN/Itza community also had to immigrate to new lands. Here it is where the great continent that is today called America arose, but the original name of these sacred lands for us, the Itzaes of tradition, is TAMAUNCHAN. Before settling in these lands that we inhabit today, the Itzaes traveled to many places, among them are mentioned the sacred lands of today's indigenous Kogis.

"When the indigenous Kogis-Taironas arrived in the high lands of what are today the countries of Venezuela and Colombia, the forests of today in the country of Brazil did not exist. This fact indicates to us great antiquity. These indigenous

brothers settled in the high lands of Sierra Madre of Santa Marta; these are geographically located between the western part of Venezuela and the eastern part of Colombia. What is today the Yucatán Peninsula, México, and the lands of Central America were under the waters of the sea. When these sacred lands arose from the waters, then the Itzaes arrived. They already knew what would be the destiny of these new lands.

"The Magnetic Pole of Religious Education of ATLANTIHA had already reached its end; Mother Earth and the cosmos had already indicated which would be the new location. ... The Itzaes brought the sacred symbols of the inherited wisdom of ATLANTIHA to deposit here.

"The Itza brought the knowledge of ATLANTIHA, but being in these new lands of TAMUANCHAN, developed more spiritual knowledge together with the Maya.

"In this manner, the Maya inherited the knowledge of the ATLANTIHAS; for many thousands of years this Magnetic Pole of Spiritual Education was in the power of the Maya. They, with what they learned from the Itzaes in their time together, developed this cosmic wisdom even more. Then they created with their sacred language the word of HUNAB K'U, so that with this word they would represent the great concept of the creation of the universe"

Later in his paper, he reminds us of how we recall "*a little of our Mayan cosmic solar memory*" and understand so little of what we forgot.

Some readers may regard Hunbatz' writing as mythical because there is no physical proof of Lemuria or Atlantis. Yet it makes sense; therefore, this writing must be factual.

The second reason for the Maya Elders re-connecting with the outside world is introducing the Maya teachings and stressing the importance of 2012 to global communities. The Mayan people also have predestined leaders; the *Wise Ones*, who learn their calendrical astrology, interpreting the messages and passing them to their people. After that, they guide their people toward appropriate life adjustments. In this way, they heal the planet and free the people. Native people historically know the significance of listening to the oracles. It seems the Western world is just beginning to understand this importance of their teachings. Mayan ancient messages and teachings still apply to modern society. One effective tool is the 52 Full Moon.

The GRAND MAYA ITZA COUNCIL created this list of sacred sites where leaders complete healing work through the 52 Full Moon Ceremonies taking us to 2012. This means that five initiate people from the indigenous of the world take spiritual journeys to sacred sites around the globe.

When Mayan Elder Hunbatz Men gave permission to include this data, he included the gentle reminder that we "need to remember our ancestors' past so we can understand our future". Participating in a spiritual journey that assists in Earth healing, does not require our presence at a specific site, or being part of the Council. Simply focusing on the location allows energy from each person to flow. The more we participate, the greater the benefit will be to everything on the planet.

Many of the chosen locations historically suffered wars and battles; however, they still carry the *light* of the Universe. The Council members carry memories of their past and work with spiritual leaders of each community to complete a healing similar to the *light healing* of long ago. Respect for the Full Moon is universal. It is a key of unity. To share in this healing, follow these simple steps at each Full Moon date listed in the table.

Four steps for participating in Full Moon Ceremony

1. Find a quiet location where you can meditate without interruption
2. If possible, wear white clothes.
3. Lie face up with your head pointing north
4. Clear your mind. Think on the location, sending love and peace to the current location, healing all wounds.

Elder HunbatzMen's introduction to the Full Moon ceremony Calendar is:

"…The GRAND MAYA ITZA COUNCIL feels proud to distribute this list of sacred sites to all the Initiates and Workers of Light from all around the world. These sites must be used to do the work of returning of the Great Spirit in order to prevent our mother Earth from the unfortunate events foreseen to happen in the year 2012.

"We the MAYA ITZA people are very aware of the bad news and disasters that are going to occur in the year 2012 as foreseen by many people. According to many of them, the world will come to an end due to phenomena like the ones mentioned in the Apocalypse of the Christian Bible.

"We the Mayans who have not been cultured by the Western Culture do not agree with all the negative things our sacred calendars have been involved in. That is the main reason why we are distributing this list of sacred sites where we are planning to do our spiritual work.

"Every Full Moon we are going to make a spiritual journey to every one of the sacred sites on the list, starting our first ceremony on November 13, 2008, and continuing that way until carrying out the last ceremony on December 28, 2012, which is the actual date when our Sister and Mother Moon is going to perform the big change on the mankind's mentality.

"The ancient Mayas used to make these spiritual journeys to the ancient ceremonial centers in order to activate all the sacred sites from all around the world. This is the best to contribute to the salvation of our Mother Earth as well as the sacred human race and all the living beings."

The Full Moon ceremony schedule:

SACRED SITE	COUNTRY	FULL MOON DATE
CUNAGUA	CUBA	AUG. 06, 2009
CHACO CANYON	UNITED STATES	SEP. 04, 2009
CHICHEN ITZA	MEXICO	OCT. 04, 2009
DEBRECEN	HUNGARY	NOV. 02, 2009
ESFAHAN	IRAN	DEC. 02, 2009
GRAN PIRAMIDE KEOPS	EGYPT	DEC. 31, 2009
GUAYAMA	PUERTO RICO	JAN. 30, 2010
HATOR DENDERA	EGYPT	FEB. 28, 2010
HELFRANTZKIRCH	GERMANY	MAR. 30, 2010
IZMIR	TURKEY	APR. 28, 2010
JIBHAFANTA	MONGOLIA	MAY 27, 2010
KALACMUL	MEXICO	JUN. 26, 2010
KRAPINA	CROATIA	JUL. 26, 2010
KURUMAN	SOUTH AFRICA	AUG. 24, 2010
LATAKIA	SYRIA	SEP. 23, 2010
LHASA	TIBET	OCT. 23, 2010
LUBAANTUN	BELIZE	NOV. 21, 2010

MACHU PICCHU	PERU	DEC. 21, 2010
MALAKAL	SUDAN	JAN. 19, 2011
MAORI	NEW ZEALAND	FEB. 18, 2011
MEXIANA	BRAZIL	MAR. 19, 2011
MIXCO VIEJO	GUATEMALA	APR. 18, 2011
MOUNDVILLE - AL	UNITED STATES	MAY 17, 2011
NAMPULA	MOZAMBIQUE	JUN. 15, 2011
OLLANTAYTAMBO	PERU	JUL. 15, 2011
PARANA	ARGENTINA	AUG. 13, 2011
PIRAMIDES DE GÜIMAR	SPAIN	SEP. 12, 2011
SERPENT MOUND	UNITED STATES	OCT. 12, 2011
SILBURY HILL	ENGLAND	NOV. 10, 2011
SIPAN	PERU	DEC. 10, 2011
STONEHENGE	ENGLAND	JAN. 09, 2012
SURAKARTA	INDONESIA	FEB. 07, 2012
TAJ MAHAL	INDIA	MAR. 08, 2012
TANGER	ALGERIA	APR. 06, 2012
TAZUMAL	EL SALVADOR	MAY 06, 2012
TEOTIHUACAN	MEXICO	JUN. 04, 2012
TIHUANAKU	BOLIVIA	JUL. 03, 2012
TIKAL	GUATEMALA	AUG. 02, 2012
TONGARIYAMA	JAPAN	AUG. 31, 2012
TUCUPITA	VENEZUELA	SEP. 30, 2012
UXMAL	MEXICO	OCT. 29, 2012
VAASA	FINLAND	NOV. 28, 2012
VIJAYANAGAR	INDIA	DEC. 28, 2012

Mankind needs to remember both the objective and our goal.

The objective of the GRAND MAYA ITZA COUNCIL is stimulating sacred sites all around the world. The goal of our participation is activating a big change on mankind's mentality.

This information comes from the predestined leaders of the Mayan society's Elders who decided that stepping out of seclusion would benefit all mankind. This is only one step. Other steps include introducing key tools such as the Mayan calendar, the crystal skull legacy, society rules, spiritual as well as healing remedies. The Maya teachers exemplify the knowledge of the owls, the peace of the doves and the transformation of the butterfly. A rewarding outcome of their stepping out is giving the Caucasian people an overview of the three *white wing* images from the Maya perspective.

The Mayan culture teaches the significance and importance of settling near pure natural springs and volcanos. We find ancient Mayan ruins in or near mountain ranges; the most famous region being the Yucatan Peninsula. Today, the peninsula appears quite flat with small mounds scattered throughout, leaving no physical evidence of the powerful volcanoes energizing societies long ago. The mounds suggest the possibility of old, dormant volcanoes but the key geological proof is in the cenotes. Cenotes are a type of the freshwater-filled limestone sinkhole predominantly found in the Yucatán and Caribbean region. For the ancient Maya, they are the only resource for fresh water and frequently provided entrances to underlying cave and river systems. Consequently, millions of years ago, this was the travel route used by the Mayans through the country. They are magical, enigmatic and sacred places of the Maya.

Here are several facts pertaining to their formation.

First, sinkholes or cenotes usually form quickly through the collapse of surface soil and rocks, sometimes with underground rock giving way.

Second, cenotes contain pure groundwater and are usually found in areas where there are few surface rivers available to provide pure water to a community.

Third, cenotes can exist for thousands of years, occasionally fluctuating in size, depending upon the spring water feed.

Fourth, they may stabilize and become a permanent lake or pond in the community.

Lastly, in cenotes, we discover underground caverns providing a new fresh water source or other ancient wonders.

Elders keep r*itual* cenotes separate from *domestic* cenotes. Domestic cenotes provide the drinking water for a community, necessitating purity. However, spiritual leaders at ritual cenotes call in God support and cosmic messages. Leaders use ritual cenotes for the global Full Moon ceremonies. The Maya recognize the importance of keeping their water supply uncontaminated; over the millennia, there are times when these cenotes were the only resource for fresh pure water. Perhaps this is where we learned the significance of unpolluted water sources. The Elders recognize the need of resource management in times of drought. They know major settlements require access to fresh water supplies and often built their cities around these natural sources. Eons ago, residents in cenote regions did not understand how these mysterious formations came to be and the cenotes acquired a spiritual air. To honor the Gods, inhabitants credited spiritual energy to these mysterious water sources, and they became the known ritual sites. It soon became essential to the communal balance of life that sacred cenotes remain separate from the community. The Maya believe these pools are gateways to the afterlife. For this reason, they toss valuable items into the sacred locations as well as sacrificial ritual beings.

At these ritual cenotes, the Elders and Shamans appeal to their Gods -- God of Rain, Thunder, Lightning and Wind. Members of local communities, go to nearby ritual cenotes calling for sacred blessings for the Full Moon ceremonies

These days if we get an opportunity to go down into the cenotes and wander through the ancient wonders, we see majestic stalagmites and stalactites throughout caverns; frequently taking them for granted. The only illumination comes through small holes in the ceiling. Residents honor this light.

The *Crystal Caves* in north-central Mexico are not accredited cenotes but we find selenite (gypsum) points estimated as being more than 600,000 years old. Hydrothermal (hot water) fluids flowing from the volcanic emissions of the Earth formed these crystals. Life forms have been on the earth longer than 600,000 years. Therefore, if humans lived on the earth at this time, is this when we began using hot water in our daily life.

This information is pertinent to modern living for several reasons. We need drinking water. We need pure, unpolluted water. We need alkaline, not acidic water, more natural the better.

Archeological evidence of settlements such as Chitchen Itza shows us where dormant and flowing underground spring water source exist. We learn how to check out natural resources, paying attention to the cenotes, or sinkholes that provide special links between the Earth's surface and groundwater resources.

Today, modern people deal with polluted resources and continually search out unpolluted sources. Rural and isolated communities already have a pure water supply that is alkaline, not acidic. The remainder of the population depends upon technical knowledge, adding chemicals to achieve the desired stage. Ritualistic sites and sacred supply centers exist around the planet. We just do not know where to look for them. Our ancient settlers did not have to search for, or produce, pure alkaline water. They knew what regions had the abundance of spring water and volcanoes. I feel that the original settlements on this planet were where the water and warmth was at its premium. Mesoamerica is one region where people settled.

Throughout this text, we refer to four settlements. Two timekeepers and spiritual leaders correspond to these. First, Gerardo Barrios Kaanek, a Mayan Timekeeper of Guatemala, includes in his creation story of the planet, four continents and four locations.[44] He gives the four *earth* continents as:

1. Kax Uleu – Atlantis, located in the Atlantic Caribbean Islands from Florida to Venezuela
2. Sak Uleu – Yis, located at the North Pole
3. Akab Uleu – Mu, located south of Africa
4. Rax Uleu – Lemuria, located between Australia and the islands north-east of present day Australia.

We view them as:

1. Kax **Uleu**, the red earth;
2. Sak **Uleu**, the white earth;
3. **Akab Uleu**, the black earth
4. Rax **Uleu**, the yellow earth.

Another writer, Aluna Joy Yaxk'in defines these earths as races. Yaxk'in is an internationally known spiritual speaker, writer and a spiritual guide to Peru, Mexico, Guatemala, and the Southwest USA. Her published books and articles, available world-wide include *Mayan-Pleiadian Cosmology.*

These earth races read as:

1– Kax Uleu, -- the Atlantic, Caribbean location (red race)

2– Sak Uleu -- the Arctic region, (white race)

3 - Akab Uleu -- Mu, Australia, South Africa, India (black race)

4 – Rax Uleu --, Asian, Polynesia, Australia (yellow race)

Here we have three independent definitions of four settlement sites; A Mayan timekeeper (Kaanek), a spiritual guide (Yaxk'in), and channeled wisdom of the *four* initial locations for colonization. The channeled data of the four initial human residencies goes back many years.

Kaanek describes the vortices on the planet, as *four centers of light* for future settlements of knowledge. His definition of a vortex matches the energy spots or the hot springs and volcanos. His description includes global vortices with ancient settlements nearby. While Kaanek refers to vortices in Mexico, Greece, Egypt and Tibet, homes of the ancient cultures on our planet, his publications concern only those identified by Maya explorers. These Kaanek's vortex regions correlate with the archaeological theories of the Olmecs' ancestral settlements. The African link correlates with Egypt. The Asian link correlates with Tibet and the Australian Polynesian link correlates with Lemuria. These ancient settlements surround ancient volcanoes on our planet and out of these regions came three societies matching the theoretical physical image of the Olmec.

There is a continual debate and mystery about the origin of Olmec people. Modern historians credit the Maya with many accomplishments, suggesting these accomplishments evolved out of Olmec society. If this knowledge transfer did not occur, why are the Maya people patterning their teachings after a society without any connection to their heritage? The Maya had writing around 2300 BCE and used their writing skills to record knowledge they learned. They successfully learned how to combine life recording and the benefits of incorporating ancient wisdom and knowledge of *their* ancestors into routine activity. It seems that people today do not analyze what our ancestors learn and just what will work in our modern society. Many traits will work and enhance today's social living.

The Olmecs did not have any apparent starting point. They just seemed to "be". Around 1862, archeologists revealed one of many extremely large head in Veracruz State of Mexico. The origin continues as a mystery and source of speculation. Their title originated in the language spoken in south-central Mexico -- Náhuatl. The head creators earned the name **Olmecs**, meaning *country of rubber* after the large quantity of rubber trees in this region. No more artifacts surfaced but some occasional disconnected data surfaced.

Researchers have so many unanswered questioned.

- Where did they come from?
- Why was there no evidence of children?"
- Why was everyone in the region older than ten years old?

Scientists finally deciphered the language and writing systems of a mysterious civilization name was Xi (pronounced Shi).

XI or SHI is similar to the Chinese word "CHI or QI". We are all residents of this planet, united as one. Therefore, it makes sense that two cultures on opposite sides of the globe would refer to themselves as *"the natural energy of the Universe."* This is the Chinese translation of XI.

The similarity of these names explains the spiritual beliefs of two worlds. The energy, though natural and physical, carries a spiritual or supernatural component and is part of a metaphysical belief system. According to Chinese philosophy, this **prana** or life force is in all living things. This belief exists in many cultures around the globe. This connection brings the spirituality of Chinese and Mesoamerican worlds together.

The latest culture in Mesoamerica, the Maya dates back approximately 4500 years. Historically, the Maya are distinct and powerful, incorporating rituals and beliefs of others as they traveled their migratory journey. They *inherited* the inventions and ideas of earlier civilizations and developed innovative steps forward. They may have modified or streamlined many inventions but invention credit involves more than one culture. There is more than one source of the evolving truths of the region. There was no consensus amongst researchers except for one point. The Olmecs alone have the title *Mother Culture*. The modern custodians of these gifts are the Maya people.

Conquering nations or tribes assimilate portions of dominated cultures, producing grey areas in history. In each diverse culture, the Zapotec, Mixtec, Toltec, Aztec, and Maya, even the conquering Spaniards, you will find Olmec characteristics. Conquering societies either destroy the evidence, or adopt and modify practices and beliefs of the subjugated people. This last approach is a proven way of getting a conquered people to accept the aggressor.

When the Spaniards arrived in Mesoamerica, they brought their own calendar but after looking at the existing calendar, they chose festival dates on that calendar to become holidays.

Most indigenous cultures of the world center their lifestyle on their personal beliefs and Gods. The Maya are no exception. They believe humans have an inherent responsibility to the Gods who make continual human existence possible. The Gods guide the Sun and Moon on their voyage across the sky. Evil Gods threaten this journey which is why the Maya believe planets and stars need help from the earthly humans. Consequently, the Maya continually perform sacred rituals, usually led by a killing or sacrifice. This is the price for the continued existence of the universe, inconsequential if it guarantees the survival of the universe. Thus, according to their philosophy, a ritualistic death is a privilege that ensures immortality.

Just as so many other indigenous people, call upon the planets and stars, to improve the wellbeing of our planet and individual immortality; the Maya people are no exception. Religions and philosophies of today place less emphasis on the care of our planet and more focus on the individual. We forget we have a planetary assignment for caring of all life. The repeated cycles of creation and destruction as described in Maya mythology are reminders of the consequences when humanity neglects their obligations to the Gods. While it may not be necessary to diligently follow the Mayan Calendar, an understanding of each phase, the end and beginning reminds us of the potential destruction of the world and brings us back to the center, into balance.

Maya Calendar

Based upon this Mayan calendar, the beginning goes back to 3113 BCE. Carl Johan Calleman asserts that the timeline is "unambiguously true."[45] In his book: *Mayan Calendar and the Transformation of Consciousness*, he includes evidence supporting this statement. The Maya culture rose to prominence around 250CE, spanning numerous countries in Mesoamerica then began a decline around 900 CE. The Maya today bring us the laws and guidelines of most Mesoamerican cultures.

Although historians assign the calendar to the Maya people, it originates with the Olmec People. Experts consider it the oldest and only calendar of this type in existence. We find evidence in Maya, Zapotec and Olmec cultures. The Olmec culture gives us the earliest evidence of all. The overview below provides an overview. It clarifies the wisdom dating 25,000 years and how it applies to our society even today.

Tzolkin and **Haab** calendars combine forming the **TUNBEN K'AK** calendar. Tzolkin and Haab are energy cycles, the Spiritual and Physical cycles. Tunben K'aK known as new Fire Ceremony honors the passing of the Pleiades through the zenith at midnight.

The **TZOLKIN** cycle tracks the *Spiritual* energy over 13 cycles of 20 days each (totally 260 days). This information sets the energy of the year for your spiritual growth and progress. This interacts with the other calendrical intersections for a complete and accurate reading of your strengths or identity. Unlike other astrological systems, it includes specific day information. Should we choose to adopt their wisdom, we see the significance of the day count and its effect on our daily actions,

2001 is the year of the New York disaster. On July 11, 2001, we receive the energy of forgiveness, compassion and tolerance bringing in the wisdom of harmony and resonance. Various societies illustrated this compassion and tolerance when questioned about this disaster.

As well, **Tzolkin** and **Haab** calendars observe the four compass directions. When we understand how these spiritual energies work with daily activities, we become aware of our soul growth journey in this lifetime.

The Day keeper for each community has the exact details of the calendrical interaction for each resident. This interpretation provides an overview of the day's strength and illustrates the approach. Just as we need to honor the Owl, Dove and Butterfly energy in modern living, each day of the Mayan calendar provides the strengths giving us this ability. **Tzolkin** and **Haab** illustrate the Owl knowledge or ancient wisdom. They show us how we bring the peace of their culture forward to our time and lastly, help us transform this knowledge into personal usable form. This description indicates three facets –

One - an animal or other physical strength such as monkey, road or rainstorm

Two -- a compass direction

Three - a strong personality trait

Calendar	Animal or physical strength	Direction	Personality trait
IMIX	Alligator	East	New Ideas or projects, primal instincts
IK	Wind	North	Spiritual day, power of communication, positive ideas
AKB'AL	Night	West	mystical dreamers, bringer of the dawn
KAN	Seed	South	Sensual, magic of germination
CHICCHAN	Serpent	East	Intense instinctive wisdom
CIMI	Death	North	Sign of cycle of Life, Death, Rebirth, psychic ability
MANIK	Deer	West	Spiritual, peaceful, concerned of welfare of others
LAMAT	Rabbit	South	Abundance, fertility, Luck
MULUC	Water	East	Fluid, dynamic, gives more than receives
OC	Dog	North	Collaboration, fidelity, reliable, bravery

CHUEN	Monkey	West	Creativity, variety of talents and skills
EB	Road	South	Conductor of destiny, devotion to others
BEN	Reed	East	Authority, respect, spiritual authority of elder
IX	Jaguar	North	Death, healing, ruler of jungles, plains and mountains
MEN	Eagle	West	Intermediary between Heaven and Earth, brings hope and faith
CIB	Owl	South	Wisdom of ancients
CABAN	Earth	East	Connection to natural cycles
ETZNAB	Flint	North	Purity of truth, insight intelligence
CAUAC	Rainstorm	West	Giver of life
AHAU	Light	South	Completion

The **HAAB** Cycle tracks *Physical* Energies over 18 cycles of 20 days (totaling 360 days). It links directly to the Sun's energy, passing to all physical forms of life and intellect. Sunrises and Sunsets are important to the Maya. At night, you are closer to Hunab Ku, the creator. Therefore, you thank him at sunset for what you received during the day. At sunrise, you get the information and spiritual direction needed for the day.

Because of the connection to daytime activities, this energy is important for food growth and growing seasons. At the equinox and solstice, the Maya hold celebrations at the end of each season, the solar cycle. The Western world does not. Perhaps this would be beneficial adoption.

The **Tunben K'ak**, or calendar round, covers the period of 52 years. This flows from one cycle to the next and *if recorded*, future generations copy and absorb into daily routines.. The Tzolkin and Haab relate to solar and lunar cycles of days, but a 52 year cycle remains unclear. 52 year cycle is longer than their average life expectancy. What the gods granted the people could apply to the next generation. After the 52 year cycle, we move to the 260 year cycle known as **K'ALTUN.**

The **LONG COUNT** is approximately 5,125 years long. This method of dating seems to belong to monumental carving. Dr. Ronald Bonewitz noted the oldest dated monument found so far dated in a long count went back to the equivalent of December 7, 36 BCE. [46] As a geologist and archeologist, he made several other comments which are worthy of note.

First, he says the calendar was pretty much in its final form in the 1st century BCE, suggesting it originated from another culture, perhaps the Olmec. Next, he proposes a possible royal link to the gods, explaining the backward calculation to 3114 BCE. This explanation of royal linkage separates the society from a solar analysis. The solar analysis continues over 5,000 years, clarifying the phase of elliptical light periods as explained in the photon band theory.

If people around the world use similar calendars, this suggests there is more interaction than scientist and archaeologists present. Four communities from Africa, Asia and North America use calendars based upon the stars, solar and lunar cycles. These communities are: – Dogon in Africa, Tibetan and Vedic in Asia and North American native nations. We expect people around the globe observe what they see, the stars, sun and moon, track the solar and lunar cycles and note the lunar and seasonal markings but how they applied this knowledge is remarkable. Their terminology may differ but the concepts match.

This takes us back to Gerardo Barrios Kaanek, the Guatemalan Mayan Timekeeper, who mentions four continents and four locations. Many of the global communities of his continents and locations developed solar calendars. However, the Maya is the only culture that developed a calendar going back 25,000 years!

The last time we entered the photon band was approximately 23,000 BCE, or 25,000 years ago. This is when the first of five Mayan calendrical cycles began. The Olmec society, the oldest known culture from Mesoamerica, had this knowledge. How is it that the Mesoamerica people had the knowledge of the photon band? How will this knowledge benefit us in the 21st century?"

There are two possibilities.

First: The information comes from astral neighbours or came from cultures no longer living on the earth such as Lemurian or Altantean. The Maya are just one native society who acknowledges the presence of these two cultures. Once we accept their existence, we gain the wisdom from them that benefit our current society.

The second possibility is the information originally had a different purpose, evolving into a calendar.

I believe *both* are correct.

Spoken stories and knowledge pass from generation to generation. Scientists and most humans doubt information given to them in unconventional methods. There is suspicion about information dating back 5,000 - 10,000 years ago, although there is evidence. The provable Maya knowledge and other Mesoamerica data lend credence to the spoken stories and beliefs. Our ancestors use remarkable tools and give us incredible data. Trusting and accepting the data opens a book of vast information.

One example is using the first two Mayan calendrical periods, Tzolkin and Haab cycles. We already use this data in a modified form. Tracking the sun's activities throughout the year and the moon's movement throughout the month are relatively easy to understand and relate to current life. The sun cycle allows seasonal agricultural planning. A slightly shorter cycle gives the life through the birthing cycle (nine-month gestation). The lunar cycle allows people to plan for pregnancy by understanding the menstrual cycle of the female.

The two periods of 260 years and 52 years are major eras, suggesting the possibility of measuring distance and migration. During periods such as the Olmec time, the earth experienced severe global warming, flooding or ice ages. Great disasters such as these spurred eons of travel. Using the Maya calendar to track how long people traveled is a way of calculating distance. Using the astrological patterns, they were able to apply the travel calendars and historic disasters to predict the pending cataclysmic events of 2012.

Another option is the cycles take us to the same position in the photon band. Rather than worry about the 2012 *pending cataclysmic event,* it is an opportunity for us to make changes and evolve even more.

The indigenous Elders of Mesoamerica give a message similar to many other indigenous Elders. Below is a message from the Maya Elder, Don Alexandro Oxlaj, head of the Council of Elders of the Maya.

Maya Message

To all my brothers and sisters
Listening to this message
These words are not mine,
They are the words of our ancestors

The prophecy of the Maya says that it is time of
12 BAKTUN and 13 AHAU
Is the return of the ancestors
Of the men of wisdom

Let the morning come
Let the dawn come
For the people to find peace
And to be happy

So I am here with you
Leaving the message, to
Not be afraid of the world
Take this message and spread
It throughout the world.

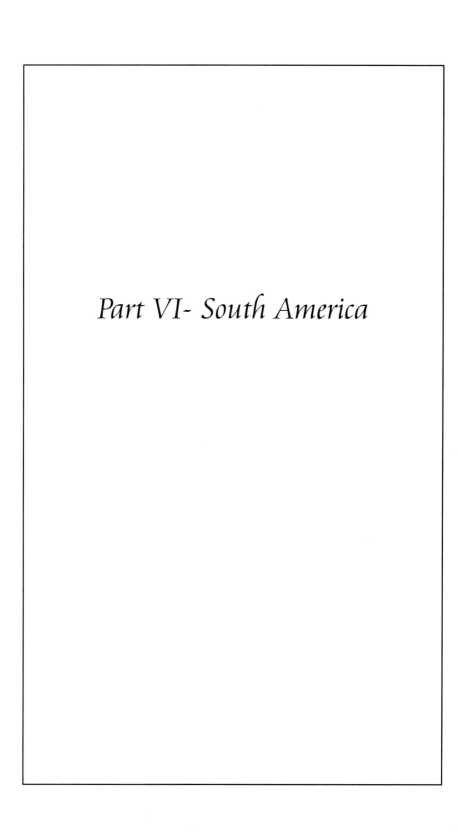

Part VI- South America

COLOMBIA

High in the mountains at the Southern end of Colombia, near the Ecuadorian border are the remains of an ancient civilization. The area is inaccessible, probably explaining why ruins still exist. We know very little about the San Agustin cultures except they are old and inexplicably disappeared. Carbon dating takes them back approximately 5,000 years ago, which places their existence between 3300 BCE and 1500 BCE.[47]

Some speculators suggest these ancient people originated in the northern part of the Amazon River, migrating down to San Agustin. Others insist the ancients lived and developed in a single location, San Agustin. Archaeological findings put their presence at back to 1500 BCE. However, carbon dating insists they are even older, 3300 B.CE.[48] This illustrates a difference between archaeological dating and carbon dating. Today, Alto de Lavapatas is within an archaeological park at San Agustin near where the Central and Oriental Cordilleras converge. Colombia has three mountain ranges; all part of the Andes Chain. The three cordilleras are the Cordillera Occidental, Central and Oriental.

In and around Alto de Lavapatas, we find many anthropomorphic and zoomorphic statues. For an unknown reason, the creators disappeared, leaving no apparent connection with other indigene in the regions.

This region of Alto de Lavapatas becomes important because of the link between 500 dolmens and statues in this area and sculptures in other parts of the globe. We have countless human and animal statues as well as combination bear/human and bear/jaguar/human sculptures. Like so many cultures, they combine human and animal for worship.

There are two volcanoes in cordilleras northwest of San Agustin. The first one is Volcan de Satara, Officially, experts class it as an active volcano but there are no known records of an eruption. It measures 4580 metres (14,436 ft). The other volcano, Volcan de Purace, last erupted in 1977. Its height is approximately 4686 metres (15,235 ft) high.

We know the inhabitants of this region honor these volcanoes and the stars. They create dolmens or megalithic tombs consisting of rock pillars, or columns, supporting a flat rock on the top.

It is unclear what the purpose and origin of the megalithic constructions is. So far, archaeologists report 13 sites from the Neolithic period, including the more popular ones in Great Britain. The first one, quite naturally is the famous Stonehenge. The remnants of Stonehenge confirm its construction date between 2600 BCE and 16 BCE. The largest stone is 7 metres (23 ft.) high, weighing 45 tons and all Stonehenge stones are void of carvings.

People from all around the globe visit this ancient wonder, and yet they ignore or downplay mysterious findings that do display carvings such as the megaliths of San Agustin. The elaborate San Agustin art incorporates both animals and humans.

Dr. Mary Helms wrote an article for BACKDIRT publication[49] in which she discusses the spectacled bear and other stone figures from San Agustin and Alto de Lavaderos. BACKDIRT is the semi-annual publication of the Cotsen Institute of Archaeology at UCLA. She refers to the late Gerardo Reichel-Dolmatoff's research where he identifies the similarities between the carvings of the bear, jaguar and human. Reichel-Dolmatoff describes the human quality of the animals; arms and fingers, not claws.

Reichel-Dolmatoff sites Indian myths of Colombia combining human and beast as a means of including the progenitor and procreator. In these myths, the human provides the social structure and the beast provides the nature, paralleling the legends of the Zimbabwe bird in Africa.[50] Both countries' carvings include human and animal parts in one figure. We know the ancient ones from Columbia stress a social structure protecting nature. Perhaps the Zimbabwe bird had a similar purpose. We know when life arrived on this planet; a basic principle developed at the same time and was consistent around the globe. This principle is:

Honor and protect all life, whether it is human, animals or plants. Myths, legends and sculptures reinforce this premise, ensuring its survival through generations of life.

This is part of different society's values. As cultures evolve, they accommodate changes in social structure but this principle remains at the core of the rules or guidelines.

The Columbian indigenous people, the Kogi are no exception. They, create statues combining society and nature. When they incorporate two forms of life in their carvings, they achieve two goals. One was a means to remind citizens of the duality. The other was protection from evil forces. Even today, societies believe protection happens when all life is valued. Many nations share this code around the globe but the three strongest in the world are the Hopi, Kogi and Waitaha. All leaders speak of the peace resulting from protecting the environment.

In 1999, the Kogi received global recognition as *safekeepers of the planet.*[51] We define *safekeepers* as people who acknowledge the interdependence among all forms of life and stand to protect it. They acknowledge continuation of life on the planet becomes threatened when people are out of balance with nature. One way they do this is caring and preserving their native culture. Their culture connects them to the environment and provides the wisdom necessary to appreciate the value of this interdependence. When B.I.O. President, Dr. Agni Vlavianos-Arvanitis, presented the award during a visit to the area, he said:

"The Kogi are a model of excellence in their perception of our role as human beings on this planet. There is no record of war in the history of their civilisation; they embody peace and global environmental harmony. The Kogi have stayed on the land of their ancestors without abusing it, and they have maintained their culture and mythos as a token of their appreciation to Mother Nature who has given them the gift of life. They protect and cherish the environment, the soil, the air, the water, and all living beings. They are an inspiration for South America and also for the entire world."

The Kogi people live in the mountains of Colombia. They came out of seclusion to give us, their Younger Brothers, a warning. It is through their mythology, we learn the teachings. The first mother gave the Kogi, through her sons, the moral, social and spiritual code of life. These indigenous people named it "the code of the mother," and it should be strictly observed by all tribes. Perhaps this explains why their elders are called *Mamas*. Mamas are in charge of verifying daily universal order and the social and spiritual order for the tribe. The Mamas have a thorough knowledge of *the code of the mother* and the universe. Through training, they become aware of all cyclical changes.

With the offerings of the mother and her sons, the Kogi let the universe follow its normal course. They believe only the Kogi takes care of life, white people do not know the law of Nature. White people only know the laws of Man.

When they came out of seclusion with their message, part of this message was a plea that we (white people) continually repeat this warning until others finally listen.

The Kogi nation is a modern branch of the Tairona people of the Colombian region of South America. Several hundred years ago, the Tairona retreated from the Spanish onto an isolated mountain formation called the Sierra Nevada de Santa Marta. The Tairona data back to the 1st century AD.

This tribe formed one of the two principal groups of the Chibcha. After their conquest, the Spaniards pushed them all into remote regions. The indigenous Los Kogui' living in the area today are direct descendants of the Tairona and custodians of this culture.

They believe Sierra Nevada is the *Place of Creation* and the *Heart of the World*. For this reason, they call themselves the Elder Brothers of Humanity and consider their mission caring for the planet. This justifies labeling others as their *younger brothers.*

The Sierra Nevada lies in a northern extension of Colombia, separate from the main continent of South America and apart from the Andes. The highest peak of the Sierra Nevada de Santa Marta is 5,700 metres or 19,000 feet. However, the Sierra is a massif, not just a mountain, a 90-mile triangular pyramid, a free-floating tectonic plate.

A massif is: a block of the earth's crust bounded by faults or flexures and displaced as a unit without internal change.[52]

The significance of this definition is that it reinforces the isolation and enhances the energy contained within a triangular mountain. Their isolation for so many years stresses the importance of their *coming out* to warn their Younger Brothers.

The Kogi chose to retreat to their mountainous sanctum rather than see, and be part of, the daily damage their *Younger Brothers* do to the planet. The Kogi knew what was here long ago when alien life settled onto the planet. Rather than be part of the increasing violence and destruction, they chose to move higher into the mountains, upholding their pure way of life.

Regardless of race or creed, we, their *Younger Brothers*, have the same heritage as the Kogi. There is no separation between races or heritage. However, people living elsewhere on the earth took a different path.

We forget our past and forget what is important. It seems that alternatively, we selfishly spend our energy trying to survive as individuals or isolated societies. We conquer everything around us for our own benefit. It seems very much like the *Law of Man* not the *Law of Nature*.

A key to our future is being "**A WITNESS**". The Kogi knew how to *witness* but they made the mistake of focusing only on the immediate surroundings. They needed to look beyond their environment and see the damage. It was only after they understood the severity and amount of destruction that they made contact with the outside world. It is not too late, if we take action now.

We frequently hibernate in our personal world, focusing on what is going to personally happen to our immediate family. We need to be a witness of everything occurring on the planet and in the universe. Everything occurring in the universe affects us; we make a difference. We may not see the universe clearly; we may not even see our planet clearly. However, everyone has a rudimentary understanding of our planet and this knowledge applies to the entire universe.

When I hear the words "**Be witness**", I also hear "**There is no such thing as a false witness.**" Distorted truths come from the desire to stay isolated within our personal world. Modern society creates the *false* witness. A definition of "false witness" is: *Taking what is observed, adapting or labeling it to suit a person's, or persons' current way of living.*

When civilizations take what they observe and apply it to the comfort of the individual, then the knowledge turns false. Our ancient ancestors have structured faiths but it does not appear selfish. Today, advocates maintain their teachings are for the betterment of all humans, yet they judge. Once we insist that someone change their approach, we judge and become false witnesses.

According to Ereira's book, *The Elder Brothers*,[53] missionary nuns tried for hundreds of years to convert the Kogi to their religion, without success. The author, Eriera, never heard of any Kogi leaving the Sierra permanently[54].

Somehow, in their core being, they carried the ability to be a witness without being a false witness. This is why the Kogi message is so important. They are not the only indigenous society who remember and apply the ability to be a witness without being false. The Hopi and the Ainu are two other civilizations who upheld their integrity.

There is a region known as the "Lost City". Tairona descendants call this development **Teyuna.** After the Spanish conquest, the Tairona residents fled, keeping this area sacred and hidden. The formal, traditional use remains a mystery but we do know it has existed since approximately the fifth century B.C.E. After its discovery in 1975, the local tribes complained about the desecration of their revered mountain. Respectfully, Colombian scientists stepped back honoring the Tairona values. When the Kogi and Tairona share their heritage with modern society, perhaps we will learn important information of the Lost City. They can teach us how to amalgamate this knowledge with our modern society. Until then, we must listen to the message from the Kogi Mamas.

In 1990 when the Mamas brought the message to the "younger brothers", they asked the Aluna, the cosmic principle of thought and potential, what they should say to their younger brother.

This was the message they received:

"*He had everything*
and Younger Brother took it all to another count

"*Now the Mama grows sad,*
He feels weak.
He says that the earth is decaying.
The earth is losing its strength
Because they have taken away much petrol,
Coal, many minerals.

"*A human being has much liquid inside,*
If the liquid dries up, we fall with weakness.
This same thing can happen to the earth,
weakness makes you fall,
weakness.

Gayle Redfern

"So the earth today catches diseases of all kinds.
The animals die.
The trees dry up.
People fall ill.
Many illnesses will appear,
and there will be no cure for them.
Why?

"Because Younger brother is among us.
Younger brother is violating
The basic foundation of the world's law.
A total violation.
Robbing
Ramsacking
Building highways,
extracting petrol,
minerals.

"We tell you
We the people of this place
Kogi
Asario.
Arhuaco:
That is a violation.

"So the Mamas say,
"Please BBC
no one else should come here,
no more ransacking
because the earth wants to collapse,
the earth grows weak,
we must protect it,
we must respect it,
because he does not respect the earth,

because he does not respect it."
"Younger Brother thinks,
"Yes! Here I am! I know much about the universe!"
But this knowing is learning to destroy the world,
To destroy everything,
all humanity.

"The earth feels.
They take out petrol,
It feels pain there.
So the earth sends out sickness,
There will be many medicines,
Drugs,
But in the end the drugs will not be of any use,
Neither will the medicine be of any use.

"The Mamas say that this tale must be learnt
By the Younger Brother.[55]

More than ten years after the Kogi's plea, and after meeting the Dali Lama, my spirit guides said:

"You have now seen a sacred land and the destruction of other lands. This is what we sent you to see. If you go again, it will be for pleasure or to remember what you learned. Our people, the Hopi, learned well but hid it. People from Sedona come up to observe but they do not learn how to forgive.

"The Navajo learned to forgive. However, they cannot forgive without getting something in return, payback as you call it. There are people in the Hopi world who have learned this but they do not believe that humans will understand that is so. You saw the Elders of our Hopi people and their sacred learning ground where they taught this important lesson.

"Students took it afar, they taught Australian Aborigines. They taught sacred people of Indonesian islands. They taught people in all corners of the world. They took the four corners of the sacred language to the four corners of the world. Now it is time for all corners to awaken, share and unite the four corners again. This will happen without your organizations or politics, as you call it, being involved. It is sad but it is also true that the corners must break away from where they are to learn what they already know.

"As you realized, the Dalai Lama and Tibet had to break away from that corner to "force" him to join with other forces, or corners. Your native people must do the same. The next corner will be in what you call South America. There are sacred people there who will be forced to break from their world to force others to join the corners you know."

This last paragraph refers to the Kogi. Their teachings tell us the Kogi escaped into the hills for protection from the Spanish and learned to become self-sufficient. It was only when they saw the devastation to the planet did they realize they must share their wisdom and warn us.

The Kogi are not the only culture or tribe to pass this information to the *Younger Brothers*. They made such a profound presentation that we need to recognize the importance of understanding how ancient wisdom shapes our present and our future. It also teaches us how to accept change, safely.

PERU

B eyond Colombia, we move into Peru and find several mystical tribes and cultures. The most famous are the Inca people, living in the Andes bequeathing their Andes legacy to us. Two of their ancestral cultures are the Matsés and the Norte Chico people. Legend has these tribes crossing the Bering Land Bridge around 9000 BCE, finally arriving in the region of Peru region around 6000 BCE. At some point, the name **Masma** came to mean a tribe of Peruvian people. However, as late as the 20th century, it suggests plateaus and communities.

Historical evidence states the Romans gave this name to an ancient tribe living in the Moroccan region of Africa. Masma also refers to the region not the people. According to Judaism, Masma was the fifth son of Ishmael.

When Asete learned of this African name duality – Masma meaning both tribe and region, he began wondering whether the tribal name came after the region, after the tribe or from a completely different source. Did these people settle in northwest Africa, later traveling to South America in search for Peru's gold?

Regardless of the mystery, the name Masma means people and region in Africa, culture, plateau and village in South America. This indicates a connection between these cultures, however remote. Independently, researchers connect the Masma culture with the Inca culture. Many ancient cultures protect their heritage and cultural values. The Inca are no exception. The Inca are a mysterious people, keeping their work in secret, sharing this secret with very few strangers. One confidant was an historian known as Daniel Ruzo

A Peruvian lawyer, Daniel Ruzo (1900-1993), spent much of his life studying esoteric topics. After discovering five towns of ruins on the plateau of Markawasi and its wonders less than 100 km from Lima, he pursued his journeys to numerous countries, successfully searching and documenting his discoveries.

The monuments around the world mark entrances to the caves and caverns, indicating the possible salvation of the seeds of humanity. Around the world, he found tunnels and caves with carvings and stone writing on their walls and entrances. These ancient monumental stone sculptures correspond with the ruins found around Markawasi. Unfortunately, many people are skeptical about the quality of archaeological research and the significance of findings. Here, credibility came from an outside source. Ruzo is a 33rd degree Mason and upholds the Masonic Order's ethical code. The Masonic Order dates back to the 18th century; the Masonic code provides the necessary creditability to his research. When Ruzo wrote his books, he compared the findings and details of ancient times and our modern era. In the 1974 introduction to one of his book, he says[56]:

"…: Observing rocks near where thousands of people lived, but they didn't see them because they lacked faith in the magic world and in the works of art left by a former humanity which created and respected this world and produced these incomparable works of art, but left no signature. The artistic work was the rhythm of life, like heartbeats, or breathing, or walking on this earth. It was a work of magic.

"Humanity has forgotten all of this and considers going to the moon much more important. It cannot explain the appearance of these genius men who break all barriers to arrive at surprising results without seeking for him, and without listening to dogmatic voices - which try to reduce to words that which has no name.

"…the carvings and the sculptures made in the natural rock, to be seen from a point of view or a certain direction, and in conditions of special lighting, give credit to a style that could only be expressed by men of profound pantheist faith. The hidden legacy carved gigantic monuments. The technique of these sculptors has not been repeated in subsequent history.

"These works are found in different places on earth, very removed from one another, repeating the same symbols, and with one thing in common: they are found around sacred mountains, temples of lost humanity, so they won't be forgotten and that they may serve one more time to purify and save humanity."

This introduction excerpt draws several points to our attention:

1. **"The technique of these sculptors has not been repeated in subsequent history."** This gently reminds us that our ancestors carved with exemplary skills, which are sometimes set aside by modern carvers.

2. **The priority has shifted**. In the 21ˢᵗ century, humanity centres on going into space instead of producing magical, artistic work carrying the rhythm of life. Ruzo revisits the ancient artwork, pleading we revisit the quality and value of each artefact.

3. **Sculptors concentrate their art around sacred mountains as a way, to purify and save humanity**. Ruzo identifies twenty-two energy vortices and their importance. From here he demonstrates the energy strengths and herbal potency.

4. While my last book, *Within & Beyond*, did not use the precise words and signs as did Ruzo, it **repeats the same messages and echoes the antiquity** and value of each sign

We find comparable statues in the Fontainebleau forest of *France,* megaliths at Stonehenge and Averbury in *Great Britain*, and an *Egyptian* granite wall behind the Temple of Thebes. The temple itself is covered in ancient sculptures. The same symbols are repeatedly found on monuments in Mexico; Brazil, The Sacred Valley of the Kings in Egypt; the Carpatos mountains in Rumania; and Kakadu National Park in Australia.

The points here are that *all* these locations provide ancient sculptures with signs or symbols that are *identical* or *similar.* It is unlikely that natural forces in these different locations could carve them and produce a similarity that is only a coincidence. Either numerous nations independently came up with the same idea at the same point in history, or travelers carried the concepts from one part of the world to another. It is more likely there must have been contact amongst the civilizations.

Through Ruzo's exploration of caves, caverns, catastrophes and ancient art, we review what "*The Theory of Life*" is.

Daniel Ruzo created a hypothesis of humanity in the 1920's, then proceeded to make it is his life's work to verify it. Ruzo researched ancient literature, ancient geological and archaeological sites.

The evidence found clarifies his belief. The theory states:

- Human life on earth has been made up of five humanities or phases.
- Each humanity cycle lasts 8,608 years and is made up of four sun cycles of 2,125 years each.
- We are in the fifth humanity.

- Every 8,608 years, the earth suffers a catastrophe.
- Following the zodiac, humanities have survived catastrophes of earth, fire and water.
- The next catastrophe will be by air and will occur between the years 2127 and 2137.

This information compares favourably to the Astrological, the Ayurvedic and the Chinese calendars. All three cultures or seers develop modern systems of analysis. Groups within the modern community use the three calendars but it seems they bypass the historical data.

When Ruzo lived on Markawasi, he took many photographs of each one. Each monument displays numerous images at the same position. For example, the main monument, the *Monument of Humanity*, has fourteen faces visible by the light of the sun and two visible only by the light of the moon.

Studying the mysterious monuments on Markawasi included other components of science, one of them being the energy vortices.

At Markawasii, There are *twenty-two energy vortices* made up of three distinct types of energy.

There are *three* of the first types found in areas of limited access on the plateau. Only those prepared to be near such powerful energy are allowed access.

The second type of cross or vortex represents the *seven* days of the week.

The *twelve* vortices of the third type have to do with the phases of the moon.

Each vortex has specific healing powers and each location is easily visible[57]. After the average person learns specific exercises and techniques, he or she will feel the energy. A disciple of Ruzo, Carlos Seclan verified the accuracy of this statement. In mid 20th century, he went to a Markawasi vortex on the full moon, learned specific movements and healed his body. This process correlates with actions of shamans and elders of the Indigenous of ancient times.

Numerous alternative healing treatments are in practice today, healing our body, mind and spirit with earth energy but they are in a minority. Popular ones today include Reiki, Yoga, Tai Chi, or, Qi Gong. Slowly we seem to open our minds to their success.

Like so many other indigenes of the world, Peruvian people for thousands of years, use plants to heal. People there believe their plants are ancient. It seems modern people must artificially create a remedy before verifying a natural plant use. They turn to teas made from:

Valeriana (Valium) for calming and stress relief. This plant is a ground cover of yellow flowers.

Margerita Silvestre's brown or yellow flowers lowers blood pressure.

Tarwi's blue flowers and leaves combat chills and fevers.

Tipta tea, made from the small leaves and yellow flowers of the plant, is useful for headaches – an altitude sickness.

These remedies are effective for visitors to this region. However, by contacting local indigenes possibly you will receive antidotes from your area.

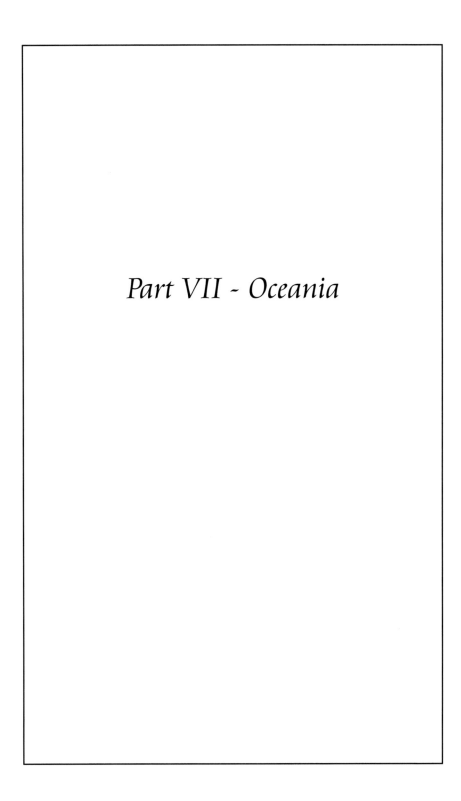

Part VII - Oceania

The Oceanic islands of the Pacific divide into three cultural groups – Polynesia, Micronesia, and Melanesia. Their anthropomorphic origins extend in four directions, into cultures of North, Central, South America, Australia and Asia. These backgrounds provide some practical characteristics of a modern world. If we combine this knowledge with our holiday image of an easy, stress-free lifestyle, we receive an optimum example of society merging the past with the present. Long ago, these people knew astrological and navigational methods helpful and applicable today. This illustrates how a society can merge the technical knowhow of the past with their *hang-loose* existence of today. Perhaps when we study their history we could create our own stress-free life, regardless of where we presently live.

POLYNESIA

The Polynesian region, or Polynesian Triangle, divides into East and West Polynesia spreading from Hawaii east to Easter Island and southeast to New Zealand. The distinctive Eastern Polynesian group consists of smaller coral islands or atolls. Each island relies on shared religion, farming, fishing, and out-rigger canoe construction. Consequently, the population of each island possesses highly developed skills, sharing their knowledge and learning how to work together. The other distinctive group, West Polynesia is home to larger communities, with bigger populations. They also share but instead of teachings, they share through the traditions of strong institutions of marriage, well-developed judicial, monetary and trading systems.

The seven main Polynesian cultures of the *Polynesian Triangle* are:

1. Hawai'i- Kānaka maoli
2. Marquesas – French Polynesia
3. Tahiti – French Polynesia
4. Rapa Nui – Easter Island
5. Tonga
6. Sāmoa
7. Aotearoa – Maori, New Zealand

The first corner is the one we are most familiar with, Hawai'i. Linguists state the Hawaiian language came from Proto-Malayo-Polynesian language of Asia 5,000 years ago. This supports the theory that the Polynesian island settlers came from Asia, spreading through the Pacific islands. We know that indigenous residents were in regions such as China, Africa, North and South America long before the Polynesian islands, giving Polynesians one of the shortest tenures in their indigenous area. Amongst the islands within the Polynesian triangle, Hawai'i is one of the most recently settled islands.

There are three vital keys to Hawaiian history.

First, King Kamehameha ruled Hawai'i until Hawaii joined the United States. Until this union, he continued the caste system of ancient Hawaiian tradition which is similar to India's Hindu system. If there had been no global communication, it would be difficult to develop organizational structures as similar as these two.

Second, the Hawaiian people, the Kānaka maoli, chose to settle on this chain of volcanic islands. Just as other indigenous people, the Kānaka maoli recognize the importance and need for volcanic and spring energy to life beings.

The last historical key is the supporting and teaching of *The 3 Ws* -- wind, waves and wings by Kānaka maoli elders. They share and support the knowledge and life of many cultures.

WIND: Plants send seeds on the wind. Animals move on the wind, illustrated by spiders and insects.

WAVES: Tidal waves take food, plant life and knowledge, carrying seeds, small animals and small boats.

WINGS: Birds eat fruit, seeds, teaching indigenous of new edible plant life.

The Hawaiian people expand upon the set of rules and proverbs accompanying their easy-going culture. It is unclear whether the Kānaka maoli people originated these or not. Regardless, we associate them with the Polynesian world. The basic proverbs and words of wisdom applicable to modern global living are:[58]

Hawaiian Proverbs:

1. E ho'a'o no i pau kuhihewa: "Just do it!" instead of worrying about doing a difficult job.
2. Hahai no ka ua i ka ulula'au: Destroy the forest, the rains will cease to fall, and the land will become a desert. NOTE: this corresponds with the Kogi warning.
3. ka makapo wale no ka mea hapapa i ka pouli: If you have no direction in life, you'll get nowhere or another way to put it is, "If you're going nowhere, you're guaranteed to get there."
4. I mohala no ka lehua i ke ke'ekehi 'ia e ka ua: People respond better to gentle words than to scolding.
5. Pupukahi i holomua: Unite to move forward. By working together we make progress
6. E lauhoe mai na wa'a; i ke ka, i ka hoe; i ka hoe, i ke ka; pae aku i ka 'aina. If everybody works together, the work will be done quickly.
7. I ka 'olelo no ke ola, i ka 'olelo no ka make: In speech is life, in speech is death Words can either be a source for healing or destruction; we need to be careful with our words.
8. He puko'a kani 'aina: Small coral heads grow into a full islands. We start small and over time, we will mature and be successful.
9. He lawai'a no ke kai papa'u, he pokole ke aho; he lawai'a no ke kai hohonu he loa ke aho: You will reach only as far as you aim; prepare yourself to reach.
10. A'ohe hana nui ka alu'ia: No task is too big when done together. United we stand, divided we fall.
11. Lawe i ka ma'alea a ku'ono'ono: Acquire a skill and make it deep. If you want to become really good at anything, you've got to study hard and practice long until it gets deep and becomes a part of you.
12. Kulia i ka nu'u: Strive for the summit, reach. Strive for the top of the mountain, striving for excellence.
13. Onipa'a: Take your stand and be steadfast in doing what is right no matter what others say.
14. Maka'ala ke kanaka kahea manu: If you wish to succeed, be alert to any opportunity that should arise.

HAWAIIAN WORDS OF WISDOM

This additional set of values resonates with worldwide beliefs.[59]

1. **Ua mau ke ea o ka ʻaina i ka pono** Preserve the life of the land in righteousness.
2. **ʻOnipaʻa**: Stand firm.
3. **E noho iho i ke opu weuweu, mai hoʻokiʻekiʻe** Remain among the clumps of grass and do not elevate yourself.
4. Don't show off or get puffed up and big-headed.
5. Be haʻahaʻa (humble). An inner self-confidence giving rise to quiet strength is far more admirable than self-importance, arrogance, and egotism.
6. **Kuʻia ka hele a ka naʻau haʻahaʻa**: Hesitant walks the humble hearted. A humble person walks carefully, so as not to hurt others.
7. Those who throw their weight around will hurt others, and eventually themselves.
8. **Nana ka maka; hoʻolohe ka pepeiao;paʻa ka waha**: Observe with the eyes, listen with the ears and shut the mouth. Thus, one learns.
9. **Ua ola no i ka pane a ke aloha**: There is life in a kindly reply. Though one may have no gift to offer to a friend, a kind word or a friendly greeting is just as important.
10. **He kehau hoʻomaʻemaʻe ke aloha**: Love is like cleansing dew. The cleansing power of aloha can soothe and heal. Hurt, pain, and suffering yield to aloha's healing power.
11. **ʻAʻohe loa i ka hana a ke aloha**: Distance is ignored by love.
12. **Ua ola loko i ke aloha**: Love gives life within. Love is imperative to one's mental, physical, emotional and spiritual welfare.

Notice the similarities between these two Hawaiian proverbial sets and current moral guidelines. Contemporary society adopts some of the guidelines and others they forget. Many indigenous guidelines of societies such as Hawaiian, Mohawk, Buddhism and Christianity teach gentleness and love for our neighbors; perhaps we can recapture and incorporate them into our lives.

Easter Island

The eastern corner of the *Polynesian Triangle* is Easter Island, made famous by the *Moai*, the unique stone heads found on the island. The Polynesian name for this island is Rapa Nui, *navel of the Earth*. As well, we know the island as Te-Pito-O-Te-Henua, *The Navel of the World* and as Mata-Ki-Te-Rani, *Eyes Looking at Heaven*. Current studies state the first inhabitants came between 400 and 700 CE. BUT, since it is close to South America and Hawaii, - 2,300 miles west of South America and 4,300 miles south of Hawaii – there is a logical association with the ancient cultures of surrounding areas, particularly the Americas such as Inca and Maya, both of which date back farther than 400 CE. Researchers such as Graham Hancock propose ancient cultures used this island for navigation and cosmic observation. These speculations include the possibility of prehistoric people living on the island, their mariners charting global oceans, and their astronomers developing their knowledge of long-term astrological cycles. This further explains the theoretical use of this location for calculating the precise grid of sacred sites. Hancock further proposes there are hints of lost astronomical knowledge similar to hypothesized Egyptian data.

These concepts might seem remote today but going back five to ten thousand years, I believe they become viable for two reasons.

First, the Maya, Hindu and Egyptian cultures developed astrological charts around this time, so perhaps other global societies did the same. Secondly, logically these cultures shared their knowledge. If the Easter Island residents were mariners, they were not as far away from these other countries as we might imagine. Again, we recall the importance of volcanoes and fresh spring water. Easter Island has three extinct volcanoes with crater lakes on the top of each one. These volcanic mountains are Rano Kau, Rano Raraku and Rano Aroi. Crater lakes contain pristine water, providing residents with the only fresh water on the island as there are no underground rivers.

Up on the sides of these mountains we find the remains of ancient Moai stone heads. We also find Moai stone heads down on the ocean shores facing inland. These heads suggest several reasons why all the Moai were constructed.

First: village guardians.

Their honored god, MakeMake (Pronounced *MAH-kay MAH-kay*) keeps them safe. He represents the creator of humanity, god of fertility and the chief god of the *bird-man* cult.

Second: protectors of water resources.

The only found pristine water is in the volcanic craters, explaining why the heads face inland.

Third: astronomical.

The heads point to the trans-Neptunian dwarf planet named after MakeMake, first identified by scientists in 2005.

Fourth: honor their ancestors.

The mythology of Easter Island, like so many societies, honors their ancient ones. This supports the scientific hypothesis which justifies a land based explanation.

These ancestors knew the importance of protecting their water supply and the existence of a trans-Neptunian dwarf planet, centuries before our astrologers discovered the planet. Once more, this reveals the wisdom ancient people had much earlier than we have in the 21st century.

We see the stone heads and possible uses in their culture but speculation continues regarding their origin. Many authorities guess initial residents came from South America, but scientific details tell a different story. Linguists maintain the first inhabitants came over from Eastern Polynesia to Easter Island around CE 400. Archaeologists maintain the inhabitants settled between CE 700 and 800, four centuries later than the linguistic estimations. This scientific research seems definitive and complete when we look *only* at Easter Island data. However, when we look at societies living on different islands and further afield, we see different possibilities.

We have evidence that as early as 7500 BCE, Melanesians were voyaging in boats and trading in the obsidian found in volcanoes. This hard stone is useful for carving and sculpting, particularly projectile tips and cutting edges. Since these people knew how to read winds, tides and the stars allowing them to travel great distances, it becomes reasonable then that mariners with this knowledge would be motivated to settle on this ideal remote island. Should people from distance places settle here, then a solid communication base is paramount. They need a method of teaching their history and beliefs to their young, preserving their heritage. An innovated system for passing on this wisdom evolved. Part of this method might have been the Moai and the other part would be rongo-rongo, the hieroglyphic script tablets of Easter Island. The order of the script tells us *how* they wrote it but we do not know what it says. The tables are undecipherable.

It is unclear how long the inhabitants of Easter Island had a written language. Researchers found more than twenty wooden tablets but their age is unknown. Instead of writing upon stone, the inhabitants freely formed tablets from forest resources. This island, once heavily forested, provided citizens with an unlimited supply of wood, not any more. Many global indigenous elders warn us regarding the damage we are doing to the earth. Easter Island, illustrates what the earth might look like if we do not pay attention to warnings and take responsibility for earth preservation. Long ago, this was a forested island. Many writers refer to a lush, forested land and when settlers originally arrived, it still was. Then Polynesian records ceased and the Moai construction stopped.

While the environment was dense woods and lush vegetation, strong farming skills were not required, people freely took what they wanted and devoted their time on ceremonial activities. This meant unfortunately, the citizens had no regard or concern for the planet. They cut trees down for housing, agriculture, cooking or whatever else was required. Not only did the forestation disappear but the soil nutrients disappeared.[60]. By the time Europeans arrived, the settlements were impoverished and the people backward with little evidence of any sophisticated skills at all.

An overview of Easter Island matches warnings we receive today from modern indigenous societies, but we seem to ignore them. It is not too late. We possess extremely powerful tools for tracking potential cataclysms and we have the option and ability for using our resources in a way that is best for both us and the planet. We have a choice.

The last corner of the *Polynesian Triangle* brings a warning from the Waitaha nation, an ancient indigenous people. The Ngāi Tahu people, from the same island also share their principles and remind us of what we once valued.

NEW ZEALAND

New Zealand is a delightful yet mysterious country forming the Southern point of the Oceanic triangle. This information about New Zealand comes from 3 sources: personal communication with the Waitaha elders, published literature and websites of New Zealand nations. Three indigenous nations of this island country include the Maori, the Waitaha, and the Ngāi Tahu.

Literature and technical sources tell us the Maori are the indigenous Polynesian people of New Zealand (Aotearoa). Maori people use the term *tangata whenua,* meaning *people of the land,* applying to themselves for the entire land. They assign different terms identifying families and communities and their relationships with a particular area of land. For example, a tribe functions as *tangata whenua* in one area, but not in another. These people gradually taught visitors from other lands to use this term instead of *New Zealanders.* As a result, we find a vast amount written about the Maori excluding other nations or the groups they class as Maori tribes.

On the Southern tip of the South Island are a people known as the Waitaha people. The Waitaha elders insist they are a unique people with no connection to other nations or tribes. When specifically questioned about the Waitaha nation, some New Zealand scholars claim the Waitaha are either an extinct tribe or one that never existed. Other authorities soften the statements by merging the tribal names, calling them Waitaha Maoris or Maori Waitaha.

In 1988, Geoffrey Clark, Department of Archaeology and Natural History, at the Australian National University in Canberra conducted a study looking into the mystery of both the Maori and Waitaha origin. According to his Waitaha source, groups containing non-Polynesian and Polynesian elements first settled New Zealand more than 2000 years ago.[61] This makes Waitaha the oldest nation on these islands. However, the debate continues. Some claim the Waitaha nation is one of the Ngāi Tahu bands[62].

These Tahu tribal members trace their ancestry back to Tahupōtiki, the founder of both the Maori and Ngāi Tahu nations. From them, we hear legendary stories speaking of their ancestors coming from South America, Africa or Asia. They also tell us that their Polynesian ancestors migrated to New Zealand about 1500 BCE, making them younger than the Waitaha.

According to the Ngāi Tahu legends,[63] when their ancestors arrived on the south island of New Zealand - Te Waipounamu - the Greenstone Isle, they found it uninhabited, yet blossoming with a wonderful food source. Since the Waitaha chose a secluded life, it makes sense there would be the food source but no sign of human activity. Instead of finding human evidence, the Ngāi Tahu find moa and sea-mammal hunting resource and an ideal farming climate.

Archaeology verifies this is the case; the original settlements were predominantly on the coast, near to their major food source, the ocean. Then, after their population increases, 500 - 800 years ago, people move inland and settlements became more widespread.

As word spreads about the plentiful resources of Te Waipounamu (South Island), others abandon their northern homes and move south into this lush haven. Legend tells us they came from the east side of the North Island; they came from other islands of the Oceanic South Pacific. According to the Ngāi Tahu nation, they eventually merged with the resident Waitaha and took control of the south island of New Zealand.

While nations on other continents lived peacefully, in harmony, the Ngāi Tahu records indicate these sub-tribes, became the first population group that exercised tribal democracy. While there is evidence of weaponry from the earlier years, the important lesson coming into the 21st century is tribal democracy can occur peacefully, it does not have to come through war and supremacy. Their visions ensure they are culturally enriched, leading the future, living long and living well. As well, their values closely match modern declarations of current societies. I feel the "white wing" images of our gifted animals remind us of this ancestry. It takes a long time to acquire this level of trust and integrity. Once more, we get gentle reminders of what we need in our society, thanks to the animalistic representation. Reflecting on the values brings us home to our century. Their values are:

- Mā te tuakana e tika ai te teina, mā te teina e tika ai te tuakana.
  Through relationships and respect we can find the way forward
- Whākana ki ō manuhiri i tō kāinga. Mana is upheld through ful-

filling roles and responsibilities
- Mā te mōhio ka mārama, mā te mārama ka mātau. By discussion comes understanding, through understanding comes wisdom
- Kāi Tahu, tītī ā-kai, tītī ā-manawa. Ngāi Tahu, gatherers of resources, resources of lasting endurance
- Aoraki matatū. Holding firm to what defines Ngāi Tahu
- Ko te amorangi ki mua, ko te hāpai ō ki muri. For leadership there must be support

Most modern nations and religions include these basic values, incorporating respect, responsibility understanding, wisdom, endurance and leadership support. Some nations might have more of one than another. When questioned, people of our world would agree these are prime values applicable to their religion or culture. Should the questioning continue, can they confirm they *live the values?*

The world has known about the Maori and the Ngāi Tahu of New Zealand for some time. However, over recent years, the world became aware of the Waitaha Nation, acknowledging they did not belong to either the Maori or the Ngāi Tahu group. The Waitaha people are an independent society whose leaders realize it is time to tell the world their story.

In 1988, Te Pani Manawatu, of the Rangitane tribe within the Waitaha Nation, asked Brailsford, university lecturer, historian and archaeologist to tell their story, sharing their teachings and ancient knowledge with the world. While Brailsford carries the support of many Waitaha nation leaders, there are some who still choose secluded living, believing it is too soon to share the knowledge. This debate continues and we thank Barry Brailsford for adhering to Manawatu's request to share the information. We are richer for it.

Ancient explorers heard the name *Waitaha* but since they never came across villages claiming to be Waitaha communities, they assume it was a mythical tribe. Over time though, stories of the Waitaha nation leak out and we learn of a society living without weapons and creating trading systems that moved industrial stone the length of the country. Today, the Waitaha are a peaceful confederation of over two hundred Iwi.[64]

On the website - http://www.waitaha.org.nz/, Waitaha elders, define themselves as:

...a people of peace, which we hold onto with all our might and mana as we follow in the footsteps of Rongomaraeroa. She gave to our original ancestors the caretakership of the foods of the noble ones, the kumara, the uwha, the taro and

the peruperu. We have honored the sacred covenants given to us, and she has honored us in giving us land in which to plant and to keep our people safe in peace and health.

The Waitaha, like many other indigenous tribes, store their lessons and history in songs. This method protects the accuracy of their legacy. For example, one published song relates when the Waitaha arrive on Earth. It states: "*Waitaha is older than old. Much of the history of this land is our history.* [65]

Waitaha people, living up to their name, *Carrier of Water*, perform rituals around water and know how to search for pure, healthy and peaceful water. They establish the *Rules of Life*, each leading into the next. Brailsford records them as:

- We kept safe the knowledge of the Tides of Life that flow from Marama, the Moon.
- Our Star Walkers joined the stars to the land.
- Our Water Seekers explored the rivers and tested their waters, and the remotest mountains knew the tread of their feet.
- Our Water Carriers planted kumara vines to clothe the nakedness of Papatuanuku.
- Our Stone Shapers brought Pounamu to the peoples of the land and others beyond the distant horizons.
- Our Sea Gardeners nurtured the many children of Tangaroa.
- We are the Tāne Mahuta, and
- We follow Rongo Marae Roa, the God of Peace."[66]

These people chose to remain isolated, keeping their beliefs private until the Elders decided it was time to record their oral history. Then, we learn their truth. Other ancient nations, Kogi and Hopi for example, decided to share their wisdom and warnings at the same time as these people. This is when the Earth enters the **photon band.** It is also the beginning of the Age of Aquarius; a time of awakening.

Although scientific records date the Waitaha back to approximately 2,000 BCE, the Waitaha people tell us they are members of a peaceful culture dating back almost 500,000 years. They are a society with high values, who remained hidden in the mountains at the southern tip of New Zealand's south island for thousands of years.

When the Elders gave permission to include their teachings in this publication, they gently said:

"*Their hearts and yours will resonate with answers when the time is right.*"

They further went on to say

"*We encourage you to continually ask the questions that you sense are requiring answers that would benefit studentship and help in guiding others into the spirit truth. We would suggest, with a great deal of love, that you let the answers come in their own time from the Teachers who, in their time, lead and guide you and those attracted to the spirit of the ancient ones..*"

With this guidance, ponder all information coming to you and ask your own questions. Other nations carry similar wisdom regardless of their age. When we understand the scope of knowledge, we "*…will resonate with answers when the time is right.*"-- given by the teachers.

After summarizing their legends and stories, the *rules* arose. Before long, my spirit friends or guides gently reminded me:

"*We also are Ancient Ones. We carry the kete (basket) of many Gods. Each kete contains a song of a world and it is time for these to blend in harmony. For so long the ketes have been kept separate and those carrying them assumed they had the biggest and best. There is no difference in the ketes. All ketes carry a message or KAWA that is for all nations. It is time to blend and sing a united chorus.*"

This message becomes a key point of ALL modern societies and a key to peace. In *Song of Waitaha* glossary, KAWA means *customary way*. This message emphasizes the importance of discovering a KAWA that compliments or binds members of the entire world together. No single culture or belief system should dictate a lifestyle or attitude. Essentially, the KAWA of cultures, whether ancient or modern, say the same thing and therefore become interchangeable amongst societies.

The *Song of the Waitaha* book carries messages and guidance from their Gods, reinforcing the importance of maintaining peace and balance in our current lives. Within these songs are many prophecies, teachings or *rules*.

- All born of the stars were brothers and sisters, kin within one family." [67]
- Honor them, as you honor the ancestors down through the ages. Humility brings true strength. [68]
- Every aspect of all life is important. There is a
- God for each part of life.
- We must honor our sacred promise

- Remember we fall because of our inner weaknesses not because of the strength of the Gods [69]
- Accept responsibility for your mistakes; do not blame others
- Respect and protect all trees and products of the earth[70].
- A young mind bends to the curve of the magic jawbone. [71]
- Healing brings responsibilities. [72]
- Sadness, pain and anger have no place beside those who tend the plants. The calm mind is the growing mind[73]

The introduction of the *Song of Waitaha* carries the Elders' personal message and becomes a binding prophecy stating:

"Walk in the shadows, hide in the waters, move in the mists, step behind the rainbow to save the taonga (treasure). Protect our ancestors. Hold the truth close and warm it with brave hearts, for pain will consume the land and the circle of our dreams will be broken. And all will seem lost beyond recall.

"Kia Kaha! Be Strong! And the day will come when the taonga will be revealed once more. And we will walk tall with the knowledge in the kete and find joy in the colours of the rainbow.

"And the fires of truth will burn into the hearts of all people of the land.

"Kahuri te Ao…the world turns. And the circle of our dreamtime takes a new shape for a new dawn. And people of all colours join to bind what was broken and live in hope."[74]

These accounts are similar to other aboriginal warnings we hear today. The Waitaha elders further say their truth may not be our truth. They remind us that we each have our own journey and there are many trails leading to wisdom, as they state in the first teaching listed above.

All born of the stars were brothers and sisters, kin within one family.

We truly ARE brothers and sisters; kin. It is wrong to confine or harm *any* creature. This family includes wildlife and other life species, plant life and other cultures. The guidelines apply to ALL life on this planet,

The Waitaha elders divide their teachings into two pieces of truth. The first, called the *Upper Jaw* is a pure stream of knowledge. The other they call the *Lower Jaw.*

The *Lower Jaw* carries stories within stories. The saga method of teaching is a technique which seems to have been lost in recent times. These stories open the doors to true knowledge. For example, since Waitaha means *water carrier*, these people understand how an individual carries his or her own water impacts their world. Do they keep their water peaceful, let it stagnate or do we fill it with anger?

The *Lower Jaw* stories are *pu rakaus* or seedling stories. Not all seedlings prosper; therefore, we need to learn the best way to handle the seedlings. We want them to grow and become part of the *Upper Jaw*. Storytellers look for examples that a child of his culture understands. These *Lower Jaw* stories relate important lessons.

Each person has the Upper Jaw or the *Canoe of the Gods* within. This means we have the truth within. The Waitaha are not the only nation reminding us that we must listen to what our bodies tell us. It seems to be a basic criterion of aboriginal lessons. Unfortunately, it appears that modern commercial societies tend to forget these lessons. We can still recapture them.

The songs of the Waitaha frequently refer to the Sting Ray, portraying its importance. If the Waitaha nation did not exist, then why is the north island of New Zealand called *Whai Repo*, the Waitaha name for the Sting Ray? In Southern Pacific waters, islands are numerous, an invisible shape 2,000 years ago, unless you are looking down from the sky. These stingray-shape islands are either in the Tonga trench, near the Pacific and Australian plate junction or part of today's infamous Ring of Fire. All of these locations have volcanoes and earthquakes, taking us back to the original settlement theory. In spite of ice ages and flooding, the Sting Ray shape remains a dominant island shape of the South Pacific. For example, Ofu Island in the Samoan Islands, Christmas Island in the Kiribati cluster, Moorea Island of Tahiti and Tongatapu of the Tonga islands are all Stingray shape. Since we only see these shapes from the sky, I ask myself, "How did the Waitaha people know that any of these locations were Sting Ray shaped?"

The second guideline suggests that the Elders know of people around the planet and are aware of the planet's diversity.

Honor them, as you honor the ancestors down through the ages. Humility brings true strength. This reminds us of: *We are all born of different colours.*[75]

They further elaborate: -

"Uru Kehu are the children of Kiwa, the golden ones, the short people with pale freckled skin, blue eyes and fair or red hair. They came out... of the rising sun. Known as the Starwalkers they skillfully read the geometry of the stars and guided people to this land.

"Maoriori looked back to Hotu Matua (mountains), for they were a dark skinned, very tall, big boned people with dark eyes and long black hair. Their trail began in the lands of the setting sun. At 6 feet, many called the Maoriori- giants. They also excelled in gardening.

Kiritea were small and fair skinned and had long black hair and green eyes. Their features carried the marks of the tallest of all mountains and the enduring qualities of stone."[76]) The Kiritea, also known as the Stone people, came from Asian lands and carried the greenstone over mountain passes.

This wisdom tells of the original colonization and the travels around the globe. The only location criterion for residency on our planet is the proximity of volcanoes and spring water. Explorers know that both volcanoes and spring water give the breath of life. Water at a healing spring is approximately 4-8% lighter than ordinary water. Today, many people, particularly in the Western world, ensure they drink uncontaminated water. This water is pure, healing and more stabilizing to the body. This knowledge exemplifies what we glean from ancient times; somehow, we recall this today. The volcanoes regularly contribute fresh, fertile soil. We consider this inherent wisdom. Each new village requires three skills. It requires exploration and gardening techniques and what I call *stone knowledge*. These Stone People have the skills necessary for constructing buildings and preparing communication tablets which makes the labeling plausible. However, the problem with this principle is once these labels become accepted, they generate misconceptions and untruths amongst the population.

The third guideline does not give modern society a new concept, but it is a reminder. It is a concept common to many 21st century religions: *Every aspect of all life is important; there is a God for each part of life.* Whichever religion or spirituality path you follow, we can look at this ancient wisdom is a reminder of HOW we should live our lives.

The Waitaha people have multiple gods honoring all life and so do other indigenous nations, only the names change. The *Peace Maker*, Rongo Marae Ro, heals the wounds left by the parting, bringing hope to the living. The *Life giver*, Tāne Muhuta, made the forests, the birds and all creatures of the land. We are kin to all. The *Peace Maker* implies that it pertains only to the dying but I believe it brings forward the strengths of all, ensuring peace. The *Life giver* protects all life.

- We must honor our sacred promise
- Remember we fall because of our inner weaknesses not because of the strength of the Gods[77]

The Waitaha teach that human failure (breaking promises) occurs because of OUR actions, not by a lack of strength of the Gods. Today, people tend to worship or support only one god, making him/her omnipotent. It seems to me that individuals think it is much easier to blame a single, all-powerful entity when things do not go as expected.

When *many* gods share power and strengths evenly, it is easier to accept their wisdom. We cannot fathom many Gods making mistakes when the individual focus of each one is small and directed. Once the indigenous of the Southern nation followed these guidelines, it opens the way for another lesson.

Accept responsibility for your mistakes; do not blame others. Perhaps vowing to honor their Gods, honoring the sacred promises and accepting responsibility for their own mistakes explains why the Waitaha are a peaceful nation. The Waitaha Elders stayed in seclusion for a length of time, avoiding the weaknesses of our modern world. As they come out of seclusion, they fulfill their teaching roll. They remind us to listen to our heart, or inner voice.

Respect and protect all trees and products of the earth[78] The Waitaha are not the only indigenous nation who values trees and products of the planet. This guideline shows the importance of the forest to the Waitaha. Fire is important to the daily life of the Waitaha. Their Gods told them what trees burned effectively. In return, they promise to respect and protect these trees. Over the millenniums, we cut down an increasing number of trees, destroyed the forests, mined for oil and minerals, gradually destroying the earth and its ecosystems. Whether the Waitaha learn the *importance of reforestation* at the same time is unclear.

Half-way around the Earth, the Kogi of Colombia knew the importance of the earth's ecological balance and warned us about the forest decimation.

Here, the Waitaha include details of waka (canoe) building to illustrate the respect and details for future generations. For example, they would not use a fallen tree to build since it is more important to allow the decomposition of fallen tree to re-nurture the earth. They chose only trees close to the shore, minimizing the destruction of the plant life along the "drag" route from source to ocean. For every cut tree, they planted 15 seedlings. Reforestation programs do plant more trees than what was taken since not all grow. Some of the seedlings will rot and return nutrients to the earth. Unfortunately, modern reforestation programs do not appear to re-nurture the earth to the degree of our ancestors.

A young mind bends to the curve of the magic jawbone. [79] The lower jaw analogies were tools for the young. Many cultures utilize tools for body analogies, teaching the young lessons.

Healing brings responsibilities.[80] Indigenous nations protect all creatures they consider healing animals. They also protect their shamans or medicine people. In turn, shamans and their medicine people take responsibility for their people.

Two ancient adages of the Western world come to mind.

"If I save your life, you are my responsibility." AND

"I saved your life; therefore you are responsible to me."

We seem to have lost the impact of these adages over time. Whoever gives or receives healing, must accept a responsibility. Western medical doctors take responsibility, as they perceive it. As an example, some doctors will honor "Do not resuscitate" requests. Veterinary doctors follow *their* oath and take responsibility for animals. Pharmaceutical staff protects the animals and plants that produce remedies. This limits the accountability to these three categories of professions. Ancient people and pioneering settlers take responsibility to heal all life in whatever manner possible.

Sadness, pain and anger have no place beside those who tend the plants. The calm mind is the growing mind.[81]

This guideline corresponds to other indigenous guidelines. In Western society, we begin understanding how our emotions carry energy. When we feel sadness, pain and anger, we pass this emotional energy to other life forms. Other cultures, particularly those of India and China have known the importance of this concept for many centuries. Therefore, they allow only healthy and peaceful humans to touch the water or garden. All life and objects carries the emotions of the person who polished, constructed or harvested it. I believe this calm mind is necessary for growing, building and teaching. This is another ancient wisdom current residents are beginning to utilize. I wonder how different cultures developed a common base of life rules.

When Däniken studies the Kiribati Islands in *Pathway to the Gods*, he refers to Dr. Robin Watt's research. Dr. Watt, an ethnologist, who hypothesizes voyagers might know of faraway islands and travel in their direction. The residents could then direct them farther afield. If this is the situation, then perhaps the following is plausible.

The Waitaha Elders talk about traveling for thirteen nights and going to an island called Waitangi Ki Roto. The name and description does not conform to a specific island today. Possibly, the land they call Waitangi Ki Roto is no longer in existence or they use a mode of transportation unfamiliar to us. If the unknown transportation method was astral, then this explains how they knew the Sting Ray shape of the North Island.

This mysterious speculation of astral transportation or vision helps explain how multiple societies around the globe know of the Red Star, called Nibiru. Nibiru comes into view every 3600 years. The Waitaha knew about it, the Sumerian, Dogon, and Egyptian people knew of this *Red* Star. How did this happen, if there was no astral travel or vision?

India's Ayurvedic knowledge and Chinese health programs emphasize instructions for the types of food to eat and times for consumption. The Waitaha songs and sages also carry this knowledge. The detailed information specifically brings the individual body and the environment into balance, healing the body. Ancient sagas relate details about food as a ritual and energy builder. Prior to setting sail in an outrigger canoe, they ate specific foods for seven nights. Then they fasted while they worked. Exerting heavy effort without food cleanses the blood and allows increased energy to flow when needed. The scientific details may be unknown but they knew the importance of individual characteristics. One difference though is they observe and remember the result.

We base so much of our lives today on the observation of our ancestors. This is how we know what to plant, when to harvest and what to eat. The Waitaha ancestors observe wildlife and discover what is edible, simply by watching what they ate.

Waitaha teachings, tell us what berries are edible. If the forest lives today, the guidelines still apply. They state:

Orange berries could be eaten but had to be steeped in water and roasted. Red ones were good unless they had a kernel or hard centre. The dark colours such as purple, blue and black were deadly, except for <u>tawa, taraire</u> and <u>tanekaha</u>. <u>Tutu</u> is edible if you avoid the seed. [82]

The Tawa and Taraire are from the *Beilschmiedia* (Laurel) family. Tanekaha is from the *Podocarpaca* family, otherwise known as celery pine. Today, we know

Tutu as Sumac Coriaria, Rhus Coriaria or Sumac Spice. Not that long ago, these plants supplied the dart poison in South America. Today, we use it as a spice and decorative plant. The Waitaha know what parts were safe and how to use it.

Poppy, Gotu Kola and Ginkgo Biloba are all therapeutic remedies but used incorrectly, are hazardous. Sometimes publications post warnings without clarification or further advice. This is when being an informed consumer is mandatory. Like other indigenous nations, the Waitaha learned methods and remedies for successful gardening. They learned how to utilize modern technology to move in harmony with the natural systems of our planet, rather than against it. One example is the importance of matching our energy to the regional energy of the planet. Foods from distant places carry challenging energy which may damage our energy. It seems we damage the entire planet when we ignore the local natural forces.

According to *Song of Waitaha* sagas, the ancients repeatedly travel a specific ocean root, returning many times to Waitangi Ki Roto. At one time, they saw all the stone statues toppled and finally, hearing about huge waves hitting the shore causing much damage. When the inhabitants came down from the hills, the travelers discovered how much was lost. These tall statues in this saga suggest ruins similar to Easter Island.

There are other possibilities. One is the famous sunken city, Nan Madol on Pohnpei Island. Necker Island, a part of the Hawaiian chain of islands displays many heads atop a cliff, reminiscent of Easter Island. Tongatapu Island exhibit large structures, gate-like and backrests, all believed to be spiritual.

Here we discover a number of islands with similar artifacts, all linked to New Zealand. These islands are all on major ocean current paths and home to many volcanoes. The huge waves could have been a Tsunami caused by an earthquake or volcanic eruption. It could also have been the sinking of an ancient land. We do not need to have all the details of the catastrophic events to realize the importance of the Waitaha warnings. The magnitude of the evidence we do have is sufficient to realize the significance of the warnings we receive.

If you choose to go beyond the sacred spring in the mountains of its source, remember who made them, and respect the secrets within. And think of the ancestors who traveled far to their final rest within the stone.[83]

The following four axioms do not include comments but this does not reduce their importance. They are:

1. Only those who walk without anger and serve others may receive gifts. Put aside the rage.
2. Learning comes from the smallest of creatures.
3. We are ever aware of the need to understand before the need to act.
4. Follow the teaching of the hawk. It favours those in greatest need. The young and old eat first.

One Waitaha song, still applies today. It is:

No one knows today will be followed by tomorrow.
No one is sure the seed we plant will grow.
No one is certain life continues.
Everything is a gift. [84]

It is a useful reminder that messages applicable today go back thousands of years.

MELANESIA

The next island grouping, Melanesia, has a diverse mix of cultures. The large island of New Guinea north of Australia and south of the Philippines splits into two regions - Melanesia's New Guinea and Indonesia's Papua Barat; formerly called West Irian Jaya. As expected, the Melanesian people know no boundaries on their islands; political boundaries simply did not exist.

We have archaeological evidence of people living on New Guinea Island as far back as 35,000 years ago[85]. These people left behind tools for farming, building and environmental management. Archaeological study of these miscellaneous tools show that even then, our ancestors knew the importance of environmental management and forest preservation.

During the Last Glacial Age, New Guinea was part of Sahul or *Greater Australia*. Jim Allen, an archaeologist at Australia's La Trobe University and Peter Kershaw from the Department of Geography and Environmental Science at Monash University, Melbourne confirms

"New Guinea was fully integrated with the Australian Continent."[86]

There continues to be speculation and archaeological debating whether these people were in any way connected to Australian aborigines. The Aboriginal culture does not show the technical advancements we find on Sahul, yet cultures from both regions display sophisticated astronomical wisdom. Russian historian Boris Frolov notes:

"...indigenous tribal peoples as far afield as North America, Siberia and Australia all called the Pleiades star-group the 'Seven Sisters.[87]

It seems an unlikely coincident that the same knowledge could evolve around the globe in the same era. Once more, there must have been communication.

Richard Rudgley notes in *"Lost Civilizations of the Stone Age"*

...a tradition of communicable knowledge of the heavens that has existed for over 40,000 years, since a time roughly coinciding with the beginning of the Upper Paleolithic. This is something that is extremely awkward for most widely accept views of history of knowledge and science – in short it is far, far too early for most people to accept.

Unfortunately, it seems many of the earth's 21st century population lost the knowledge of Sahul and New Guinea's environmental management, forest preservation and usage of the astronomical data. Future generations may pick up and adapt portions of the basic concepts but it does not seem that the full lesson is picked up and expanded upon. This is the key of our ancient wisdom. They gave us basics, taught how it evolved and then left it to people in future generations to expand and build upon ancient premises.

Contrary to the New Guinea proof of humans being there 35,000 years ago, Fijian residents insist the Lapita people from Fiji's Viti Levu Island are the earliest-known people to have lived in the region. DNA and legendary stories point to a common ancestor or native of the entire region, predating Austronesians, Polynesia, Micronesia and Melanesia The ancient Lapita people live in six Melanesian locations: 1)New Caledonia, 2)New Guinea, 3)Solomon Islands, 4)Samoa, 5)Fiji and Tonga, and 6)Micronesian territory, Kiribati. If you ask about their origin, the Lapita people will either tell you: "We have always been here." or "We came from the sky."

After hearing this, a challenge arose as scientists, anthropologists and historians sought a single explanation. Out of this came several contradictory opinions.

According to the Metropolitan Museum, these people originally came from Southeast Asia, and then moved east into the Oceania islands.[88]

Scholar Jim Allen insists he located the origin of the Lapita civilization in the Bismarck Archipelago off New Guinea. He believes it was first colonized 30,000-35,000 BCE[89].

In the last theory, archeologists identified unique pottery near the community Lapita on New Caledonia Island, thereby assigning the name – *Lapita* –to these people. This evidence only takes them back roughly 3,000 years. We find remains of used earth-ovens, providing evidence of aquatic, land and animal farming. Confirmation of their lifestyle is on many islands and coastlines telling us they were a seafaring people who navigate the oceans with ease, settling on varied shorelines. This also explains why there is a versatility of culture. People settling on varied lands and developing various fishing or farming techniques create their own cultural style.

In 2005, 1200 miles away on the island of Efate, Vanuatu, thirteen headless skeletons turned up in an ancient cemetery going back to 1200 BCE. This is the oldest graveyard ever found in the South Pacific; 200 years earlier than when anthropologists thought the Lapita arrived on this island. Based upon this find, they believe the first humans to live in Vanuatu was this tribe..[90]

After this amazing find, Alex Bentley, an anthropologist at Britain's Durham University conducted extensive research. Two years later, in 2007, Jeanna Bryner of Live Science Magazine wrote an article.[91] Resulting from the anthropological discoveries and analysis, Bryner states the Lapita people initially buried the deceased with heads attached. Later, after the flesh had rotted away they dug up the graves, removing the skulls and keeping them in sacred places. Bentley surmises that:

"It is a sign of veneration of the senior individual. The skulls of all those buried were removed during the mortuary process and presumably curated somewhere else."

One intriguing piece of this research is learning most of the bodies were immigrants but one skeleton had three skulls of local bodies lying upon his chest. Bentley speculates that burying a local alongside traveling immigrants implies Lapita's respect, usually respect for their ocean travels. Bentley justifies this by noting that the burials were for Pacific mariners, some of the best navigators on earth in over 3,000 years. This further suggests admiration of sea-faring people's long-distance traveling abilities.

Most scientists believe they were from East Asia. Bentley did not support this.

Lapita people had both a terrestrial diet and marine food diet. Depending upon where the site was, inland or coastal, a corpse confirms which diet type and lifestyle they lived. Sometimes a village has access to both locations. This illustrates how the body successfully combines both terrestrial and marine food, reaping the benefits required by the body. Observing this evidence shows modern societies the benefits.

The Lapita people's history is versatile and creative. Written research demonstrates how these people avoid floods and storms by living in villages of stilt-legged houses. They survive floods, storms, and other anomalies of nature, adapting their eating habits according to availability. They knew how to survive. Today many lands endure floods and storms, forgetting the creative home building of these ancient people. Even though evidence of Lapita residency is strongest in the Melanesian islands, different sources substantiate their residency in many Oceania islands. This spreads the wisdom throughout the islands.

MICRONESIA

Micronesia means 'small islands'. This grouping of islands includes over two thousand tropical islands scattered across the Pacific Ocean between Hawaii and the Philippines. Humans lived on these islands for more than 5,000 years. DNA analysis indicates both Micronesians and Polynesians have a Southeast Asian ancestry, suggesting humans migrated from Asia to Philippines and Indonesia and from there to the Micronesia islands.

Many Oceania islands are void of ancient artifacts or ancient people. The one exception is Kiribati, an island cluster in the Micronesia regions. Kiribati is a group of sixteen small islands. It is here that we find the island Arorae stones or maraes. This finding suggests the possibility of a prehistoric spiritual or meeting place Even today, residents of the Kiribati islands honor their family and social traditions. After a Kiribati resident told Erich Däniken about the mysterious objects, he traveled to these islands to see these maraes.

Here he discovered monolithic stones the size of a man or larger. On Arorae Island, he discovered two stones consisting of granite, a rock formation absent from this island. He then found three others formed of volcanic stone. Geologists tell us that Pacific atolls are typically the residue of extinct volcanos. Yet some of the small islands in the Kiribati cluster display no evidence of ancient volcanos. Here we have two anomalies on these islands formed with non-existent stone. What happened five thousand years ago remains a mystery.

Explorers, archeologists and anthropologists frequently refer to these well-known stones as the famous *Arorae Navigation Stones*. Native navigators around the globe use night stars to maintain a set course. They use landmarks to set a canoe on its course during the day. At night, the directions to the nearby islands relate to certain stars. Some ingenious ancestor hit upon the idea of setting up the stones as permanent sailing directions. They could then check on the star's position and movement before a voyage began.

When you plot these directions onto a chart, you discover four of the directions pointing to the three nearest islands have a constant error of five degrees. The following is a drawing of how the ancient Micronesian residents, perhaps the Lapita nation, may have used the stones or slabs for this purpose.[92]

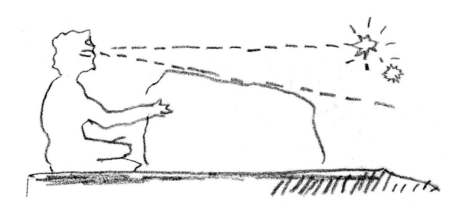

There is no scientific proof of this use. However, our imagination reveals an image of someone sitting beside the stone projecting a trip through correlation between the stars and a slab. Researchers accepted this plausible use.

In addition to the *Arorae Navigation Stones,* Däniken found solidified footprints in stone beds outside the village of Banreaba, Kiribati. Each one measured 1.37m (4.5 ft) by 1.14m (3.75 ft.). Some prints indicated six toes while others showed twelve.

Also in *Pathway to the Gods* Däniken includes details the resulting three direct lines of megalithic stones. The first one points to Niutao Island, Tuvalu, 1,800 km away. The second line points to the Fiji islands, 1,900 km away. The third line points to the Tuamotu Islands 4700 km away.[93] All three point southeast. The longitude difference from start to finish is approximately 7°, 2° and 45° respectively. It is uncertain whether Kiribati was the starting point or the culmination point of the travels.

Today, the natives of the Oceania remain conservative and resistant to change. Conspicuous displays of individual achievement or wealth are discouraged. Once more their ancestors AND ours had these traits which we can easily blend into our Western lives.

Part VIII - Eurasia

PHILIPPINES

There are fourteen known tribes in the Philippine islands. Where they came from we do not know, their ancestry is a mystery. One suggestion is they travelled the oceanic paths of the Jomon, Polynesians or Micronesians. Another suggestion is that people crossed an Ice Bridge from Asia 30,000 years ago. Graham Hancock, author of *Underworld*, describes the Ice Age as lasting 5,000 years occurring sometime between 123,000 BCE to 15,000 BCE.[94] During this era, a land mass known as "Sunda Land" spread around Malaysia, Indonesia, the Philippines and north to Japan. This creates a larger bridge quite different than the Bering Bridge between Asia and North America. Through Hancock's research, he discovered:

Around modern Malaysia, Indonesia and the Philippines, and stretching as far north as Japan, lay the endless plains of 'Sunda Land', a fully fledged antediluvian continent. It was submerged very rapidly sometime between 14,000 and 11,000 years ago.

Up until about 12,000 years ago, the three main islands of Japan formed a continuous landmass.[95]

If we rely on the bridge theory, then we face an unusual dilemma. How did the Stone-Age humans arrive prior to 30,000BCE? It might explain the Austronesian-speaking people arriving between 4,000BCE to 2,000BCE, but not the continuous occupation of the Tabon Caves by hunter-gatherers for almost 50,000 years. There are more than 200 Tabon Caves in the Palawan province of the Philippines. In 1962, Dr. Robert B. Fox unearthed a 22,000 year old skull cap in one of the Tabon Caves. Researchers verify Negritos fit into this ancestral chain from the Tabon Man down to the current Aeta tribe. Whether Tabon Man links to other tribes is uncertain. Thanks go to the late Dr. Fox who recognized the important implication of these discoveries to countries throughout the Pacific and Southeast Asia. These cultures benefit from the learning based on wisdom gained from knowing about the historical development of the Tabon people. This clarifies why we need to learn about wisdom of long ago, giving us excellent examples of ways to blend good traits from our past into our present way of life.

Based upon the Tabon Caves history, we know the Aeta tribe lived on Pinatubo Volcanic Mountain until 1991 when the world experienced one of the worst eruptions ever. These people still prefer mountain living, resisting change and adaptation whenever intruders arrive. They make adjustments in certain areas but resist change in others.

In World War II, the American soldiers landed on the Philippine islands with no jungle or survival training whatsoever. When the troops were suffering from thirst, one of their Aeta guides went into the woods, took out his knife and made a cut in one of the tall plants. Out of this plant flowed enough water to fill the troop's water bottles. The Aeta people continue teaching survival techniques to servicemen of all countries. They explain which plants were edible, poisonous or medicinal. They also taught how to use bamboo for pots, spears, or fuel. These remedies and solutions are still useful for modern western society. Unfortunately, we restrict our imagination and rely on chemical solutions rather than looking to nature and working in harmony with it.

The Aeta people deserve our admiration. They choose living on volcanic mountainsides although volcanos destroy most of their world; they are resilient enough to rebuild their communities. They bring forward their skills and knowledge, teaching others the ways of their past while learning and adopting new abilities. In addition, Aeta people willingly share their knowledge with others. What was once a remote jungle is now a protected conservation area. A navel harbor is now a diving resort.

This nation, the Aeta people, moves forward into the 21st century with pride and integrity, preserving their traditional beliefs. It is unclear whether the Aeta follow the same traditional laws as the other tribe - the Apayaos. If they do, their legends survive with confidence, since the Apayaos teach their young history and many of their traditions.

There are two branches to the Apayaos' roots. One came down through Indonesia via Southeast Asia. The other is Mongolian via Central Asia. Their physical traits eventually amalgamated, producing the people living on the island of Luzon.

The Apayaos people are kind, hospitable and generous. Those who know them also attribute other traits to them such as: courageous, freedom loving and protecting others. Their life rules include:

- If a man steals, his wife will leave.
- If you acquire money unfairly and buy rice, the rice will not give strength.

I believe these seven common laws are still in practice.

- Must not steal
- Do not tell false stories
- Do not court another's wife
- Respect the rights of others
- Give food to visitors
- Teach children old legends and customs
- Honor and learn the complete system of social etiquette

The smallest tribe is the Tasaday. The Tasaday appear to be Stone Age people living in the 21st century. This is not surprising if a nation chooses to follow the beliefs and practices of ancient times, carried from their ancestors.

In the late 1960s, experts and governmental officials told of an ancient tribe, the Tasaday, who remain hidden in the jungle, avoiding contact with the modern world. In 1971, television and magazine reporters interviewed them. Then, fifteen years later, experts on David Brinkley's television program claimed the entire Tasaday portrayal was a hoax.

Originally, David Brinkley and several qualified scientific experts describe the Tasaday as an ancient Stone Age people who remained isolated in the jungle for thousands of years. Around the same time, National Geographic magazine photographed and interviewed the group. Then in the mid-eighties, Swiss reporter, Oswald Iten and Rizal "Joey" Lozano, hiked into the jungle and uncovered the deception. They declared these people were not living primitive lives; they dressed in modern clothing and were not even ancient.

Speculation continues until the present day. Possibly, they are a small tribal group who prefer living an isolated life high in the mountains or deep in the jungles. If so, they would appear prehistoric. They might move from the hills through necessity. It is also possible that the country's political leaders found a small remote group, bribed them and dressed them up, cueing the appropriate actions as an attention getting method.

In the late 60s and early 1970s, there was a small group of indigenous people *discovered* on the island of Mindanao, the large south island of the Philippines. They remain secluded in the jungle for months, perhaps years, at a time. It was only when a helicopter pilot reported seeing them in a clearing below that government officials and anthropologists pursued their identity. We do not know this impact on their size; they are a small group.

Their name **Tasaday**; pronounced *TAW saw dye* or *Ta SAH dye*, comes from one of the nearby mountains. Anthropologists, Robert Fox confirmed their language, Manobo, was distinct from the other languages in the area.

Beginning in 1971, American television specials, narrated by Jack Reynolds, relate stories of a small native group suddenly exposed to modern technology. They refer to a loss of innocence and the loss of a sacred haven away from wars, traffic and violence. They are content with their food, healthier for it and live a life without worry or want. This description parallels reports from other secluded cultures.

In 1991, the Kogi people from Colombia, South America warned us about environmental damages in the film "Heart of the World". Another warning comes from a sect of the Hopi in the United States who adopts a secluded life, rejects modern technology, and follows traditional beliefs and practices. These three ancient cultures protect the veracity of their society by hiding from the modern world.

Generally politicians and external societies honor the wishes and leave isolationists alone. It seems wealthy and political leaders of remote countries shape events of their land to meet their needs. I believe this applies to the Tasaday lifestyle.

From 1971 forward, documentation refers to a Philippine Government minister, Manuel Elizalde, known as Manda. Manda carries a dubious background but we acknowledge his help for many indigenous groups in his country. Elizalde encourages minorities' to have pride in their heritage and beliefs. He moves groups to remote locations, or villages, where they can practice their traditions in relative security[96]. Some reporters view this as an altruistic action. After discovering the Tasaday, he formed an organization known as the PANAMIN – *Private Assistance for National Minorities*. The creation of villages in the Philippines during the 20th century is similar to North American reservations during the 19th century. The only difference is that one location allows maintenance of beliefs, the Philippines. The North Americans outlaw traditions and "force" adoption of the modern western way.

Manda visualizes the primitivism of locales and insists tribal people in their special communities adhere to his perception. Possibly, this is what leads to the criticism and speculation of the Tasaday hoax. When scientists find the people dressed in western clothing, living in modern huts and working with contemporary tools, the media immediately declare "they were fakes". Did they put on a facade? Possibly, they simply conform to a leader's demand and adopt some of the modern lifestyle practices that were unique and different.

In exchange for the *gift,* Manda insists they put on a façade or show when strangers appear. Naturally, they return to the newly discovered products and way of living when the show ends. Since visitors require permission to visit the Tasaday, Manda controls the exposure to the Tasaday.

Elizalde was a powerful man, albeit misguided. He controls each reporter's visit, what relics they saw. As a ruse, on one of the jungle trips, Robert Fox introduces fellow anthropologist, Jesus Peralta, as a scientific illustrator rather than his official title of a Paleolithic archaeologist. Peralta saw a man using a 10,000 years old high-angle opaline quartz scraper[97] identical to Stone Age tools he had excavated in the Cagayan Valley in Luzon.[98] When he told Manda of his finding it, Manda quickly confiscated it. It never resurfaced. This illustrates where combining 20th century tools and Stone Age scraper is productive and effective.

Prior to 1971, archaeologists had been exploring various caves throughout the country. The relics from these caves were carbon dated tools at approximately 22,000 years old, more than twice the age of the opaline quartz scraper found by Peralta. Writers Fox and Hemley claim that this 10,000 year old opaline scraper found by Peralta is the oldest one still in use. Manda may control what the public sees but he cannot completely control what anthropologists report and document.

Speculation continues about this lost group. Rather than view them as a fraud, let us look at them as descendents of an ancient people, carrying forward the ancient way of life. They are peaceful, do not seem to want for anything and are satisfied with their life.

Another anomaly that keeps appearing when studying the Philippine population is the rice story. The Tasaday "bribe package" included rice. Apparently, they ate the rice raw; as this was their first exposure to this food. These people live on the Mindanao Island, the Southern end of the Philippine islands. One thousand kilometres away, on the Northern Island near Luzon are the famous Banaue Rice Terraces, more than 2000 years old. Why would residents in one location know about growing and cooking rice while residents in a nearby location do not? It is possible that the Tasaday remain secluded, deep in the jungle away from the rice growers from Banaue.

It appears at some point in history, their ancestors chose secular living like the Kogi, Buddhist and Hopi nations. Around the planet, people search for a lifestyle harmonious with their beliefs. The Tasaday said they live in the forest and that is all they know. Written reports confirmed this statement. Their ancient tools meet their needs. They do not need modern machinery. Their diet does not require rice as does the Banaue diet.

Unfortunately, these people no longer live a life without worry or want. They depend upon the new styles and fabrics. After trying the new clothes, they can no longer return to their former garments. According to the stories that came down through time, the Tasaday people lived an idyllic life, very different from ours, maintaining the balance and integrity of time long ago. Now stories leak out about this tribe being, manipulated and then simply abandoned.

We need to look closely at their historical way of life, decide what components and values we can incorporate into our world and then let them live as they choose.

INDONESIA

In December, 2004, a major Tsunami and Earthquake disaster measuring 9.0, struck areas surrounding the Indian Ocean, including Siberut Island, just west of Sumatra Indonesia. This is the home of an ancient people called the Mentawai. Prior to this disaster, they lived in seclusion but after the disaster, they began interacting with other societies. Like the Kogi of Colombia, the Mentawai Sikereis, Medicine Men, ask their outside contacts to give the world a message:

"Tell the world, we are Mentawai and this is our culture. As long as we have forests, the Sikereis will always be."

Archeologists and indigenous songs tell us the Mentawai arrived on the islands somewhere between 2000 and 500 BCE. They journeyed south from the north island, Siberut, down to the southern islands Sipora and the Pagai. They remained isolated until 2004. After the tsunami and earthquake catastrophe, many people came out of seclusion and they began offering tours through their land, talking about their culture and spiritual practices. Preservation of their culture is mainly for the integrity of the tribe but tourists benefit as well.

According to their mythical stories, the world began when a young boy transformed himself into the first SAGO tree, the *Tree of Life.* This transformation ensures that his people would never run out of food. The Sago Palm is very old. Legend tells us it has been around since the days of the dinosaurs, evolving over millions of years. The Mentawai, like other cultures, consider it a local sacred tree worthy of their honor. The Maya of Central America, for example honor the Seiba Tree; the Haida of Canada honor the cedar tree. Mentawai Shamans believe it is important to maintain the harmony with the spirits of the forest. One way they do this is tattooing a Sago Tree on their body.

Inner Bridges, an earlier publication, stresses the importance of living locally, consuming products produced and grown close by. This keeps us in harmony with the Earth and the living beings of your global region. The Mentawai Sikereis say the same thing, which is why they have a local sacred tree. As spiritual leaders and healers of the community, they know the antidotal plants growing nearby and in the same region. They know it is unnecessary to go far from where you live to harvest the remedy plant. They tell us the healing properties of every plant, what is deadly, what heals and what is antidotal. By listening to the Sikereis, learning the herbal history of their past and incorporating it into Western remedies, we gain important knowledge.

The Mentawai live and stay in the dense jungles while other tribes socialize with coastal visitors. When the 2004 Tsunami came, many tribal people left the island, but the Mentawai people stayed behind in the tropical forest. Now, researchers and historians express gloom about the Mentawai future. By learning and exploring their histories and remedies of the past, we initiate a connection into modern times, preserving the culture. Anthropologists predict extinction within ten years if left unaided. This doom corresponds with the Maya calendar's predicted ending. However, if we learn from this culture, we can incorporate it to modern lifestyles, making it a positive event preserving their future.

After 2004 tsunami, the Mentawai citizens began telling us of the importance of their forest and the devastation forewarning. Their precise words may differ from the Waitaha, Kogi and Hopi, but all nations broke their silence. In the late 1980s and early 1990s selected representatives spoke. Brailsford spoke for the Waitaha and Alan Ereira spoke for the Kogi. Then in 1994, Graham Hancock visited the elders of the Hopi nation and received their warning[99]. When leaders from ancient cultures such as these, speak of disaster, perhaps we should take heed. It is important that we understand that life itself will not end. Our life, as we know it, may adjust but it does not mean there will be total destruction. These predictions are not new; they are similar to ones from long ago and the world did not end then.

JAPAN

The beauty of this land and wisdom of the people leaves gentle warmth within many of us as we search for answers to multiple questions. One question is "How did they get there and where did they come from? Many people believe the earthenware known as "corded pottery" originated in Japan. If the Ancient Ones traveled from the Americas and the Oceanic islands up to Japan, navigating via the Pacific Currents, we begin understanding how the knowledge of pottery making traveled through the lands. We see how these patterns originated in the Americas with Japanese Ainu people expanding the technology, molding it into a unique technique.

Ancient explorers proved eons ago that maritime routes from the Oceania islands followed the Pacific currents heading north toward the Asian continent. Depending upon the currents and winds, these currents connect the islands, allowing citizens to share knowledge and new skills. This becomes one more pathway around the globe; another avenue for knowledge to open doors of wisdom.

A key indigenous tribe of Japan is the Jomon people. Jon Turk, adventurer and author, wrote an exploratory report about an ancient man, the Kennewick man.[100] This introduces them and I began studying their unique history. He learned of this skeleton in the late 1990s and began wondering; how such an ancient skeleton of Asian ancestry could end up in Washington State, USA.

In 1996, hikers discovered a skeleton in the muddy Columbia River near the town of Kennewick, Washington State. Scientific testing estimated he died sometime between 9,300 and 9,600 years ago. But who was he? Where did he come from? Initially, scientists assumed the skeleton was Native American. Later research proved his cranium matched both the Polynesians from the South Pacific and the Ainu of Japan, disproving the North American theory.

Although the Ainu today live on Japan's northern island, Hokkaido Island, a straight line from there down to Fiji, 7500 km or 4500 miles long reveals a range of possible homelands, Kiribati, the Marianas or the Philippines.

In 1997, Loring Brace, Professor of Anthology at the University of Michigan, declares the Kennewick skeleton was Jomon, one of the original people of Japan. Another expert, James Chatter, a forensic archaeologist, corroborates this ancestry. Chatter's studies include South America research where Chilean co-explorers identified ancient skulls found there were also Jomon. These excavations included pottery fragments matching Jomon pottery. We now have three locations, Japan, Chile and the United States linked by these skeletons and pottery pieces.

Stepping back in time, we might understand how cultures spread. Approximately 10,000 years ago, the Jomon people were a nomadic, hunter-gatherer tribe. They learn about their island environment including wildlife, seasonal plants, and the skills necessary to harvest, process and store whatever they needed. Their invention of earthenware, allows them to store seasonal products, trade and establish a more sedentary lifestyle, but they never lost the mobility of their heritage. They know the characteristics of items such as specific trees and apply this knowledge toward construction of canoes, homes or other articles. By keeping their heritage current in each generational life, they were able to carry this knowledge into societies around the globe.

Prior to the discoveries in Chile and the United States, scientists assumed the Jomon people were secluded to the Japanese islands. During this time, the shorelines of Asia and Alaska merged over the Bering Strait. After evidence surfaced in the Americas, the assumption arose that the Jomon people wandered across the Bering land bridge away from their home in Northern Japan into the Americas. Later historians suggested they developed sailing skills strong enough to handle the currents across the Pacific into the Americas, leaving behind the Kennewick Man in North America.

Although Jon Turk speculated about the origin of the Kennewick, he was not as interested in historical theories as he was in the feasibility of the travels. Therefore, he applied his expert kayaking skills to retrace a potential route heading north from Japan to Koryakskiy and across the Bering Strait. He proved migrating along this route was viable for ancient cultures. Did they travel across the Bering Strait, south through North America and Central America into South America? Was this the best route for the Jomon getting from their original Japanese homeland down to Valdivia, Ecuador, the Fijian islands or Washington State, USA?

Another unanswered question concerns the corded pottery. The only recorded evidence of matching "corded" pottery links northern Japan and Valdivia, Chile. If they were simple hunter-gatherers, as many assume, why did they create the pottery with the corded pattern? This was excess baggage for their migratory lifestyle. Or did they migrate at all?

Graham Hancock, author of the Underworld[101] introduces another possibility. He speculates that over time, strong ships carried them through the currents of the Pacific Ocean. This vehicular possibility answers many theories. These could take the pre-Inca, pre-Moche, and the Olmec into the Polynesia regions of the Pacific where they would have met the Waitaha of New Zealand, the Jomon of Japan, or the people from Africa. The scope of this speculation opens the study of the significance of cross-cultural trading.

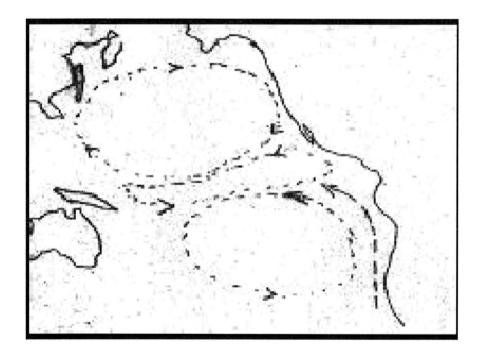

Pacific currents

This drawing illustrates an overview of the three main Pacific current patterns. First, the currents in the Northern Hemisphere flow clockwise, moving north from Japan to the Bering Strait and down the North American coastline.

Second, the North Equatorial current flows away from the Americas connecting with both the Kuro Shio (past Japan) and the Equatorial counter back to the Americas.

Third, the other prime currents are the Humboldt and Peru currents. They head north along the South American coastline becoming the South Equatorial current, flowing past Valdivia, and the Fijian islands.

The first evidence supporting the ocean current theory concerns the Pericú people. Archaeological records for Pericú people in Baja California Sur, Mexico date back about 10,000 years ago. Their distinctive "long-headed" skulls match those of Polynesians, Jomon and Ainu. This correlations gives credence to the theoretical explanations of the Jomon travels.

Secondly, the Valdivia pottery matches the Jomon pottery, dating back more than 10,000 years. This rough calculation of time corresponds with the Pericú migratory estimates. The Humboldt/Peru Current runs from Australia across to South America and up the coast of the continent flowing back across the Pacific Ocean at the Equator. It is a long oceanic journey but the archaeological evidence confirms the feasibility of these voyages.

In the scientific world, debate continues, leaving unanswered questions and unsubstantiated hypothesis. Unfortunately, 10,000-year-old cultures leave us little evidence behind satisfying the scientific criteria. It seems, skeletons and pottery are quite sufficient. Scientific evolution is fluid, as evidence and scientific study evolves, opinions change. Consequently, we base historical knowledge and opinion on both evidence and faith.

When we *cross the threshold* and begin taking things on faith with the realization that events happen or exist beyond current comprehension, then we have options. Once we accept the precept that the Jomon, or intervening cultures, traveled across oceans and possibly, around the globe, we need to look at who else is in this connective chain. In Jon Turk's book, he sites only two indicators of the Jomon excursions, the Kennewick Man and the "twisted cord" pottery.

In contrast, Graham Hancock expands beyond the Kennewick Man and the Jomon into the Pacific Ocean, where *many* cultures existed. One of these cultures is the mythical Lemurian society who dates farther than the Jomon/Kennewick existence. Researchers speculate the Jomon culture was simple, contributing very little to subsequent societies. Yet, in 1998, Graham Hancock's trip to the Jomon site at Sannai-Muryama, near the north tip of Honshu Island, Japan,[102] told an alternative story.

This ancient site reveals evidence of a pottery-generating civilization including public buildings, wide streets and planned sanitation, paralleling the time and life in Egypt, a benchmark for Western society. In addition to the buildings and sanitation, they found pyramids similar to the Egyptian pyramids with symbolic burial patterns. Rather than preserving stories of an ancient nation of hunter-gatherers *evolving* into a social society, legends tell of a society suddenly *emerging* and settling into the region.

Here, according to legends, we have a culture, the Jomon, who suddenly appear. If they were descendents of the Lemurian society, they give us lessons from a sophisticated advanced culture. Geological evidence indicates a continent sank rapidly in the middle of Pacific around the same era as the archaeological Jomon dates. It is certainly plausible then, survivors fled to Japan, Valdivia, Ecuador, the Fijian islands or the Philippines, traveling with the oceanic currents.

Since the Philippine tribes are along the theoretical migratory path of the ocean's currents, potentially they genetically link to the Jomon. There is an ongoing debate about the people of the Philippines crossing a land bridge from Asia 30,000 years ago, before the Ice Age. Graham Hancock dates the Ice Age as sometime between 125,000 and 17,000 years ago.[103]

In all these lands, we find archaeological evidence of technological skills matching, or superior to, humans' current expertise. If we could slow our pace of life, we would have sufficient time to study ancient technology discovering secrets applicable to the 21st century.

Richard Hooker from Washington State University – WSU, summarizes the history of the Jomon and Yayoi peoples of Japan. An article states:

"Although the Japanese do not settle Japan until the third century BC, humans had lived in Japan from about 30,000 BCE."[104]

Flint tool remnants confirm this data. The archaeological world acknowledges the Jomon are the oldest pottery-making culture. They were also a distinct, homogeneous group. Although many archeologists categorize these people as hunter-gatherers, their life practices go beyond. Their crop planting provided a reason for pottery. Approximately 12,000 years ago, they created pottery to hold their rice - not a typical accomplishment for hunter-gatherers. For 14,000 years, one culture, one language and one religion stayed intact.[105] Hooker, a former professor at WSU, notes the Jomon, in isolation from Egyptians, Sumerians, and China's Yellow River (Huanghe) people, created pottery, villages, and earth religions.

Hancock and Hooker found a rationale for the Jomon extinction theory. Societies are anxious to preserve their inherited knowledge of ancestral wisdom and teachings more than their tribal identity. They absorb names of other cultures while they pass on the teachings. This realization came when all the local residents Hancock researches and explores in Northern Japan are Ainu. Today, they are the only acknowledged indigenous people in the region. Perhaps the Jomon are not extinct, simply a group of people who adopt another name. In current times, we find societies, based on languages, adopting the cultural name of others. For example, Celtic describes the cultures of Ireland, Scotland, Wales, Cornwall, the Isle of Man and the French region of Brittany. Yet, historians hypothesis their origin is the Ukraine region north of the Black Sea.

Hancock discovers the Ainu people are a culture and religion who:

"...lived in harmony with their environment, used an intelligent mixture of strategies to ensure comfortable survival and security for the future, who avoided the pitfalls of militarism, materialism, conspicuous consumption and overpopulation, The civilization remained intact and flourished, decently, humanely, and generously for more than 14,000 years."[106]

14,000 years ago, this civilization learned the significance of a lifestyle without *the pitfalls of militarism, materialism, conspicuous consumption and overpopulation.* They teach us to "live simple, live local" a statement similar to the message of *Inner Bridges.*

The physiology of the Jomon, Ainu and the intermediate race, the Yayoi, differs from one another, yet there are sufficient Mongoloid and Polynesian similarities supporting possible connections. Authorities view them as distinct, separate and unique from the Japanese people today. One piece of evidence is the Caucasian fair skin. This description supports speculative links and ancestry, including Aryan, Basque, and of course, the Kennewick Man.

The Smithsonian National Museum of Natural History states:

"Recent DNA research shows that the Ainu are descended from the Jomon people. Physically, the Ainu differed from Japanese and other nearby Asian peoples in language and especially in appearance. Their eyes are deep-set, the bodies muscular and hairy.[107]

Dr. Rein Kilkson, a physics professor from the University of Arizona, found similarities in both language and handicrafts between his homeland, Estonia, and the Ainu.

When we look at Ancient Wisdoms, we focus on the wisdoms evolving in ONE location at one time. The dilemma between Jomon, Philippines, Kennewick and Ainu spreads across the Pacific, into Estonia, Europe and over 14,000 years. We learn of cultures who once worshiped a goddess, later becoming animistic. Over centuries, they learn techniques of living in harmony with their environment, then passing this knowledge to future generations.

The Ainu facial features support claims that the Ainu are descendants of the same prehistoric race that produced the indigenous Australian aborigine. These features conform to the indigenous of New Guinea and Australia.[108]

Lastly, the Ainu link to the Jomon. Steve Olson, author of Mapping Human History, bases his comments on research on fossils as old as 10,000 years.

The outcome of this data gives us two triangles. The first one – the corded triangle - links Chili, Ainu of Japan, and the Kennewick man of Washington. The other triangle - the ancient life triangle -- includes Ainu/Jomon, Australian aborigines and Tibetan ancestors.

Today, the Ainu live very secluded and private lives off the northern island and like other global indigenous people; they keep their beliefs private, sharing with no one. Perhaps they will soon see the need and share them like the Kogi and Waitaha people.

CHUKCHI

While many people knew of the Chukchi people, they received world recognition after National Geographic presented the DNA research from Spencer Wells' book, *Journey of Man* in their television series. Through his DNA research, Wells confirms the link between the Chukchi people of Siberia and the San people of Southern Africa.

The Chukchi people lived in Eastern Siberia as early as 45,000-40,000 BC.[109] Archaeological evidence connects Southern and Eastern Europe, Central Asia, and Mongolia. DNA and mitochondrial DNA (mtDNA) confirms additional links to other regions of the world. There are many cultural bonds existing amongst cultures regardless of how long ago people migrated. Bonds such as these are not limited to Arctic societies. These societal bonds include healing practices, similar ceremonies or a preferred lifestyle of an isolated life. Today, cultures such as the Ainu, Kogi, Hopi and Chukchi respect cultures of others and expect others to respect theirs. Unfortunately, it seems many modern communities forget this instinctive integrity. Mysticism amongst Eastern cultures requires protection so members of Western societies can learn from it when the time is right.

This community's name originally came from the word *Chauchu* meaning "rich in reindeer". They traditionally divide themselves into two groups. The *Maritime Chukchi* live on the coast, relying on ocean animals for food and clothing. In contrast, the *Reindeer Chukchi* live on the tundra and their resource is reindeer. As a means of distinction from the Reindeer Chukchi, the Maritime Chukchi call themselves "the sea people". Chukchi literally means "true person".

Officials named the Sea above the Bering Strait linking Asia and North America the *Chukchi Sea*. Researchers theorize the Chukchi nation crossed the land bridge into North America spreading their knowledge, thus earning the right to this name.

Since Wells' DNA research confirms the link between the Chukchi people and many people of the globe, we know their ancestors migrated great distances. Therefore, it makes sense they could also migrate across the land bridge into the Americas.

Today, this society lives on little subsistence, adapting their lifestyles according to where they live, in reindeer land or near oceans. These people survive on very little and live in severe cold weather. Other Arctic societies, such as the American Inuit people follow similar life routines. These cultures pass this wisdom down to their offspring and will teach us, if we are willing to listen. This includes learning local healing methods and techniques for combing them with their sparse lifestyle.

The indigenous people of the North are traditionally animists. This means spirits of the sky, earth, and water affects our lives. They produce images of these spirits in human or animal form. Sacrifices to these guardian spirits in the form of animals and other food products were common in the past. Today, sacrifices come through the Community Shaman mediation between their people and the spirits of the other worlds. The shaman performs religious and healing ceremonies, healing sickness, predicting the future, and delivering the souls of the deceased to the world of the dead. Although many indigenous people officially converted to the Russian Orthodox Church during the revolution, the ways of shamans and religious healers still exist. Throughout many indigenous settlements and migratory journeys, we encounter healing methods and religious ceremonies that merge effectively with the religion of your choice.

The spirits of the Chukchi ancestors are still present. They have been the driving force for their survival throughout the centuries.

Their Charter of their Association begins:

"We, the indigenous peoples of the North, Siberia and Far East of the Russian Federation, believe that:

-The Air, the Land and Water are blessed;

-Nature is the source of life;

-Man is but a drop in the whirlpool of life;

-The river of time is but a reflection of the past, present and future and that how our ancestors lived in the past is how we now live and how our offspring will live in the future..."

The Chukchi people existed for centuries in what we perceive today as inhospitable territory. They survived and lived in peace. These people are intriguing, gentle and wise people with many lessons to teach us. The key point here is their harmonious living with nature. They know how to cope with extreme cold weather, without complaint. Many communities complain their global region is getting colder. Here is an example where we can apply this knowledge to our world and future societies and generations can incorporate the Chukchi lessons. It does not matter where we live, all humans around the globe benefit.

THE SÁMI

"*Nature abounds in plants and animals; the world fills with different languages and cultures. We, the Sámi, see ourselves, as part of this nature.*" [110]

These are words spoken by the Sámi Elders.

Scientists identify the Sámi (formerly Saami) as the oldest postglacial inhabitants in the arctic region of the world. The titles Laplanders, Norse and Sámi are interchangeable. Historical records of the Sámi people only take them back to the first century CE, but by archaeological evidence substantiates .their predecessors, the Fosna, Komsa, and Hensbacka cultures go back another 10,000 years.

The most recent of these cultures live in Northern Norway. Approximately 6,000 years ago, around 4200 BCE, this culture, the Fosna, ostensibly carved more than 5,000 petroglyphs near the town of Alta. This society of hunter-gatherers lives almost exclusively at sea. We also know they are competent shipbuilders and fishermen.

The primitive carvings match stone engravings found in the southern parts of the Norwegian coast, opening a connection amongst northern coastal nations. They also tell us this skill existed in all coastal societies.

We also find evidence of the early Fosna/Hensbacka people in Sweden. These two cultures came from a similar era initiating the merging of these two names. The Hensbacka settlements are in Bohuslän along the Swedish west coast, not far from the Fosna settlements.

Exactly where the Komsa, Fosna and Hensbacka came from is unclear. Some say from the south – Europe. Some say from the east - Chukchi territory and still others speculate they came from the west – Inuit of North America. Their oceanic lifestyle suggests feasible ancient connections in any direction.

The Chukchi people of Eastern Siberia are also ocean dependent and their culture dates back as far as the Norwegian cultures, 10,000 years suggesting explorers may have travelled either east to Siberia from Scandinavian lands or the opposite way, to the west. All these societies are comfortable with the Arctic environment.

Whichever direction their travels took them, literacy existed. Scandinavian cultures used petroglyphs as writing, communication, and directional tools. The Komsa and Fosna people improved these tools, incorporating them into significant messaging systems useful amongst other cultures on their ocean-going adventures. Over time, as the Sámi society evolved, literacy increased in importance and in sophistication. Primeval Norwegian and Swedish people utilized the skills and left behind scant historical recording from this period. The Sámi and Viking people accepted the writing system, ready to pass it on to other countries. The Runes, similar to the petroglyphs are one ancient lettering form to evolve, but exactly where it came from is unknown. When the seafaring Vikings traveled to faraway lands, they took their system of writing with them, leaving runic inscriptions in isolated places such as Greenland.[111]

Traditionally, Sámi spiritual views are animistic, with shamanistic features. They believed that everything in nature has a soul. These beliefs confirm with beliefs of all Arctic people. This is quite common amongst indigenous societies and many of these entrust a Shaman or Elder with the guidance of their beliefs and "taking care of" all souls whether they are in human, plant or animal form.

Numerous indigenous cultures hesitate to share specifics about their spiritual beliefs. One possible reason is the inherent need to protect their values, keeping them away from the people they perceive would manipulate and destroy their culture.

Like many nations, the Sámi people went to their shamans for prophecies, magic, healing and protection. The Sámi shaman is not a prophet as we interpret it today; he is an Oracle. Today, we use the term *-Prophecy-* very loosely. Modern prophets tell you what to expect. A Sámi shaman does not do this; he leads people toward living a fuller and purer life. This corresponds to the objectives of shamans from many ancient cultures and most indigenous tribes.

When you hear the warnings from the Kogi, the Waitaha or the Hopi nations, for example, you will understand the message of an oracle. Today, other tribes also state their warnings in the hopes that we save the Earth from imminent disaster. Should individuals pause to listen to ancient wisdom and warnings, possibly modern societies will take heed.

Throughout time, Sámi skills display gifts of witchcraft, similar to the gypsies aptitude that we see in middle Europe. Christians are not unique in their fear of the unknown. They feared the Sámi's powerful magic and forced their conversion to Christianity. Like so many conquered societies though, the oppressed group put up a front and followed their personal beliefs behind closed doors. These subjugated people developed similar routines as other societies such as the Maya of Mesoamerica. After Spanish domination, the Maya retreated in a similar manner. Maya Shamans kept their teachings private until recently when the right time came for open teaching. The Sámi began some time ago. These illustrations demonstrate the commonality of shamanic wisdom. Tribal elders knew when to keep their values private and when to publicly acknowledge them. Studying their judgment provides the knowledge for contemporary people. We all have truths we are reluctant to share.

If you ask the Sámi people where they came from, their answer would be something like "*We fell from the sky*". Numerous indigenous nations define their origin in a similar way, "*Always been here*". Various ancient cultures around the globe may not repeat these exact words but they convey the same truth in their language, invariably stating that hot springs have always been in their lives. Hot springs and saunas are anomalies of the earth where at some time in history healed bodies and gave humans vital information. The arctic land introduces humans to the principle and benefits of the mineral water of saunas and hot baths. People from many eras claim their healing powers.

Interestingly, throughout northern lands we find hot springs, but the points of a particular land triangle, called *The Triangle of Springs*, takes us to the points of three cultures: Sámi, Chukchi and Buryat. This triangular journey takes us from Norway East to Siberia South to the Mongolian border. It is a very cold and frosty triangle but with resort springs at each peak. Sámi and Chukchi people live along the coast and the Buryat live at Lake Baikal in the Russian Federation near the border of Mongolia. All of these cultures, particularly the Buryat, may resort to living in distant cities but they always return to their homeland. It is fundamental to their beliefs, as so many others, to return to the source of knowledge and energy of their native soil. Unfortunately, modern cultures no longer stress this importance.

You may well ask, "Why is this important?" Indigenous people know they are born with specific energy from a specific earth region. This energy keeps us healthy. By returning to their homeland, individuals stay healthy longer.

THE HIMALAYAS – TIBET AND NEPAL

The first culture, the **HUNZA**, of this broad region, comes out of present-day Pakistan. They live high in the Himalayas. People in Western society dream of long lives but pass it off as an elusive dream. BUT, when they learn about the Hunza people reaching 130 to 140 years of age, the Western imaginations stirs again. We may never achieve comparable legendary long lives. This does not stop us from adapting life patterns and lessons that makes a longer, healthier life a feasible goal.

The Hunza are not the only social group who routinely attain ages of one hundred or more. Six cultures claiming centenarians keep appearing. Interestingly, all live in high mountain ranges or near extinct volcanic islands. For each cultural group, pure alkaline water is easily accessible and is their normal consumption. This takes us back to the theory of life evolving where there were volcanos and water springs.

These cultures are:

1. Hunza in the East Pakistan region of the Himalayas
2. Japanese of Okinawa, Japan
3. Tibetans in Western China
4. Armenians who reside between Iran and Turkey
5. Titicas in the high Andes near the Peru-Bolivian border
6. Vilkabaumba in the Ecuadorian Andes.

The last four pass on their heritage verbally to their descendents, eliminating an accurate documented proof of their longevity. Since the Hunza society gives us both verbal and recorded evidences, we will concentrate on these people.

HUNZA

The Hunza people carry an air of mystery and live in a remote valley at the Western end of the Himalayas. This isolated valley is approximately 9,000 feet above sea level and is one of the main routes through the Himalayas linking the surrounding countries.

Travelers and authors describe these people as happy, healthy, agile, enthusiastic, serene, fearless, good-tempered, cheerful and possessing boundless energy with remarkable endurance. When questioned, they tell us youth lasts to 50 years, and middle age is around 80 years and people enjoy plenitude or abundance for the remainder of life.

Dr. G.T. Wrench quotes Robert McCarrison as saying:

"These people are unsurpassed by any Indian race in perfection of physique; they are long lived, vigorous in youth and age, capable of great endurance and enjoy a remarkable freedom from disease in general." [112]

We read so much about attitude and outlook on life; these people are an excellent example. In our Western world today, old age is thought of as an end to productivity and usefulness; a time of illness and pain. In contrast, the Hunza consider it an age of *plenitude.* Plenitude is a time of completeness and abundance. To the Hunza culture, it is time for reaping life's rewards.

A key to their life style is not having any *retirement* as we understand it; they simply modify their work and travels. Like many indigenous cultures, they consider it as being a time of respect and wisdom. Unfortunately, this does not apply to the western society. For them, as they evolve, they improve technology; simplify the work load and lifestyle. However, instead of respecting community elders, it seems a perception emerges that older people become incapable on every level - mental, physical and often spiritual.

The Hunza origin is a mystery, unconfirmed. A heritage of suitable life habits does not appear to have come from another culture. Consequently, these Hunza, during their mountainous residency, noted the nature of the mountains, developing an eating pattern and daily routine suitable to their environment.

Many of these patterns apply to people around the world, regardless of where they live. If we choose, adopting some of their teachings and lifestyle expands the average human life span. The most concise resource supporting this option is an e-book - *Health Secrets of the Hunzas.* [113] Their eating habits surprise me. Their daily routine did not.

They live in the high mountains with short seasons and yet their diet consists primarily of fresh or dried fruits, vegetables and very little meat. The Hunza dry their food in preparation for the cold, dark months. One of these fruits is the apricot. It originates in regions of China more than 5,000 years ago. Sources refer to utilizing the complete crop, sun drying, storage, skin, meat, even the pip. Apricots are low fat, cholesterol free and high in Vitamin A and C. Dried apricots contain much higher quantities of the nutrients than fresh ones.

Other mountain societies consume mainly meat and starch, utilizing the fruit and vegetables provided only in season, when it takes minimal effort. These societies do not appear motivated to cultivate and harvest the products.

Unlike people in neighbouring valleys, the Hunza take the time to harvest a varied, natural food source. The Hunza discovered the importance of these foods. Their bodies are remarkable proof. The Hunza display very little ill health, little cancer, bone or tooth decay.

Dr. Wrench speaks of a group called the Ghizr living west of the Hunza. Unlike the Hunza, the Ghizr are a lazy nation, not bothering with food storage for winter and end up starving at the end of a long winter. Another nation, the Ishkomanis, from another neighboring valley, is also poor, undersized and undernourished.[114] There are numerous tribes living in neighboring Himalaya valleys. Most have comparable traits to the Ghizr but a few have characteristics similar to the Hunza, but they are the minority. All these nations have access to alkaline water, a key of physical health.

There are several reports and articles referring to glacial alkaline water. Since the weather and seasonal patterns are consistent throughout the Himalayas, this means all native residences of the Himalayas receive the same benefits of glacial alkaline water. This becomes a *heritage lesson* since they learn how to collect alkaline water and store it for traveling or severe weather. This ancient wisdom came from their ancestors and its use spans the globe. We have a choice of applying it in our community.

In North America, we only recently discovered the importance of alkaline water. Scientists in the early twentieth century received Nobel Prizes for water research. It is only recently that adjustments to people's water drinking habits were encouraged. The Hunza intuitively knew the importance but not the details. One point that started scientists thinking is the Hunza people know instinctively, they do not need to drink as much water as Westerners think.

Research shows that when water is alkaline, the body only requires half the quantity of water. Alkaline water produces more oxygen in the body, reducing the acidity of the cells and blood stream. When we develop acidic blood or acidic cells, we destroy the healthy cells. Glacial alkaline water cleanses, rejuvenates and keeps you health and young.

After discovering the longevity of the Hunza people, Dr. Henri Coanda, born in 1886, a Romanian father of fluid dynamics, spent sixty years studying the Hunza water trying to determine what was in this water and why it benefits their body. Together with Dr. Patrick Flanagan, he learned their water had different viscosity and surface tension. Their water had a high alkaline pH and high active hydrogen. In other words, their water was *living*.

Consuming alkaline water, the body increases its ability to absorb water because of the low surface tension. This *wetter* water flushes waste and toxins away. When water has too high a surface tension, the nutrients cannot get into the cells, killing the cells because of waste products.

The 1912 Nobel Prize winner, Alexis Correl. Carrel, kept a chicken heart alive for 37 years, insisting that a secret of life is feeding and nourishing the cells, then letting them flush their waste and toxins. Our body needs water with a low surface tension. If the surface tension is NOT low, the nutrients cannot get into the cells and the cells die of their own waste products. He found that water was the appropriate medium for this. If the surface tension is too high, waste removal is inefficient.[115]

Further research shows the Hunza water carries colloidal silver particles. If colloidal silver occurs in alkaline water at 5 parts per million or higher, it kills numerous infectious bacteria, explaining why their teeth and bones are healthy, with no cancer or decay. Ancient societies intuitively knew what was required. They did not require the scientific details that modern people demand. We have a choice, we can choose to intuitively follow their practice or follow the research of the modern curious mind. If we choose intuitive trust, then alkaline water is the first step. The scientific mind has also proven the need for alkaline water.

Although other tribes have similar attributes, it seems that the Hunza nation are the only people who chose to retain and follow the legacy of their past. Seasonal selection and quantity of food are characteristics common to *all* tribal nations. The Hunza daily regime consists of

1. Drink glacial water
2. Early rise
3. Eating two meals, with the first at midday. Their meals were frugal and consumed for necessity, not pleasure

4. They meditated regularly. This could be their way of coping with the thin mountainous air. With thin air, they need to rest approximately every hour. Instead of a non-productive time, their spirituality led them into meditation.

5. Possibly, because of the mountains, they climbed or walked regularly.

Hunza Diet

The Hunza society consumed white meat only on special occasions - a festive food. They recognized the importance of animal protein and consumed large quantities of milk and cheese, limiting the quantity of solid meat fiber. Yogurt, also an animal protein, was a major portion of the food consumption. Citizens of other cultures enjoying longevity also consume yogurt.

Their main grains are barley, millet, buckwheat and wheat. Other grains were available and, from these, they produced their main bread, Chapatti. Did they adopt it from the Hindu people or the reverse? China is a close neighbour of the Hunza and although rice is a Chinese staple, it was not in the Hunza diet. Perhaps the climate is too cold and too dry.

During harvest time, they ate the fruits and vegetables raw and dry the excess crops for the remainder of the year.

The Hunza dietary lifestyle, matches the way of life of our western ancestors hundreds of years ago. If we break it up into *dietary rules*, we may not live 140 years but we *can* live longer. These rules are:

Frugality. There is no need to consume the quantity we do. Restaurants serve one person the quantity for two or three.

Make fresh fruits and vegetables, from your local area the main part of your diet. [116], Reduce meat and avoid white bread.

Fast regularly

Indigenous people, including the Hunza, eat what is around them, fruit, vegetables and meat. Their way of life, including diet, follows the basic principles of Ayurveda, an Indian *Science of Life*. The Hunza have been around for approximately 2400 years; Ayurveda has been around twice as long. Both the ancient cultures of India and the Hunza people pass this knowledge down to us. For clarification, go to *Ayurveda Demystified.*[117]

It is the diet *and* the exercise that creates this amazing people. We do not suggest that Western people have to adopt identical patterns. However, when we study their routine and develop a prototype, we can then review our lifestyle and absorb the techniques useful for us. This illustrates how ancient wisdom effectively merges with the technology in our lives.

The Hunza live high in the mountains and routinely go out of the valley for supplies. A daily walk of approximately 20 kilometers is normal. After returning from the usual hike down the mountain, the average person would work in the field for several hours. Walking up and down the mountain at a fast pace was no effort. This is an excellent and complete form of fitness.

These people understand that the necessity of relaxing their bodies throughout the day is a fundamental part of living. How this became a basic precept of their lives, we do not know. Today though, it is customary for farmers to pause in the field, perform yoga breathing exercises and meditate for short periods several times a day. These respites extend their work day resulting in a slow, steady work pace, unlike our hectic workday.

Enjoying the plenitude and respite are normal ways of living for these people. In North America, we will enjoy this as we observe activities at Senior Centers or Senior Games, but participation seems limited. The Hunza live slow lives, eat local food, exercise and meditate regularly. Perhaps we can do the same.

BUDDHISM

While the Hunza civilization focuses on the physical wellbeing of the individual, Buddhism focuses upon on our spiritual and mental wellbeing as formulated by Siddhartha Gautama.

Siddhartha, known as the Buddha, lived between 563 – 483 BCE. Since Siddhartha came from the Hindu faith, many of his teachings follow Hindu beliefs.

Gautama Buddha teaches us that suffering is a part of living that mental and moral self-purification will overcome. Originally, Buddhism is the religion of eastern and central Asia but it grew into a global way of life followed by people around the world. Our Ancient Ones believe compassion and understanding is the way of living and sharing.

The legend tells us Siddhartha's knowledge developed after sitting under a Bodhi tree in northern India. For a tree to carry the wisdom of the universe, it must have been near a sacred underground spring or underground river. If we took time to pause and meditate under a local tree today, perhaps, we could receive universal teachings from sacred springs.

Siddhartha Gautama lived in regal luxury, witnessed corruption, extreme affluence and severe poverty as the ways of his country. These experiences polluted all his original Hindu teachings. Because of this background, it took time to comprehend the humility and simplicity of the Buddha teachings. Once comprehension occurred, he devoted his life to sharing the Buddhist teachings and helping others.

Today, we understand the impact of human experience upon our learning. Siddhartha illustrates how this perspective alters thinking societal lessons are firmly ensconced in his mind. He gave four gifts we utilize in current times is
hearing the lesson,
appreciating the importance of learning,
observing the results, and finally
sharing the new knowledge with others

Siddhartha Gautama did not believe there was a Higher Being or Power controlling man's destiny; he believed each person owned their own fate. His teachings show a way to rise above the poverty. This is contradictory to most new religions. Most founders of religions claim to be God, his incarnate, or a direct messenger. Consequently, they create and encourage fear in their followers. Buddha did not; he only taught what he had discovered to be true.

There are three resources for the details on Buddhism. One written source, one spoken and one channeled.

The book "What the Buddha Taught"[118] is not new. Rahula gives us an uncomplicated summary and explanations of his teachings.

In 2001, the Dalai Lama presented a 3-day workshop in San Francisco.

Questions taken into a meditation resulted in channeled answers.

A major Buddhist differences lies in the foundation of the belief. The basis of Buddhism is the "Theory of Emptiness"; while for other religions, it is "Busyness".

Indigenous nations several hundred years ago had a calm, serene presence. There was no such thing as a state of *busyness*. Some time and somehow, modern civilizations began teaching that *busyness* is GOOD. The following comparison illustrates this difference. Christianity accounts for one-third of the global population. Therefore, when we compare it with Buddhism, we see:

Buddhist beliefs:	Christian philosophy:
Non-creator, non-focus	*Creator - theosophical*
Denies Atman	Atman, Soul Theory, Eternal
Rebirth	Non-rebirth
Spiritual freedom	*Salvation*
Mental State	*Physical Plane*

Everything in this list makes sense except the second belief (Atman). According to Webster's Collegiate Dictionary, the Hindu word, Atman means, "*the innermost essence of the individual.*" It can also mean breath or soul. Rahula, author of *What the Buddha Taught* defines it as:

"*If there is no permanent, unchanging entity or substance like Self or Soul (atman), what is it that can re-exist or be reborn after death? Before we go on to life and death, let us consider what this life is, and how it continues now. What we call life, as we have so often repeated, is the combination of the Five Aggregates, a combination of physical and mental energies. These are constantly changing; they do not remain the same for two consecutive moments. Every moment they are born and they die. 'When the Aggregates arise, decay and die, every moment you 'are born, decay and die. Thus, even now during this lifetime, every moment we are born and die, but we continue. If we can understand that in this life we can continue without a permanent, unchanging substance like Self or Soul, why can't we understand that those forces themselves can continue without a Self or a Soul behind them after the non-functioning of the body?*

When this physical body is no more capable of functioning, energies do not die with it but continue to take some other shape or form, which we call another life."[119]

Earlier, Rahula clarifies his meaning of "mind" as it differs from spirit, soul, or matter. Buddhism does not. Rahula emphasizes that the mind is "*only a faculty or organ like the eye or ear. It can be controlled and developed like any other faculty.*"[120] Other philosophical schools separate spirit and matter into distinct parts.

During a meditation, I received the following channeled information:

"*All truths are valid. It is important to remember that religions are to guide human beings and give them a sense of being and togetherness. When we look at Spirituality, it is the movement of the Soul BEYOND the Earth Plane. Religion, on the other hand, is to give human beings or any other species a way to cope or survive the Earth Plane. Ideally, the religion will also include spirituality so that the spirit can evolve. You have seen at other times that the human being cannot copy or understand a greater life. We are sure, for we know that many leaders understand the spirit or essence as you do. They know that the essence lives on. How can you accept rebirth without soul life? To say there is no "I" is only one way to try to justify the religion.*"

Telling a following that there is no "I" or "SELF" helps mold moral practices on the Earth Plane. However, how can you separate the "I" (Soul, Essence) from the good for the Universe?

All life is connected. This means there is no "I" but there is the TOTAL. Many humans do not understand or accept this, yet they talk about the aggregation of atoms or particles. Is this not the Total?

Mind is the Ultimate Total, including the knowledge each requires on each Earth Plane and in each life.

This information is not contradictory to the Buddhist teachings but explains the emphasis of two, divergent ways of thinking. With this clarification, the Buddhist teachings take on clearer meaning.

The complete original wisdom of the indigenous people of our planet states:

- Do no harm,
- Honor all life,
- Respect dead and ancestors, and
- Honor all cultures.

Buddha emphasizes these points by re-introducing the equality and peace, initially shared by all living. His bias comes through a desire to ease the suffering around him.

Buddhism is a complex study divided into three sections demonstrating the physical, earthbound focus. They are:

The Four Noble Truths

The Middle Path

The Aggregates

The Four Noble Truths:

1. **Dukka**: Suffering or imperfection, emptiness
2. **Samudaya**: Origin of suffering. Thirst, desire, greed, craving, and manifestation, which leads to all forms of suffering.
3. **Nirodha** (Nirvana): Cessation from the continuity of suffering
4. **Magga**: Way leading to the Cessation, the Path.

The Middle Path:

- Right Understanding
- Right Thought
- Right Speech
- Right Action
- Right Livelihood
- Right Effort
- Right Mindfulness
- Right Concentration

Five Aggregates which are part of the First Noble Truth:

1. Matter
2. Sensations
3. Perception
4. Mental Formations
5. Consciousness

A major factor of Buddhism philosophy rests with reducing suffering *within* the self. For Buddhists, this means *withdrawing* from society.

In each generation since Siddhartha, there has been a Dalai Lama, chosen by reincarnated birth, who leads his people through peace. Traditionally, his monks withdraw from society to reduce suffering. The circumstances of the Chinese revolution and Tibetan takeover have altered this. Our present Dalai Lama is much more visibly active in society today. He elaborates upon the teachings of Buddha and uses them in his plea for world peace. Buddha, like so many of our Ancient Ones believes compassion and understanding is the way of living and sharing. These traits become the first step to the world peace sought for by our Dalai Lama.

After the Communist takeover of Tibet, Buddhists facing oppression and violence fled to India in 1959. Authorities and supporters smuggled the 24-year-old Dalai Lama into safety.

Today, when we reclaim our heritage and the values of ancient cultures, we realize how they help our present and future communities. All Ancient Wisdoms of this planet teach us to value and honor life, including the planet itself. The Dalai Lama went farther than many indigenous societies because he was able to travel teaching Buddha's truths, easing suffering and sharing compassion.

In 2008, there was a march for peace and freedom. We see a merger between ancient teachings and modern living, including a cry for past ideas being allowed to come forward. This demonstrates how societies, if they choose, will bring ancient teachings forward. It displays the three icons of this book. The Owls carry wisdom and teachings, we should listen to their call. The Doves carry the peace and spread the teachings. The Butterflies transform it into a useable form such as a peace walk, popular in the 20th century.

The following note comes from a peace-walk participant, expressing the information and emotion reinforcing the truths of Tibetan, Buddhist values. Clayton Di Chiro's notes illustrates how we can take the Buddhist values, their *Philosophy of Life* and apply them to our present society. We replace irrelevant sections with "…" These excerpts illustrate the Tibetan truths and the passion of current participants. He wrote:

"…*During my first 10 days in Dharmsala, the home of the exiled government, or more specifically McLeod Ganj,*[121] *I attended lectures from His Holiness, the Dalai Lama on Buddhist philosophy, a real experience for me as I have always respected and revered this man, who, in the face of adversity has always led with compassion… A passion was instilled for the injustice these people have faced from Chinese rule since right after World War 2.*

"…*Those Tibetans not fortunate enough to escape into India or other nations have faced brutal living conditions in their own Homeland… for up to twenty years they are being arrested for simply displaying a Tibetan flag or carrying an image of the Dalai Lama.*

"…*Against all this pain and injustice, the Tibetans have been struggling to bring about non-violent revolution for justice and equality to the people of Tibet who have been subjected to gross human rights violations… I have been swallowing and pushing away for a long time, the idea of standing up for what we know is right. Standing up for our rights as people, looking beyond nationalism and saying: "No more will I stand by and intellectualize human suffering!"*

"…*Luckily, this personal breakthrough lined up perfectly with the beginning of a march through India to Tibet of 100 core marchers mostly monks and other Tibetan activists. March 10th 2008 marked the 50th anniversary of the first Tibetan uprising and the beginning of the march to Beijing to protest the human rights violations of Tibetan people and culture… You can only deny people freedom for so long before they will do anything for it. Yet on March 10th, this was all still to come.*

"… *They took my passport information, registered me and gave me an official "support marcher" card. At this point, I really had no idea what I was signing on for. Once the march began I found out that this walk was going to take 6 months and for those who may not know monks are some focused and in shape men and women!!! I never said answering "the call" always felt good or made sense, but there I was amongst nearly 5 thousand Tibetans guitar in hand, big Tibetan flag strapped around my back, knowing that I was exactly where I needed to be and I laughed as I thought about my dream of the Dalai Lama. "Here we go" I thought "another grand adventure."*

Today's Earth population may not be in a position to walk as Clayton walked. However, mankind is in a personal situation allowing them to express their values. The initial walk began with the majority of Tibetans living in McLeod Ganj and consisted of about 5 to 8 thousand people screaming "Victory to Tibet!" and other slogans in Tibetan. Clayton saw the look of pain, suffering, anger, frustration wiped away with hope. The lines of sadness evident on the faces of an exiled race, yet the passion flowing from the mouths and eyes and hearts of these people gives sound to the notion of Freedom, gives Justice a voice with a universal language. This walk reinforces the wails of all who suffer today, every slave, every man woman and child, every one throughout history who has known the pain of persecution, the sting of injustice, who stared down the face of hate.

"…He thought of the people who tasted freedom, grew passive and docile with respect to what so many fight and died for. He saw images flash through his mind as the color of the Tibetan flag mixed with the red and yellow of the monk's robes and the green of the youth's shirts, and the sweat and popping veins on the foreheads of those yelling in a language foreign to my ears but whose message he understood clearly.

…He realized he was exactly where he needed to be."

This expression of Clayton is a key expression. So many people ignore this cry for help and by-pass the call of others.

"…He cannot tell us what he felt at this moment because words only cheat the moment. He thinks it is Freedom. …What he recognizes is the understanding of why people die for this feeling. **To have freedom and know freedom are two completely different things.** *Those who have freedom seem not to know it as intimately as those who are not free."*

This is key knowledge from our ancient ancestors. So many people carry the heritage forward in time. Unfortunately, it seems so many people living today do not understand the difference between *having freedom* and *knowing freedom*. People conduct peace marches and individually express their power.

Clayton is one of these people. As he continued through this march, singing and playing his guitar, he stated: *"Let the healing of this planet begin and let it begin with me, and you and you and you and you too. Just watch the power of action!!!"*

The last statement he makes is:

"… What will fix this world are individuals KNOWING that they are empowered to make change. <u>YOU</u> ARE SO POWERFUL! We must individually understand

that as big as a problem may seem there are so many of us out there just like you and TOGETHER we can do anything, solve any problem. Do not wait one more day. Do not think that the fruits of freedom are yours alone or believe the myth that this freedom is only available to you at the expense of another person or nation. We are ONE and together the world will know peace when each of us individually decides that we want it."

-- End of Clayton's comments

The key messages given throughout this note is *having* freedom and *knowing* freedom are **two completely different things.** This reminds us that our ancestor's wisdom frequently displayed this freedom and it is relevant to our modern cultures. It does not matter what an individual's faith is, this message applies.

Buddhism is more recent than many other societies but when we study them, there is an historic echo. It is a gentle reminder for us to find the peace of freedom. Our Ancients found it.

NAGAS

The Naga civilization is high in the Himalaya Mountains northeast of the Bay of Bengal.

In 2005 Johann Landes,[122] author of *The Future Code* included comprehensive research by James Churchward. Churchward spent many years writing about the lands of Mu and Lemuria, lending credence to speculations about the undocumented travels of ancient people. Throughout his studies, he uncovered an ancient people that he came to know as *Nagas* of 15,000 years ago. With the help of an Indian priest, Churchward deciphered the ancient Naacal Tablets stone slabs late in the late 19th century. Based upon data derived from these tablets, Churchward describes the Nagas as:

"...straight forward people, honest, hardworking, sturdy and with a high standard of integrity. They are lacking in humility and are inclined to equate a kind and sympathetic approach with weakness. The Nagas have a very strong sense of self respect and would not submit to anyone riding roughshod over their sentiments."

This describes an advanced and highly respected society, but unfortunately, physical evidence of the ancient Nagas vanished long ago, leaving us only Churchward's interpretation. His research tells us both the Naacal and Naga peoples existed up to 15,000 years ago. If they died out so long ago, why are people in this region still going by the *Naga* name?

Because of the limited data, determining their origin becomes a dilemma. Some say they came from the Maya community, currently in Central America. Others say the opposite, the Maya people originated from the Naga currently living in the Himalayan Mountains. Although today the Nagas follow Hindu beliefs, a connection exists between the Hindu beliefs, their way of life and the Maya world of Central America. Here are two cultures living on opposite sides of the planet with amazing similarities.

Hunbatz Men, a Mayan Daykeeper, includes information about the Hindu and Nagas in two of his books on the Mayan people, illustrating their joint history. According to the main Hindu scripture, Mahabharata, the Mayas were a tribe that left the Indian subcontinent. This scripture defines the Nagas as members of a Naga-Maya tribe, a mysterious, ancient people originating in Tibet. Hunbatz Men includes details from the *Ramayana* and the *Mahabharata* books, two of the sacred books of India in his writing.[123]

Even though the fact that Hunbatz Men includes both approaches, he asserts the Naga Maya took their religion to India in approximately 2700 BCE. He refers to the Naga as "people of the high mountains."[124] Whether they lived on the high mountains or in the Indus Valley, accessed through high mountains, we do not know for sure. Both regions were home to ancient wise civilizations.

To Tibetans, Naga *means* serpent. Many citizens, both Tibetan and Indian, describe the Nagas as the "serpent spirits of the underworld". There are many locations throughout India named after them; Nagapur (or Nagpur) and, Nagaland, for example.

Whether the Naga moved from India to the Pacific Islands, traveling on to Central America or the Maya culture came from Central America, migration occurred. The point here is we need to analyze what each culture left behind for modern society. Over almost five thousand years, two distinct societies successfully merged knowledge and we now have the opportunity to use it.

The language similarities of these distant societies illustrate one connection. For example, the early Mexican word *nagual* means sorcerer and medicine man. Today in rural Mexico, *nagual* or *nahual* depicts someone who we perceive as a witch. The Theosophical Society describes the first Nagas of India as serpents of wisdom. In modern American society, Nagual often refers to a spiritual leader. This one word can mean: serpent, sorcerer, medicine man, witch, or spiritual leader.

Numeric systems may vary but the numeric names for numbers one to ten in the Maya and Naga languages are almost identical. They are:[125]

	Maya	**Naga**
1	Hun	Hun
2	Ca	Cas
3	Ox	Ox
4	Can	San
5	Ho	Ho
6	Uc	Usac
7	Uac	Uac
8	Uaxac	Uaxax
9	Bolom	Bolam
10	Lahun	Lahun

Another vocabulary example comes from the languages of Naga, Tibetan and Maya people. All three cultures consider "K'U" a sacred word or word-ending. To Mayans, K'U is the generator of thought. Tibetans define K'U as our essence. We find K'U in Tibet, India, and Mexico, recorded in ancient times. In their languages, important names, personage or Gods, receive the ending "KU".

Most of the cultures of the Indian Subcontinent such as Tibetans and Hindu left us with records and understanding that spans time. One exception is the Harappans. Who are these people? Iravatham Mahadevan, an eminent Indian scholar studied theories and analyzed artifacts found in the Indus Valley, Southern and northeast Indian peninsula. He found remnants of a little known people. He did prove commonalities of Harappa and Dravidian languages but little else.

[126]5,000 years ago, a civilization now called Harappan lived in the Indus Valley. We know very little about them since there are no deciphered written records. There is a writing system but nobody could interpret it. Iravatham Mahadevan studied this writing system but could get neither confirmation nor agreement from other scholars. However, through his extensive research on Dravidian text, he verified a connection between Harappan and Dravidian. In a May, 2006 website article, he analyzed words fitting the cultural criteria of two diverse cultural people.[127]

Part of his analysis includes the symbols found on the stone celts dating back to around 2000 BCE. Observing the images of these symbols, helps us understand his description. He verbally describes one symbol (below) for **muruku** as:

"…a skeletal body with a prominent row of ribs, shown seated on his haunches, body bent and contracted, with lower limbs folded and knees drawn up. This seated god represents destroyer, killer, one of the Harappan deity."

There is no correlation between these images and others found in the Indus Valley or any specific meaning eradicating the mystery of the images. From the archaeological evidence of Harappan cities, we know they were a sophisticated and symmetrical people.

The ruins show:

Whole assortment of seals used to identify goods for trading, and brief inscriptions intended for the clients. These Harappan seals, similar to those turning up in the ruins of Ur (between the Tigris and Euphrates River), Vaisali and Bihar in northeast India, indicates there is widespread trading with neighboring societies.

The cities are made of mud bricks, baked in ovens. The streets are well-planned and well laid out, wide enough for oxcarts to pass each other.

These streets are equipped with elaborate gutter and drainage systems and the houses supplied with bathrooms.

The enormous swimming-pool-sixed baths, known as the Great Bath Complex has an intricate well and drainage systems. This system ensures a continuous flow of clean water. .[128]

Each city has a double-walled citadel of unknown use, similar to the walls found in Zimbabwe ruins.

Author and historian John Keay comments on the similarities and distinctive characteristics of several hundred Harappan sites. He says:

"The ubiquitous bricks are all of standardized dimensions, just as the stone cubes used by the Harappans to measure weights are also standard and based on a modular system. Road widths conform to a similar modular; thus, streets are typically twice the width of side lands, while the main arteries are twice or one and a half rimes the width of streets. Most of the streets so far excavated are straight and run either north-south or east-west. City plans therefore conform to a regular grid pattern and appear to have retained this layout through several phases of rebuilding. In most cases, the ground plan consists of two quite separate settlements, one apparently residential and commercial ('the lower town'), and the other elevated on a massive brick platform ('the citadel')." [129]

Based upon archaeological evidence, Keay presents these key points:

1. The Harappan settlements are perhaps the world's first, planned cities and townships.
2. The Harappan tools, utensils and materials confirm an impression of obsessive uniformity
3. Keay expresses: "the uniformity in technology is as strong as in the town-planning, and so marked that it is possible to typify each craft with a single set of examples drawn from one site alone."[130]
4. From the evidence, it seems that these people pioneered cotton spinning and weaving spreading the knowledge throughout their trade routes.
5. Perhaps the Harappan people were first in the world to use wheeled transport. [131]

Although there is no readable script found from the Harappan era, archaeologists found hundreds of individual characters of the Indus script on pottery, and other artifacts. These characters point out the vastness of their influence, including the advancement of their products. Throughout the texts, authors repeatedly state Harappans built cities over the remains of former cities, following the same pattern. This shows us a cluster of people who recognize successes of their ancestors, apply the wisdom to their current lives, then pass the wisdom onto future generations. When archaeologists research ancient cities such as Edinburgh, they find evidence of historical ancestors but the evidence is limited. It is beneficial to copy these structures as we move through time.

Scanty though the recorded evidence may be we discover the linking facts another way. These come through other archaeological findings.

1. Finding the Harappan seals in both Vaisali and Bihar cities in northeast India, suggests possible trading links between the Indus Valley cities and northeast Indian cities.

2. There is no archaeological evidence of trade between Indus Valley and Central America yet cultures in both lands incorporate the ending of "KU" in sacred words.

3. There is a definitive connection between the Nagas, Maya, Mu, and Harappa. We see the characteristic outcomes from one society in one era carried over to later ones; hopefully the good traits.

The Indus Valley people remain a mystery. We know sophisticated cultures built lifestyles emphasizing earth-based religion, plant and herb harvesting. During the studies of the Indus Valley, we find references to the Harappan people settling there in 3012 BCE, the Maya initializing their calendar there in 3113 BCE, designed to end in 2012 CE and finally the Ayurveda Health System beginning in the Indus Valley around 3000 BCE. Both the Maya calendar and the Ayurveda Health System survive into present day. A question we need to ask is if a sophisticated calendar and a progressive health school endured, then why didn't the cultures? [132]

It seems that modern society ignores the finer points of many ancient cultures. The traditional way of tracking time is simply observing sun, moon and stars. These observations tend to be basic; - sun rise or sun set. It is only recently that we realize people began noting the energy shifts accompanying planetary rotation and the effect on us. Ancient societies, including the Maya, were studying this for eons.

A more in depth overview of the Maya calendar is in the earlier section on the Maya culture. Five thousand years ago, the Maya based a calendar on the universal energy affecting human life, either spiritually or physically. Around the same time, the creators of Ayurveda health system designed an entire system based upon life energies. They identified three universal energies essential for the body: *VATA* (the energy that manages all movement), *PITTA* (the energy that handles processing), and *KAPHA* (the energy that decides storage).

Ayurvedic physicians and elders recognize ALL life requires ALL three but the quantity varies according to the individual structure, the time of day and season. A key outcome of early research is discovering each body has the three energies in unique proportions; one body may have more movement and very little storage whereas another body may have dominant processing and storage with little movement energy. These components affect things like physical structure and illnesses.

How humans maintained their health two thousand years ago is unclear. But, thanks to our ancestors, individuals today can easily manage basic control over their personal health by first discovering their dominant energy and second, learning the tastes and life patterns appropriate for their body.

In order to maintain physical health consistency, three approaches depend upon the dominance of energy within the body. *MOVEMENT* energy needs sweet, sour and salty tastes. *PROCESSING* energy needs sweet, astringent and bitter tastes and the *STORAGE* dominant requires pungent, astringent and bitter tastes. Unfortunately, in the busy Western society, people tend to ignore simple dietary planning that accompanies good health.

For more information, either refer to my book, *Ayurveda Demystified* or the Appendix in this book.[133]

CELTIC PEOPLE

The Western edge of Eurasia introduces the Celtic race. These people, a subset of Indo-European people, go back approximately 5,000 years. They inhabit an area from the British Isles, south to Spain and into Asia Minor. Over time, the definition of Celtic narrowed down to six specific nations which forms a *Celtic Crescent* consisting of the following regions (Celtic names in italics):

1. Scots - *Alba*
2. Irish - *Éire*
3. Isle of Man - Ellan Vannin or Mannin
4. Welsh - *Cymru*
5. Cornish of Cornwall - *Kernow*
6. Breton from Brittany - *Breizh*

The Celts have close ties to the earth and all nature, sensitive to the world around them and the psychic and spiritual flow of nature's energy. They demonstrate this closeness to the earth through use of herbal healing, earth circles and menhirs.

This culture carefully preserves the Celtic clan system, their astronomical stone tools and passes them down to our generation. As they explore foreign lands, they share their wisdom, establishing bonds with indigenous societies around the globe. For example, in North America, Celtic communities merge with other societies in locations such as Saskatoon on the prairies and Cape Breton Island on the East coast in Canada. Residents discover the clan system's functionality, descendents made use of it and while we do not see the system in much use today, we have the knowledge to employ it again, if we choose.

Originally, clan systems were methods of dividing the land holdings amongst offspring. This concept is similar to the feudal system with one difference. In the feudal system, the senior male remains the supreme head of the community with *many* bloodlines. However, in the clan system, a clan originally only has one bloodline. We find different last names evolving from a single name.

As these people move into different locations such as North America or Australia, we discover alterations in last name spellings. The curious-minded with Celtic ancestry can log onto the internet, type in the surname to discover the clan. For example, people with last names of Andrew, MacTier, and Taggart all belong to the Ross Clan.

Larger clans have regular *ceilidhs*, or gatherings, in larger centers. Historically, the ceilidh did not include dancing but instead was a get-together where elders related stories and tales, poems and ballads, and songs. At these informal parties, clan elders teach the young their ancestral social order, ethics and traditional rules. This teaching appears to be lost today, tales and ballads lost their impact but gradually new dancing styles developed and today we have the well-known STEP dancing made famous by the Riverdance troupe. Even today, in a close-knit Celtic region, the size and locale of a family is still valued. When a clan or family got too big for one location, offspring settled elsewhere.

Around the world, every society considers its teachings, prophecies and history important and search for a lasting medium. While they are not unique in the world, stone monuments meet these criteria for Celts. The carvings may wear down over the years but messages survive regardless. One benefit of paying attention to our ancient wisdom and honoring the data is the innovative result when a nation observes historical carvings and blends new information into traditional data.

Explorers carry their cultural knowledge around the globe, providing information to cultures thousands of miles apart. Celtic circles and stone formations in Northern Scotland meet these criteria. Then, in Däniken's book, *The Pathway to the Gods*[134] Däniken introduces us to the Kiribati *empty* circle. This circle corresponds to the circles of Northern Scotland formed more than 5,000 years ago. Here are two societies, 8,000 miles apart who formed message circles known as Celtic (Scotland) and Kiribati (Pacific Island) circles. They have comparable physical layout and comparable symbolic design.

One of the Celtic circles is the *Callanish Stone Ring* on the Isle of Lewis in the Outer Hebrides, dating back to 3400 BCE. Three thousand years later, island residents carved inscriptions on stones in Scotland in three styles, cuneiforms, runes and ogham, connecting the ring data to regions elsewhere on the planet. Cuneiforms originate with the Sumerian culture in the Middle East around 1400 BCE. Rune creation bonds with the Norse, Germanic or Anglo-Saxon people. Lastly, the ogham alphabet dates to ancient Irish, Scottish, and Celtic peoples.

As the Celtics and Romans traveled throughout their Celtic homeland, they carried the ancient pictographic writing systems with them, showing us how knowledge of one culture effectively transfers over to other cultures. An interesting note is people do not always connect artifacts on lands 8,000 miles apart but they accept similarities of items found within a 2,000 mile radius. Humans question the synchronicity of Scotland and Kiribati but will not question similarities in Europe.

Most of the stone rings found around the globe open gateways of speculation; the Callanish Ring is no exception. In the center of this ring is a cross of thirteen stones, matching the Southern Cross formation. Paleoclimatologic studies drew this similarity to our attention. Suggesting it is an astronomical device is not as remote a possibility as we might think.

Over time, the planet's orbit shifts, the ice melts and shorelines shrink or expand. If we visualize a shift of the planet's axis, then what societies see in today's night sky differs from what their ancestors saw 3000 years ago. This does not stop us from learning from the tools of the past. We know earthquakes affect the rotational axis of the planet. Planetary shifts depend upon the celestial changes, however small they might be. This is where we merge the wisdom of the ancients and the scientists. Scientists apply laws of physics as they analyze the skies of the planet. Patrick Geryl, writer of several books, researched, studied and explored many of these topics. He examined cosmology through interpreting hieroglyphs, deciphering codes, studying maps and exploring archaeological finds.

The result of his expansive research is:

1. Sudden and regular reversals and pole shifts are natural to the Earth.
2. The reversal of the poles results from the harmonic cycle of the magnetic fields of the sun.
3. Calculation of polar reversals resulting from the sunspot cycle theory or the magnetic field theory. The Maya and the Old Egyptian records reveal more details, many preserved in sacred pyramids.

Perhaps creators of the Callanish Ring did see the Southern Cross in a Northern sky. It is unknown whether there was a polar reversal at that time. The Maya calendar goes back to 3000 BCE, around the time of the Callanish Ring so who knows what happened on the earth plane and what knowledge needed preservation. We do know ancient navigational techniques, including this star no longer match what travelers require in the 21st century. It is important to understand that even though the axis realigned, climate adjusted and requirements altered, this should not stop us from studying the methods and merging them with our modern technology.

Once more, we see a connection between societies. Geryl found hieroglyphs and codes in the Labyrinth Hawara in Egypt. The Celtic people carved messages on the stone megaliths for future travelers. Now we leave messages for our descendents in whatever method seems appropriate. Because the Southern Cross is no longer visible in the 21st century Hebrides sky, skeptics question whether we saw the Southern Cross from Scotland 3000 years ago. These correlations refute this hypothesis. The cross in the center of the Scottish Callanish ring:

1. Aligns with the Pleiades position in 1330 BCE.
2. The ring accurately marks the 18.6-year cycle of the moon, like Fajada Butte in Chaco Canyon, New Mexico.
3. Aligns with the Metonic cycle of Greek and Babylonian cultures. The Meton's Greek cycle is quarter of a year off the cycles of Chaco Canyon and Scotland

The Metonic cycle originated in approximately 440 BCE when Meton, a Greek philosopher, discovered that 235 lunar months adjust approximately every 19 years. This sequence became the basis for the Greek calendar until 46 BCE. Sometime later, the Greek applied the Callanish lunar knowledge to create a calendar.

What we have when we look back in time are stone configurations on opposite sides of the globe presenting similar data. Descriptions such as 18.6 year-lunar cycle, 235 lunar months or 19 year cycle compare to the complex Maya calendar going back to 748 BCE. Formations similar to the Callanish Ring correspond to remnants from societies in Scotland, Greece, Central America and North America. Here are cultures anywhere from 1,200 miles (2,000 km) to 6,000 miles (10,000 km) apart having the same data at their fingertips. How did they have the same information? If Celts, Greeks, Egyptians, Chinese, and the Olmecs could all produce mathematical and astronomical theories around 300-100 BCE, then why could they not devise methods of communication and travel? Each one made their own contribution.

Other Scottish-Celtic rings 230 miles away in the Orkney Islands date back to approximately the same time, 3,500 BCE. They carry similar noteworthy historical evidence. For example, in the village of Sternness, we see three megalithic stone groupings known as (1) Ring of Brodgar, (2) The Standing Stones of Stenness, (3) Ring of Bookan. Each one carries inscriptions comparable to others around the world. The most significant and largest, the *Ring of Brodgar*, was built around 2500-2000 BCE. Today, only 27 out of the original 60 stones remain. It seems residents used the ring for approximately 3000 years prior to historic carving, archaeologically dated to around 400 AD. The ring has four imprinted stones in the northwest, each one with different markings. One stone has a runic inscription, another has a cross, another has an anvil carving and finally, the fourth one has an ogham inscription. The rune and ogham inscriptions are cuneiform-based alphabets.

While stone erosion limits the quantity of data available to us, scientists successfully interpreted some astronomical data. We know this is one way shamans and spiritual leaders of the era preserve spiritual information and traditional teachings. For example, leaders include the names of gods or goddesses in the rune and ogham markings of the first and fourth stones. Regardless of heritage, the prime objectives are protection, keeping order, and ensuring no harm or destruction comes to the Earth or all life upon it. In addition, to guarantee peace and harmony continues in each land, inhabitants also sculpted a spiritual image of the cross on the second stone is either a Celtic cross, or a star configuration such as Southern Cross.

The objectives and sacred rites of these Northern residents match the purpose or *Rules of Life*, of numerous ancient indigenous cultures. There is a sense of pride when people today declare their ancestral connection. Yet, for inexplicable reasons, historians do not consider them indigenous. These people can trace their heritage back as far as other recognized indigenous people just as we see in the stone circles and carvings. Citizens of the Celtic nations share common values or *Rules* with others around the world; the only difference being is how various cultures label them. These parallel teachings recognize the importance of living in harmony and protecting all life, including Mother Earth. Since all humanity needs the peace and protection, it seems we could copy the Celtic *Rules of Life* and put them into words of our language here in the 21st century.

We assume all circles or rings have the same astronomical or navigational purpose. We take for granted all global circles are the same but they are not. Some circles are permanently void of life, such as Kiribati's circles. Other circles such as those on the Orkney Islands flow with wildlife. Grass grows, birds fly and it is a favourite grazing ground. Whenever humans enter the circle though; the wildlife leaves, returning only when it is quiet and free of humans. Animals are aware of a shift in the energy, as were our predecessors. This knowledge kept them safe and guided them to food. Three thousand years ago, wildlife and people around the globe intuitively knew of the energy shifts and accepted the ability to sense these shifts as normal. This is a key lesson for our generation. As we move through the evolution of industry and modernization, we pay less attention to the energy and shifts. We lose the intensity of our ancestor's energy knowledge. There are people today who recognize the shift but this is unusual. Perhaps if we re-examine the circles and its changes, we can re-awaken our ability to recognize changes.

One benefit of paying attention to the historic circles is noticing *where* the wildlife is active and what the environmental draw was. Is there an ample water source? Is it alkaline or acidic? Is the plant life and soil rich in natural valuable nutrients such as phytonutrients, minerals herbs, amino acids and calcium? If we answer these questions for each circle, we might re-discover the energy, find a healthy resource and perhaps notice a link between historic circles to the volcanoes and springs of ancient times. If we realize the importance of these natural sources and the importance of keeping the body balanced, we may also realize that disease cannot live in this atmosphere.

Not only did wildlife *adopt* certain circles guiding life forms, the ancient people created specific circles, or centers, according to their function of life, health and healing. Archaeologists acknowledge the specific purpose produces a calm and balanced wave of energy for the community.

Just beyond the boundaries of the circles and communal settlements of the Celtic, we find remote individual stones, *menhirs,* standing isolated from rings and sacred centers. One particular stone, *the Odin Stone* stands 450 ft (140 metres) north of the Standing Stones of Stenness. This *Holed Monolith* dates back to 3,000 BCE. Because of its position, experts believe this menhir carries the balancing, healing energy for the area. Here the curative quality of the stone itself, the design of Odin Stone and the mythical healing water of the nearby Bigswell healing wells all blend into one. This is only one example from a single extinct volcanic island in the Orkneys.

These islands continually remind us of the qualities and nutritious remnants deposited by spewing eruptions. It is difficult to visualize this area as mountainous landscape, when the only volcanic evidence remaining are the 70 dormant peaks, each one now an individual island.

The Celtic shamans practice natural healing with plants and stones. They know the power for the stone, the power of the formation and the healing of plants. It seems they understood the benefit of natural healing and consuming healthy food. We know the Celtic Odin Stone and the Bigswell properties are moderately recent, only dating back 5,000 years. The Celtic people are relatively young but it appears they succeeded in establishing practices to teach and help others. They preserved their wisdom for future generations.

Their legacy and knowledge equals wisdom found around the globe. Numerous formations in the Celtic path prove their astronomical prowess. The Harappan civilization of the Indus Valley developed advanced mathematical, engineering, astronomical systems and formed the basis of Ayurvedic Health system. The Maya developed a numeric and astronomical system ending in the infamous 2012. Let us look at the Orkney Celtic rings.

Paul Devereux, in his book, *Secrets of Ancient and Sacred Places,* discusses the Celtic ring correlations with the annual equinox and solstice. He includes a diagram created by Magnus Spence in the late 1800s (Devereux, P19). [135] For brevity, Spence and Devereux used two symbols in the diagram on the upcoming page.

L. Circle -- representing Ring of Brodgar

S. Circle -- representing Stones of Stenness

This diagram shows three scalene triangles, one with solid lines and the other two with dotted lines.

The first triangle is between Ring of Brodgar (L circle), Maeshowe Cairn and Barnhouse – solid line. The L circle – Maeshowe line extends beyond the triangle.

The second triangle is between Ring of Brodgar (L circle), Stones of Stenness (S circle) and Maeshowe – dotted line.

The last triangle is between Ring of Brodgar (L circle), Watchstone and Maeshowe – both solid and dotted lines. Watchstone menhir is actually part of the Stones of Stenness ring which sits on the second triangle.

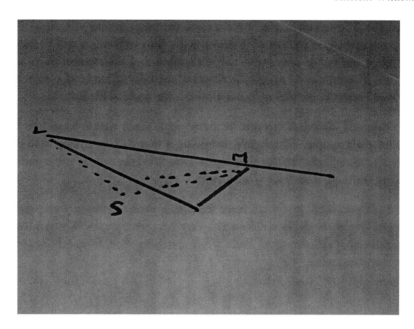

Points to consider from this diagram:

- Maeshowe (M), a connector of all triangles, contains the remnants of one of the finest and largest cairns or burial sites surviving time, indicating the importance of ceremonies and burial sites.
- The significant pathway is between Ring of Brodgar and Halloween equinox. Beltane at the Ring of Brodgar is the beginning of May, the height of spring and blooming life and Halloween is the end of October and the height of autumn, when growing ceases.
- According to ancient tradition, the rising sun represents the beginning of the end, or the first step towards a new year, life itself.
- The Ring of Brodgar has a center hole for ritualistic purpose. Because mythology alludes to passing a newborn baby through the hole, reasonably this open hole faces both Ring of Brodgar and Barnhouse, calling in the energy from the rising sun at winter solstice. It is important to give all life a strong spiritual beginning. One way they did this was pull the *energy of life* along this line.
- All extended lines point to a piece of the equinox. A society needs a connection of some form linking the beginning of life (spring) to the end (winter). This suggests belief in a form of afterlife. Therefore, they would develop a pathway for the departed souls. In this case the Maeshowe burial cairns connects all of these lines or triangles.

Spence and Devereux focused on the cairn connection where the dead lived. They acknowledged an *arm of life* between the Ring of Brodgar and Barnstone but felt it was not as relevant to the settlements and the connection to their afterlife. However, as we review the rings and menhirs of Scotland, we discover spiritual mysteries paralleling other worldly sites such as Kiribati.

Ancestors tell historical legends in many ways. Each nation knew the best way for their people. The significant point is that ALL countries have their society's *Rules of Life*. Various philosophers modified the rules of other nations, making them applicable for their people.

Since philosophical teachings from European societies began just prior to and evolving through the modern era, they became a part of Western living. Regardless they follow a set of *Rules of Life* matching those from other cultures on other continents.

Part IX - Middle East

The land linking *three* of our continents – Europe, Africa and Asia, is the Middle East. Cultures from this region have a major influence upon these continents, in fact upon our entire planet. Many tribes, cultures and societies call it home.

The political divisions are: Afghanistan, Bahrain, Iran, Iraq, Israel, Jordan, Kuwait, Kyrgyzstan, Lebanon, Oman, Pakistan, Qatar, Saudi Arabia, Syria, Tajikistan, Turkey, Turkmenistan, United Arab Emirates, Uzbekistan, and Yemen.[136] Unlike societies influencing communities nearby, they contribute to cultures *around* the globe, not just a limited planetary area. The ancient civilizations of this area create communication styles and religions appropriate around the globe, spanning eons of time.

Out of all the nations and cultures from the Middle East contributing to our heritage, three seem to stand out in their gifts to modern times and multiple cultures. These are Sumer, Babylon, and Nabataea. The estimated dates for these inhabitants are Sumerians 5,000 BCE, Babylonians 3,000 BCE, and Nabataeans 2000 BCE.

Scientists credit Sumerian culture with inventions ranging from the wheel to astronomy, earning a descriptive title of *The Inventive Society*. They came from what we know today as southern Iraq or the *cradle of civilization*. While numerous cultures in this region developed civilized systems with many inventions, this is the first society to create year round agriculture, harvesting a variety of plants relevant to each season. This process requires storage facilities, record keeping and established cities, marked by canals and boundary stones. Their cities had complex systems of sewers and flush toilets set up to eliminate waste from cities. Perhaps they were the earliest culture identifying waste and pollution.

Beyond their pollution flushing systems, a key legacy for us is their record keeping and writing system. They developed the first known syllabary writing system. Here "syllabary" means an approximate syllable or sound cluster. Because each syllable identifies a series of sounds, the system became transferable from one culture to another.

They split the hour into 60 minutes and the minute into 60 seconds. Their calendrical structure was primal; it was effective and became the basis of other culture's products. They observed solar and lunar cycles and elementary constellations.

We recognize Sumerian law codes contributions to possibly the first economic formula, contributing features we still use today in our pricing system, and interest format. For example, they designed basic inheritance rules and property taxing methods. As expected, environmental and social structure changes over time. This country's inventions and law codes illustrate how future societies apply ancient knowledge and develop modifications according to changes in their surroundings and community. Regardless of the era or location on the planet, everyone has an example at their fingertips. With the Sumerian knowledge, future societies can adopt their:

- Sanitary system
- Record Keeping and writing system
- Time structure
- Calendrical system
- Solar, lunar cycles and elementary constellations
- Economic formulas
- Law codes

Now upcoming societies have the choice of following this ideal example or creating a new system that may not work. A key to potential success is the incorporation of the ancient wisdom into upcoming social structure.

These inventions and innovations easily place the Sumerians among the most creative cultures in history. The modern world utilizes Sumerian scientific achievements. We know other global societies produce comparable configurations and we know other societies adopted them. The difference is the Sumerian population is one of the earliest civilizations who recorded their achievements and resided in the cross-roads of three continents, hence a part of the cradle of civilization.

After the Sumerian decline, cultures came and went from this region. As we review the history of these societies, we begin understanding how leaders adjust ancient wisdom or discoveries to fit *their* particular modern world. Some of these societies adjusted the legal codes according to their era. We acknowledge the global contribution of the Babylonian king, King Hammurabi.

King Hammurabi reigned between 1792 – 1750 BCE. Throughout several peaceful decades, he expanded upon the evolutionary developments of his ancestors, including the Sumerians. He brought together Assyrians and Babylonians, which in that era was the Mesopotamian civilization. During his reign, his people improved upon navigation, irrigation, agriculture, and tax collection methods. This is a situation where people adapt ancestral contributions to current environmental and societal lifestyles. They selectively chose aspects of ancient lifestyles.

These innovative advancements are remarkable, yet they are not what we remember Hammurabi for. We remember him as a great humanitarian figure. He moulded a society centering on the equality of humanity.

This is a key gift for all future societies.

Earlier we referred to the Sumerian law codes. This man, King Hammurabi, now had a choice of classifying community laws into the *Code of Hammurabi* which included the Sumerian codes. He adopted ancient wisdom. Authorities consider it the earliest legal comprehensive code known in history; influencing legal thinking even today. Hammurabi incorporated historical Sumerian and Akkadian legal systems into his Hammurabi Code.

The Code of Hammurabi contains 282 laws covering a wide range of topics including economic retaliation and fines. The precursor to *modern* thinking reinforces the concepts of presumed innocence and equality amongst humans regardless of status or gender. These ancient codes use the phrases "innocence until proven guilty" and an "eye for an eye". Three other city-states in this region created similar codes around the same time, suggesting the core knowledge came from the same source. These are: Code of Ur, Laws of Eshnunna, and the Lipit-Ishtar Code. Historians consider these four code sets as sources for modern constitutional law. Yet, the one we remember is the *Code of Hammurabi*. We remember his leadership but, it seems inconsequential to recall the nation or the location. In other global locations, we remember the nation and not the leader. In the Middle East, we have Sumerians named after Sumer and Babylonians named after Babylon, but there is no such place as a "Hammurabi" community.

In the 2nd century BCE, a tribe known as Nabataeans came into prominence in the Middle East. They settled in what we call Jordan, east of the Dead Sea. Over time, people began exchanging two names; Arab and Nabataea became synonymous. Initially the Nabatean nation was nomadic, later becoming prosperous urban dwellers settling into fortress cities. They were also literate, leaving examples of graffiti and inscriptions on obelisks and walls. Many credit them with inventing Arabic Script, the Mediterranean Arabic Script.[137] Since this is about the time the Sumerian written communication style faded out, it makes sense that this is the birth of the Nabatean writing inventions. Unfortunately, we have limited evidence of written legal documents and trade agreements.

Our ancestors knew that cooperation is a strong survival requirement. Their climate, environment and the surrounding population spawned the formation of defense, irrigation, and agricultural systems, all leading to cities. Regardless of how they built cities and defense, they made certain their fundamental values were always in place.

As part of their defence and residential protection, they carved the key city, Petra from the rose-red cliffs of southern Jordan. This city is accessible through a thin split in the mountain. The leaders optimized the use of natural formation benefits. While severe earthquakes shattered many of their settlements, including parts of this one, their leaders saved two things: the elaborate architectural carvings in the rock faces and their water systems. Thanks to the architectural excellence, today's scientists note the quality of the water used in years past. Archaeologists still marvel at the Nabataean skills as architects, engineers, stonemasons and artists.

The Nabataean people constructed amazing hydraulic systems, still functional. Ancient residents needed a method to maximize the usage of the scant rainfall they received. This earth region averages only six inches of rainfall per year. Yet, these people provide a daily fresh water supply five times the needs for a population of their city's size when their harnessed rainfall is added to the water gleaned from desert springs. They accomplish this engineering marvel through an intricate system of cisterns, pools and waterways that captured and transported water to the city.[138] This system was created more than 2,000 years ago and we still use a similar watertight system of bell and spigot joints to transport water. Arid locations could gain from this technology today. This exemplifies how ancient wisdom successfully moves forward through time.

We know how vital water is to all life. Did the Nabataeans learn the importance of maintaining water quality from other societies and then search for a method to preserve it? Or did they initiate the understanding? Did this knowledge pass along trade routes from the Hunza civilization high in the mountains? Or did it come out of Egypt, resulting in Nabataea engineering systems? These systems include water conservation systems and the dams constructed to divert the rush of swollen rivers that would otherwise create flash floods.[139] Was the technology unique to the region or did they acquire it from other global cultures? Did it travel from one culture to another?

These answers are unknown but we do know we benefit today from the hydraulic engineering systems regardless of their origin.

If it came along trade routes, then perhaps it came along one created by these innovate people. The impact of these creative people flows around the world. The Nabataeans developed the spice trade extending from Arabia to Aqaba on the Gulf of Aqaba and then up to Petra in present-day South-west Jordan. Their influence extends through the Arabian Peninsula and down the East Coast of Africa. Science confirms the travels into Africa, reinforcing a theorized link between Solomon, Sheba and Zimbabwe[140]. The Nabataeans built lavish temples and obelisks. On the sides of these obelisks, the Nabataean carved symbols which illustrate the sophistication of their writing.

Several years ago, my spirit friends showed me a new language of symbols, kept in pairs of pillars, similar to a gateway. On one tower, positioned on the left side, the symbols flowed from the bottom to the top and the other, positioned on the right side, flowed in the opposite direction. This concept matches the carving formats we find in Nabataean regions. The ancients placed images on obelisks, flowing from bottom to the top on one obelisk, reversing the order on another. Thus, we see earlier cultures' text correlating with the information in current times.

The obelisk symbols discussed previously in *Within and Beyond,* describe how the carvings of ancient times illustrate the residents' basic understanding of cosmic knowledge. We know spiritual leaders in ancient cultures receive guidelines necessary for daily living. If the guidelines of long ago came in the form of symbols, then perhaps we need an in-depth study of these symbols as researchers apply them today. During ancient times, the shamans or spiritual masters were the only interpreters of this data. Through the ages, all citizens learned details so everyone becomes an interpreter. The pyramid-shaped top of each obelisk equals one half of the **MANU NYMBA**. This brings the electrical energy down from RA, or the universe. The information provided by the pillars, or towers, is simple and forthright.

The Nabataea people lived in the lands of the Middle East sharing knowledge of their past and their leaders. Symbolic and archaeological evidence places Christianity, Judaism and Islam in the region regardless of the current spirituality of that nation. We need to remember customs and lifestyles of people change. Ancient residents were mainly herders or nomads requiring a mobile population across lands, unaware of regional status. When we review ancient cultures and apply the knowledge to the transition of historical societies, we learn that modern societies *can* work together.

For example, according to legend, Abraham is from Ur, in Iraq. Ur is on the east side of the land close to the Persian Gulf. He is the founding father in the Book of Genesis. He is also regarded as an important figure in three faiths - Judaism, Christianity, and Islam. Abraham means "Father of Nations". Note our ancestors pluralized Nation.

Another image, the Tower of Babel is in Iraq. According to the biblical account, a united humanity, speaking a single language and migrating from the east, took part in the building of this tower after the *Great Flood*.[141] We know *the wise men* were travelers, or shepherds, crossing the Arabian Peninsula toward the Jordan River into what we call Israel. Literature states they came from the East. To travel a specific route heading west, they must have originated in a country that was NOT Israel.

We find numerous references to Babylon and Mesopotamia in Christianity and Judaism literature. However, both ancient nations are between the Tigris and Euphrates Rivers which run through Iraq.

By reviewing this history, we remind ourselves that people of long ago understood the cultures and discovered ways to bring peace into their cultures. Symbolic owls and doves are in both the Arab and Jewish cultures.

Just as the owls of the northern hemisphere *carry* knowledge, the owls in the Middle East *demonstrate* this wisdom with tales of a series of successful Jordan River crossings. Thanks to the owls of the region, residents demonstrate this usage. As residents lived with this knowledge, a cross cultural cooperation program across the Jordan River successfully uses owls to keep the rat population down. This is teamwork across borders.

Our ancient wisdom reminds us that nations may go through turbulent times but our ancestors worked out peaceful, healing ways to work together, so why can't we achieve this today?

The point of including data from multiple religions and multiple counties demonstrates how regardless of religion or nation, people adopt pathways leading to similar conclusion, all pointing to safety and cultural progression.

Part X - Africa

Many people maintain planetary life began in Africa. Everywhere on the African continent, we find primeval remains, eroded mountains, faded artifacts and unexplained mysteries. As well, scientist and historians continually explore the land looking for fresh information. Two regions complimenting the scientific data are Zimbabwe, and Mali.

ZIMBABWE

Throughout the research on Africa, the name Zimbabwe and related references constantly surfaces. Even former Zimbabwean residents join our local Canadian community. This constant flux of data indicates we need a clearer understanding of the importance of this land.

The name Zimbabwe means either *dzimba dza* - Houses of stone, or *dzimba woye* - Venerated houses. The ruin of Great Zimbabwe is one of the largest relics in Africa, covering almost 1,800 acres. Consisting of stone houses and great walls, the ruins suggest a chief's dwelling or spiritual center surrounded by clusters of smaller buildings. The *Zimbabwe Wall*, constructed around the 16th century CE, is a key component of this archeologist site and now one of the wonders of the world. If we look at both aerial and land photographs of the actual Zimbabwe Wall, we understand the skill and thought behind its construction. Two sections of the structure are so narrow that visitors have to enter in single file; suggesting either a safety necessity for the enclosure or respect for a chieftain or leader.

The walls of the structure are more than 800 ft in length and 32 feet high. There is no indication of mortar, scaffolding or use of a plumb bob, yet they are virtually perfect. We do not find this style of construction anywhere today, so we need to ask ourselves - *Why Not?* Even though this style proves very effective, why did humans cease building walls without the binding of mortar or similar compounds; is there a logical reason? Is this something we could confidently adopt for use today?

We find similar walls or bastions around the world, older than the Zimbabwe ruins. We have the stone Kaimanawa Wall on the north island of New

Zealand, 7,000 miles away from Africa. We have similar ancient relics on Easter Island and Tonga, 2,000 miles northeast of New Zealand. All these walls have a dry stone construction and only three relics of similar styles exist elsewhere. But how, and why, did remote cultures build defensive structures such as these. Did they invent the same style at the same time or did they design a method to pass this knowledge from one society to another? Since researchers place the origin of the Zimbabwe relics into the Current Era, this suggests the technique travels *from* other lands *to* Africa. It seems to me that whatever the circumstances, we could re-examine the methods, applying them in construction where there was no concern about weight *on* the structure.

A unique feature of the Zimbabwe Wall is the *Zimbabwe Bird*. This magical Bird is a 12-inch carving of an eagle-like bird with human legs and four or five toes, not talons. Originally, pillars spaced down the entire length of the Wall each displayed a soapstone carving of this *Bird* on top. Today, only eight complete ancient bird carvings remain.

The Zimbabwe Bird exemplifies the strong bond that ancestral humans had with animals, nature and spirit guides. Perhaps the Ancient Ones of the Zimbabwe region believe this eagle-like bird to be *their* ancestor. If this is so, then a statue combining humans with nature appropriately symbolizes a guardian. This rationale clarifies the reverence and importance of the Zimbabwe bird and why in 1980, their citizens placed it on their newly designed independence flag. They are not afraid to assert their respect and beliefs.

These ancient artifacts of walls and birds received modern labeling after a modern political restructuring of the land. The European history and tales of a strange land bypasses the wisdom of the original tribes. There are many carvings and paintings along the length of the *Zimbabwe Wall*. They came from an indigenous people of Africa. But who painted them and what did they signify?

Some of the tribes associated with this region of Africa include Shona, Bantu, Bushman and Khoi or San tribes. They were all wanderers or hunter-gatherers, living in many parts of Africa. Did these relics come from the hands of one of these tribes?

Spencer Wells reports that San people, lived in this African region roughly 50,000 years ago.[142] Khoisan[143] occupation dates back between 40,000 BCE to 10,000 years BCE. Researchers base this estimate upon found Stone Age (Paleolithic) implements, Khoisan cave paintings, arrowheads, pottery, and pebble tools in several areas of Zimbabwe. Since there is no evidence of anybody moving them, this gave scholars the initial dating of the society.

We find cave rock or *Bushman* paintings, throughout Zimbabwe, depicting the lifestyles and beliefs as tribal society evolved. Modern Khoisan people or Bushmen learned from their elders. They still live in harmony with nature, posing no threat to wildlife and vegetation by over-hunting or gathering. Wildlife and vegetative knowledge contributes to our modern world.

This past reminds us of the power and strength of humanity. This shows us how residents in this region develop skills and strengths to withstand their difficulties. Perhaps they create a molded symbol as a reminder. They built walls that, according to modern technicians, are almost impossible. They molded birds exemplifying the harmony and power of their unification with nature. While time changes both the societies and terrain of this region, the strengths remain.

We do not know why humans moved into the Zimbabwe area. It is unclear whether we came in search of minerals or came in search of volcanos, pure spring water and hot springs. These resources provide energy and alkaline water, a basis for an historical background.

While Zimbabwe does not have active volcanoes today, the rolling hills in Eastern Zimbabwe, the Inyanga range, suggest an ancient, large volcanic range. Mining occurred in this range long before the King Solomon era. One study, based on charcoal findings, places humans there between 26,000 – 20,000 BCE. Another study by Zecharia Sitchin, dates the evidence back to 41,250 BCE.[144] It seems that the Inyanga range provides the necessary energy to the creators of the Great Zimbabwe region.

Who received the benefits of the volcanos and springs in this region and who constructed the amazing structures is an enigma. Many researchers insist there was a continuous search for gold, minerals that fulfilled the perceived *missing needs* of humanity. These resources, found near volcanic rock and hot springs, form an economic basis for much of Africa.

The Israelites and Phoenicians became important in Zimbabwe history because they traveled down this Coast of Africa toward the area of Zimbabwe/ Mozambique. Sitchin offers evidence and an explanation as to the exploratory routes of Israelites and their associates. One suggested route went through the Red Sea down the East Coast to the Zambezi Basin just east of Zimbabwe and north of Swaziland.

LEMBA PEOPLE

This clan, part of the Zimbabwe people, presents an interesting heritage for this society. According to history and legends, the people known as the **Lemba** evolved from the intermarriage of African travelers with inhabitants of the area. Even today, they insist they have Israelite heritage. There are six areas corroborating this testimonial.

First: - the Lemba's ancient legends and teachings state they migrated from the Middle East. Contemporary residents claim their ancestors built the Zimbabwe wall shortly after leaving the Middle East 2700 years ago. For generations, they insisted upon Jewish heritage while historians dismissed it because they were black and did not display the physical traits of Israelites. A Lemba song legend states: *Male ancestry originally was white people from over the sea who came to southeast Africa to obtain gold.* Their history and legends come in the form of songs instead of written text. They chose song as a simpler way to pass legend down to their young. This keeps their birthright alive, ensuring their young understand the past.

Second: - carvings on Zimbabwe ruins are similar to Middle East carvings. This society develops skillful carvers, so by carving symbols on stone ruins around Great Zimbabwe keeps the Lemba connected with the Middle East. The symbols and carving in the Middle East and Great Zimbabwe match carvings found farther south in Africa. Were they the ancient residents who inexplicably left Zimbabwe, moving farther south?

Third: - there is a DNA match. Early in 2005, the History Television Channel presented a show about the Lemba people called *The Lost Tribes of Israel*.[145] The outcome of this filming led to testing the Lemba DNA. The scientists confirmed the DNA match between the Lemba tribe of Africa and the people in the Hadramaut region of Yemen[146]. Not only did the DNA match but members of the most senior Lemba clan displayed the Cohen Modal Haplotype, a feature of Jewish priesthood. This priesthood division has stayed in effect for almost 3,000 years. The DNA testing also verified the link between Israeli Jews and Lemba people.

Fourth: - ancient maps show a city in the Middle East named Lemba. In Zimbabwe, experts found an old map from around 100 BCE showing a town called Lemba between the Jordan town of Medeba and the fortress of Macherus, east of the Dead Sea.[147]

Fifth: - Lemba words indicate a Semitic origin. This compares to studies of modern languages indicating the travels and migration of ancient societies.

Six: - according to Dr. Rudo Mathivha, Pediatrician and ICU specialist in South Africa, Lemba beliefs and practices correlate with Judaism, contrary to many indigenous African teachings. These include the following:

1. Monotheism, calling the creator God "Nwali".
2. One weekly day of praise of Nwali.
3. Praising Nwali for caring for the Lemba, the chosen ones.
4. Honoring mothers and fathers.
5. Performing male circumcision before age eight.
6. Refraining from eating pork, any foods prohibited by the Old Testament or forbidden combinations of permitted foods, like mixing milk with meat. Washing hands before handling food or cooking utensils
7. Saying grace and thanking Nwali before feasting, as in Judaism.
8. Performing special burial rituals with a Star of David on the Tombstone.
9. Encouraging Lembas to marry other Lembas. A non Lemba woman learns the ways of the Lembas if she is to marry one. She learns the religious laws, dietary laws, etc. She may not bring any kitchen utensils from her maiden home to her new Lemba home. And she is to bring her children up according to the Lemba tradition

Ritualizing animal slaughter, making meats fit for their consumption, resembles Jewish Shechita. . [148]

Many readers view these as commonplace differences. However, when you compare them with practices of local African people, they are unusual. For example, eating pork and wild meat is a normal practice to non-Lemba residents.

Unfortunately, so many societies around our world lose the heritage of their ancestors and bypass the lessons or lifestyles of their predecessors. Here, the Lemba remember their past through legends but not the skills.

The point is if future generations had the interest, they would retain the technology. It seems we utilize knowledge only when it suits our immediate interest.

The great Zimbabwe walls and carvings illustrate that 3,000 years ago, humans knew how to create structures of phenomenal magnitude. We know the Lemba people participated in the construction, but whether they initiated the creation is unknown. It seems to me that the Lemba people, through their history, show us how humans migrated, carrying skills and knowledge to other lands.

Zimbabwe demonstrates how the animal knowledge of the owl, the dove and the butterfly affects the 21st century.

The Owl reminds us of the knowledge of the Wall structure and the wisdom of the Lemba people. When we recall the harmony of the molded birds exemplifying the harmony and power of their unification with nature, we see and hear the Dove. Lastly, the Butterflies transform the knowledge into a form that people such as the Lemba use.

MALI

The review of the Zimbabwe cultures, illustrates the physical contributions passed to us, members of modern society. Then when we go over to the west side of Africa, we gain the ancient knowledge that opens the door to a more mystical reflection.

The Dogon people live in the Mali region of Africa. We know them for their mythology, dances, wooden sculpture and architecture. Their villages cluster around a stretch of escarpment, the Cliffs of Bandiagara, running along the Niger River. Like other indigenous groups, the Dogon insist they *came from the sky*. Archaeological theories and evidence trace them back to the Sumerians or Egyptians on the other side of Africa. Perhaps this explains the knowledge of the Dogon but does not provide any details. We learn of people escaping into this land around 1500 CE which historians claim were the first human inhabitants in this region. Yet carbon dating on remains from the cliffs place humans in this region as early as 3rd century BCE. This becomes a difference of 4500 years!

Three cults exist amongst the Dogon; the Awa, cult of the dead, Lebe, the agricultural or Earth God and Binu.

First, within the Awa cult – cult of the dead, the priests conduct rituals to sort out unsettled spiritual forces and reconnect the departed with his or her deceased ancestors.

Second, the Lebe priest, or Hogon, teaches the community the agricultural methods and techniques. They protect the life force of soil and plant life, keeping all food nutrients safe and nutritious.

The third cult, Binu, is totemic. Binu spirits make themselves known to a clan in the form of an animal. This animal intervenes for a clan during its formation or migration, becoming a clan's totem. The Binu priests ensure there are numerous paintings of mystic symbols or graphic signs throughout sanctuaries. Each village has a totem shared by its residences and each individual has his or her personal one. In this way, Dogons believe the benevolent force of their ancestors and Nommo comes to them.

According to Dogon mythology, Nommo is the creature created by Amma, the sky god and creator of the universe.

Amma designed Nommo as a multiple sets of twins. Each set represent one source, or/soul, splits into two, the yin /yang. These sets represent the individual, community or universe. When one twin rebels against the other, it weakens the cosmos. Therefore, a community, through ritual and symbolic design activity, restores duality balance through healing. Today, it becomes imperative to acknowledge or recapture the harmony and peace of this group. Modern spirituality and groups recognize the balance but current groups insist they are the creator or founder of this precept.

The three cults represent the harmony of communities. If we pause in discussions of current times, we find harmony, healing ourselves and a grouping of people. Like other ancient cultures, the Dogon believe in communal harmony. These ancestors found ways to bring peace into their lives, presenting two features we can adopt.

First, people praise one another and continually ask how another is doing. If the answer is *sewa*, it means everything is fine. This gives them the nickname of the *sewa* people.

The other feature worthy of implementation is the *toguna* building, meaning – 'House of Words'. Each village has a meeting building structure with a low ceiling. This prevents people from standing upright. A mad person cannot stand up and therefore cannot become violent. It is not possible to take part in a fist fight while crouching under a low ceiling. This building with a low ceiling is similar to buildings found in other indigenous communities. The *toguna* building is a viable village structure regardless of where we live.

People today, associate Dogon people with astronomical star wisdom. They bypass Dogon's *silent gifts,* communal healing or *house of words.* Oral teachings and traditions base their astronomical understanding upon their knowledge of the star system Sirius but for centuries other cultures dismissed it. Now that 19th and 20th century scientists proved this information is accurate, humans finally acknowledge their wisdom. The Dogon elders taught this information to younger generations through oral tradition, dating back 5,000 years. Now the speculation begins. How did they learn about the Sirius system? Their oral traditions say it was given to them by the Nommo. If this is so, how did their God – Amma - or the first living being, Nommo gain this knowledge.

Dr. Marcel Griaule, a French anthropologist, documented their mythology and sacred beliefs for the last 30 years of his life, including their knowledge of Sirius. He spent fifteen years of these years studying with four Dogon priests. These priests taught:

- Sirius is 8.6 light years from the Earth
- Sirius has a companion star, invisible to the human eye.
- The companion star moves in a 50-year elliptical orbit around Sirius
- Sirius is small and incredibly heavy.
- Sirius rotates on its axis.

These facts match the findings from 20th century scientists. Another incredible piece of data from the Dogon is: *The **DNA** pattern perfectly matches the elliptical orbit made by the two stars as they rotate around each other.*

This includes the identification of **three** Sirius stars. **Sirius A** is ten times larger than our sun and is twice as massive. It is the largest, most brilliant star and it is known as the blue-white star. **Sirius B** is called a white dwarf star, with the equivalent mass of our sun packed into a globe four times the size of our Earth. It completes an elliptical orbit around Sirius A in a 50 year cycle. It was discovered fifty years ago by the scientific community but the Dogon tribes knew of Sirius B more than 5,000 years ago. The Dogon call Sirius B - *Po Tolo* which translates to small, heavy and white. *Po* means smallest seed and *Tolo* means star. This name describes the size, weight and color. **Sirius C** is the third of the Sirian stellar family. The scientific community has not confirmed the existence of Sirius C, yet the Dogon knew of it by the name, *Enome Ya*. They discovered its revolution around Sirius A. The Dogon charted the Sirius star system before anyone was able to see invisible stars and celestial bodies, accurately tracking them for centuries.

The ceremonial festivities, called **Sigui,** takes place every 65 years, lasting several years. This coincides with the cycles of the Sirius stars. The next one begins in 2032. These dates correspond with the Mayan 50 year cycle, ending in 2012. Each village has a totem shared by its residences and each individual has his or her personal one.

The Dogon are not the only indigenous people who knew of stars and orbits. It seems modern people need to review the wisdom of many indigenous nations and apply their knowledge to our modern world. The Ancients knew details of stars that we are just beginning to learn.

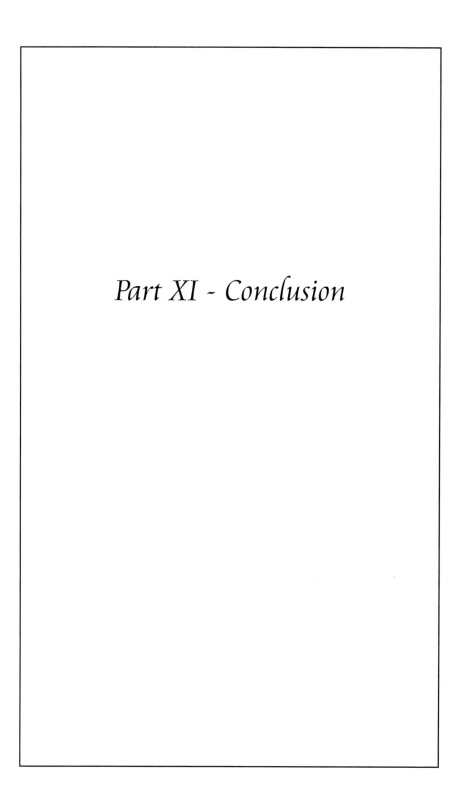

Part XI - Conclusion

THE METAMORPHOSIS

Ancient teachings from around the globe give pieces of knowledge applicable today. These pieces include gifts from our three white feathered animals; the owl dove and butterfly carry them forward through time. Even though an animal is absent from a region, we still feel the energy.

The owl carries the knowledge of time through generation, teaching us the value and meaning in current lives.

The dove reminds us of the importance of bringing peace and harmony into our lives.

The butterfly teaches us how to incorporate this wisdom into our lives, merging with our environment, thus forming a better world.

As I researched ancient civilizations, I found the wisdom of remote societies was more applicable than the culturally bound teachings of our immediate ancestors. It seemed the older the society, the more relevance it has today. One of the connections was the volcanic and spring locations chosen by the residents.

These volcanoes appear destructive but they bring forward energy and tools we need in our present and future. The Ancient Ones, my spirit guides, give lessons from our past about them and how important they are to our future. We just need to be patient. They said:

"Volcanoes build bridges. Humans tend to stay in what they call the NOW, forgetting that all time is occurring simultaneously. A volcanic eruption builds a bridge and makes changes that are for the betterment of all life.

They are a way of bringing peace and harmony to a planet. They create new springs, better (purer) water that pulls in new life from beyond your small narrow plane. In the beginning, all life realized this and they understood.

Today, there is arrogance amongst humans because they believe that only they can build things. They do not understand or accept the principle that there are other ways to create.

A volcano brings new forms of mineral deposits to the surface, which will allow humans to use and see a new potential. We do not see why all the work of digging, or mining as you call it, is encouraged. When you look at your past, you possibly will see when cultures used what was on the surface or perhaps in a cave and did not need to dig. This was very long ago. This is when the Zimbabwe bird symbolized a sense of freedom. We encourage all who read this to look into their neighbourhood and identify a region that had a disaster early in your lifetime. What did it look like and what does it look like now. What is the difference?"

The Ancients remind us of the importance of applying peace and love in personal living before communities cooperate. It seems we are just beginning to learn this, yet this is what we desperately need. The way the Mi'kmaq and Chinese shared and taught one another illustrates this teamwork.

Most regions of the world have indigenous values similar to other districts. Cultural groups who stepped out of isolated living, such as the Kogi, see the importance of sharing this data. Each segment of this book shows these similarities, imbedding most of the information. However, in some cases there are specific quotes. I include fifteen excerpts to help you see connections and similarities between cultures. If you re-read these excerpts you will see these similarities and discover how each guideline set fits into the 21st century.

1. Mohawk

Treat the Earth and all that dwell thereon with respect.
Remain close to the Great Spirit.
Show great respect for fellow beings.
Work together for the benefit of all Mankind.
Give assistance and kindness wherever needed.
Do what you know to be right.
Look after the well-being of Mind and Body.
Dedicate a share of your efforts to the greater good.
Be truthful and honest at all times.
Take full responsibility for your actions.

2. Inuit

Respect for life and wisdom
Lack of individual ownership and greed
Sense of destiny, place and freedom of choice
Commitment to live in nature's cycles.

3. Haida

"Their words are simple and their voices are soft. We have not heard them, because we have not taken the time to listen.

Perhaps now is the time to open our ears and our hearts to the words of wisdom they have to say."

4. Cowichan

Give all invited guests a gift. Residents must follow this rule for all time.
Do not kill for the sake of killing. Kill only for food.
Drink and eat sparingly.
Bathe in every clear water you encounter. This makes you strong.
Listen to all that is said and follow it accordingly.
Know your place in the world.
Treat the world with respect.
Take from the world only what you need.

5. Stó:lo

"This is our land. We have to look after everything that belongs to us.

6.   Mi'kmaq

"Stated simply, we take nothing we don't need, we waste nothing, and we offer thanks for everything we do take."

7.   Hopi

Take care of Mother Earth and the other colors of man.
Respect this Mother Earth and creation.
Honor all life, and support that honor.
Be grateful from the heart for all life. It is through life that there is survival.
Thank the Creator at all times for all life.
Love, and express that love.
Be humble. Humility is the gift of wisdom and understanding.
Be kind with one's self and with others.
Share feelings and personal concerns and commitments.
Be honest with one's self and with others. Be responsible for these sacred instructions and share them with other nations.
Simplicity
Brotherhood
Love
Peace

8.   The Lakota – Sioux

Only after the last tree has been cut down,
Only after the last river has been poisoned,
Only after the last fish has been caught,
Only then will you find
That money cannot be eaten…

9.   Kogi

Segment of Kogi message
…"Please BBC
no one else should come here,
no more ransacking
because the earth wants to collapse,
the earth grows weak,
we must protect it,
we must respect it,
because he does not respect the earth,
because he does not respect it."

10.   Hawaii

--Just do it!" instead of worrying about doing a difficult job.

--Destroy the forest, the rains will cease to fall, and the land will become a desert

--People respond better to gentle words than to scolding

--By working together we make progress

--If everybody works together, the work will be done quickly

--Words can either be a source for healing or destruction; we need to be careful with our words

--We start small and over time, we will mature and be successful

--You will reach only as far as you aim

--No task is too big when done together.

--Acquire a skill and make it deep.

--Strive for the summit, reach. Strive for the top of the mountain, striving for excellence

--Take your stand and be steadfast in doing what is right no matter what others say

--If you wish to succeed, be alert to any opportunity that should arise

11.   New Zealand – Waitaha

A.

Through relationships and respect, we can find the way forward.
Mana is upheld through fulfilling roles and responsibilities
By discussion comes understanding, through understanding comes wisdom
Gathers of resources, resources of lasting endurance
For leadership, there must be support

B.

All born of the stars were brothers and sisters, kin within one family.
Honor them, as you honor the ancestors down throught the ages. Humility brings true strength
Every aspect of all life is important.
Accept responsibility for your mistakes; do not blame others
Respect and protect all trees and products of the earth.
A young mind bends to the curve of the magic jawbone.
Healing brings responsibilities.
Sadness, pain and anger have no place beside those who tend the plants. The calm mind is the growing mind.

12.   Philippines

Must not steal
Do not tell false stories
Do not court another's wife
Respect the rights of others
Give food to visitors
Teach children old legends and customs
Honor and learn the complete system of social etiquette

13.   Samí

Nature abounds in plants and animals; the world fills with different languages and cultures. We, the Sámi, see ourselves, as part of this nature.

14.   Buddhism

Do no harm
Honor all life
Respect dead and ancestors
Honor all cultures

15.   Miscellaneous

Treat the earth well.
It was not given to you by your parents
It was loaned to you by your children
We do not inherit the Earth from our
Ancestors, we borrow it from our Children.

Love everybody with my heart and *You should also love your enemies.*

Once you accept the rights of every living thing, tree, animal or human to exist according to their place in the lifes path, it is impossible NOT to love.

A key value that came through all the research and literature is that in cultures of long ago, people lived simple and generous lives, loving and honoring ALL life. These ancient nations knew a freedom that included a degree of nonconformity.

Ancient Wisdoms give humans a simple life, allowing sharing and loving unconditionally. We do have a sense of understanding that we need to bring into our present day.

Your heart will resonate when the time is right. The time is now.

APPENDIX I– WITHIN & BEYOND SYNOPSIS

W ithin & Beyond covers the vastness of life. Thinking of *Planes* and not dimensions, *Cosmic* Pattern and not destiny, or *Manu Nymba* and not genetic material, we begin to comprehend the vastness and interconnection of life. Here is a basic overview of the principles introduced in *Within & Beyond*:

The first concept is *Planes of Reference*. Today, we frequently hear people talking about being in a specific dimension such third or fifth. In *Within & Beyond*, I re-categorize these dimensions as *Planes of Reference* or KEY sections. These are:

1. Solidity key – tangible physical world
2. Texture key – movement of energy and relationship of life
3. Identity key – survival protectiveness of self and others
4. Emotional key – discovering emotions of yourself
5. Empathy key – sharing compassion with others
6. Insight key – expanding your potentiality
7. Spiritual key – connecting to all other energies
8. Guidance key – knowing there is universal guidance
9. Council key – ultimate connection

Previously, thinking in separate dimensions implies we can only be in one dimension at a time and this span might be for several years. Now it is important that people think of dimensions as *keys* recognizing that we work with ALL the keys at once but we strengthen only specific one at any one time. All these keys are accessible simultaneously and our ancestors, particularly shamans, realize this. Different societies may carry the strength of one key more than another but they still pick up whatever tool, or key, they need at any particular time.

To illustrate, I compare this to driving a car. We see everything around us but when necessary we focus on a specific image such as a car coming toward us or a traffic light changing. The Keys of the Planes of Reference are similar. We have all nine in our concentration but may at some time center on the solidity key or the empathy key, as example. This does not suggest we are ignoring the eight other keys.

Another concept is the *Cosmic Life Pattern* or *CLP*. The CLP includes all data that is readily accessible to every life form in the cosmos. It becomes true wisdom and unconditional love. A Hindu refers to this as the Akashic Records. The difference is the Akashic is information and the CLP is energy, information *and* pattern of soul life. The Kabbalah from the Hebrew refer to the Akashic records as the text containing the sacred, secret structure of the Universe.

The third concept is the MANU NYMBA, the storage of information. MANU NYMBA means the *Nucleus of Life,* and connects the Magnetic energy of the Earth and the Electrical energy of the Universe, each is a tetrahedron forming a star tetrahedron – the Manu Nymba. This core, or Nucleus, contains the knowledge from all our past and future lives, the knowledge of the entire Universe and the CLP. In the 21st century, the accessibility to this source becomes easier. We have a choice of remembering and utilizing this wisdom or letting it lie dormant. The exhilarating link here is all the MANU NYMBA within the body stores wisdom from *the individual's* unique past, communal history and the universal wisdom. Five thousand years ago, we had access to this knowledge and integrated it easily into our lives and those of our fellow citizens of a region. Gradually, life became complicated and the community elders deemed all knowledge as sacred, revealing it only to their Elders and Shamans. This means individuals in a society function without the Shaman's knowledge. They have the data but do not know what to do with it, unless a Shaman explains it. This means there is conformity of all information whether a layman or a shaman views it. The interpretation differs. Understanding this helps us understand the phrase: *Light of our Spirit is within the body.*

While the MANU NYMBA contains universal information, it also contains the CLP records. This universal information is common to all life but how we look at it depends upon when and where we were born. Astrological charts are a form of interpretation used by community leaders. As the Earth's axis shifts, it places planets in a different position, affecting how much information comes to the citizens. The CLP then, is the etheric data bank. The attributes vary according to where and when person lives, which Planes of Reference are activated, and what lessons or information are gathered by the soul through many lives. The connection between human CLPs is spiritual since the CLP carries the universal knowledge *needed* by the individual soul.

The three principles, (1) CLP, (2) Planes of Reference and (3) Manu Nymba, take us through all the planet knowledge. When you review the focal points of a culture, hopefully, you recognize which one is the strength of a region, what is present today and what skills and knowledge move forward into current time creating a composite blend of all three.

APPENDIX II -- THE MIGRATORY JOURNEY

M any people explore human evolution but Spencer Wells, geneticist and anthropologist, used the DNA Y chromosome to accomplish the same task.[149] Wells insists that all humans living today descend from a single man living in Africa around 60,000 years ago. In contrast, the DNA of the South African Bushmen show they descend from a man over 100,000 years ago. To increase the confusion, the DNA genetic markers of these people do not match the markers of people found outside of Africa.

Paleoanthropologist, Alison Brooks, from the George Washington University in Washington DC, argues that this data does not correspond to the migratory patterns presented by human fossils. She states that Y-chromosome data gives consistently younger dates than other types of genetic data.[150]

Wells concentrates on DNA, ignoring Mitochondria (mtDNA). Chromosomes *inside* the nucleus of the cells carry Deoxyribonucleic acid (DNA). This chemical inside the nucleus of all cells carries all the required genetic instructions.[151] The mtDNA code is also in our cells but this is *outside* the nucleus.

We inherit our DNA through both parents and mtDNA only from our mother. A mother passes mtDNA to both sons and daughters but her sons cannot pass it on. Therefore, the mother-daughter chain is unwavering from generation to generation. Scientific analysis indicates mtDNA mutates about once every 10,000 years. Conversely, Y-DNA mutates every few generations. Therefore, some scientists claim mtDNA analysis produces a more reliable source of the migration story. The mtDNA mutations traveled with the woman and Y-DNA mutation stayed with the men.

Confident in his team's analytical results, Spencer Well develops a theory of potential migration. Bryan Sykes in his book - *The Seven Daughters of Eve*, presents a similar theory of potential migration. [152] Between them, they extimated that the comparable timelines for migration might be

Throughout Africa	120,000-150,000 years
Out of Africa	55,000-75,000 years
Asia	40,000-70,000 years
Australia/PNG	40,000-60,000 years
Europe	35,000-50,000 years
Americas	15,000-35,000 years
Na-Dene/Esk/Aleuts	8,000-10,000 years

This data, from both Wells and Sykes, assumes that all other strains of mankind died out, leaving only Homeo Sapien descendents. But, fossil evidence proves Homeo Erectus lived in Southeast Asia, including China and Neandertals lived in Europe. The National Geographic News article "Documentary Redraws Humans' Family Tree"[153] states the fossil records showing that a first wave of migration occurred around 100,000 years ago. This is 25,000 years earlier than Sykes' estimate.

Scientists presented a multi-regional model stating that Homeo Sapiens left Africa and modern humans evolved from them independently and simultaneously, in pockets of Africa, Europe, and Asia. Interestingly, the pattern of fossil evidence supports life evolving around volcanoes and pure spring lakes. We still face the mystery of the connection between these communities.

The mtDNA research divides homeo sapiens into twenty main groupings, situated in seven locations - Africa, Australia, Europe, Asia, Oceania, North and South America. The mtDNA evidence gives us proof of multiple origins.

They are distributed as follows:

- Africa   L, M
- Asia   A, B, C, D, F, G, M, N, Y, Z
- Australia   M
- Europe   I, J, K, H, T, U, V, W, X,
- North America   A, B, C, D, X
- Oceania   B
- South America   A, B, C, D, X

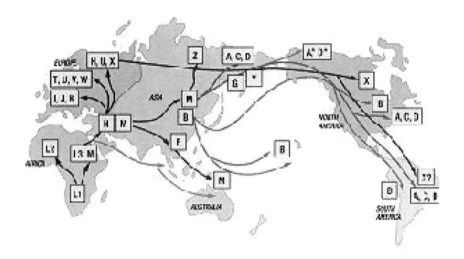

Migratory patterns according to our mtDNA[154]

This information supports the theory of "many Eves". These genetic groups share common universal *Rules of Life*. These rules provide a mysterious connection. Perhaps there was one carrier of these guidelines passing them to other communities. With many volcanoes providing essential minerals and springs providing fresh water everywhere, why would colonization occur in just one region on the planet? Perhaps, some day, we will find scientists willing to follow research on *many* sources.

APPENDIX III - AYURVEDA

Many indigenous cultures keep their beliefs private, regarding them as sacred. This health system is open to other cultures and it is up to the individual as to how much they choose to incorporate into their personal lives. It can be complex requiring a physician's hand, or a novice can learn the basics and adapt them into their lifestyle. The health system goes back approximately 5,000 years, or starting around 3000 BCE, perhaps with the resident Harappa or the estimated arrival date of the Dravidians in India.

Initially all of India practiced Ayurveda, but gradually the Kerala State in Southern India became the only State officially endorsing Ayurveda. Over time, health experts discovered the benefits of integrating this distinctive essential branch of medicine with Western technology. Ayurveda focuses upon achieving wellness of the complete body by balancing the three energies of the body's according to *each* individual body. The human body requires Movement (Vata), Processing (Pitta) and Storage (Kapha) energy for healthy systems. However, *each* body has a unique combination of the three.

People in modern India successfully combine these two healing schools. It is difficult for busy Western citizens to integrate them to the same extent, but once we understand the basic concepts we are better able to blend the general principles. It may be as uncomplicated as understanding why we get a sore throat or acid reflux.

Once we know this, we adjust our diet and lifestyle to accommodate personal idiosyncrasies. Therefore, taking the time to learn the basic principles of Ayurveda and identifying our personal constitution, we apply this ancient wisdom to our modern living. Having the capacity to correct minimal imbalances becomes elementary and reduces the need for medication and doctor visitations. It seems though that most people do not want to make the effort. Ancient Wisdom gives us a gift that blends extremely well with our modern world, wherever you live, we have the option to follow or not. The following is an introductory overview into the system, giving you enough information to decide whether you want to explore this system deeper.

The Science of Life

The simplest way to look at these two sciences is consider Ayurveda as preventative with minor corrective techniques and Western medicine as a major curative process. Ayurvedic practitioners apply natural herbal remedies according to a person's constitution. There are five ways to bring a body into balance – meditation, diet, herbs, chemical drugs and surgery. Meditation, diet and herbs are mainly preventive procedures while the use of herbs, drugs and surgery are corrective. Herbs are both non-invasive and multipurpose. Drugs and surgery are usually contrary to the human body and might cause side effects. While numerous systems follow a preventive and corrective division, Ayurveda acknowledges broad principles. It:

1. Places *equal emphasis* on our body, mind and spirit, restoring the inherent harmony of the individual.
2. Incorporates the *elements* earth, air, water, fire and ether.
3. Follows a *cyclical* system both 24 hour and seasonal.
4. Recognizes *integrated balance* must be part of our internal and external lives.

For good health, a balanced body becomes vital. The three main energies within our body provide the required stability. The English translations for these energies are MOVEMENT, PROCESSING, and STORAGE.

The first energy, MOVEMENT force is responsible for all movement within the entity. It protects the lower part of the torso, pelvic area, large intestine, bones and thighs. Pain and illness usually first occurs here. The balanced MOVEMENT force is slow, thin and irregular. Out of balance, it speeds up, becoming more erratic. We can compare it to a serpent or snake slithering away. When the imbalance is large, the *snake* moves faster, our pulse becomes rapid. Symbolically, the snake represents rebirth, initiation and wisdom.

The second energy, PROCESSING force looks after digestion and the fire in the body. It protects the middle part of the torso, small intestine, stomach, sweat glands and blood. A balanced PROCESSING force is strong and lively. Out of balance, it seems like a jumping *frog*. The frog represents transformation. We must transform, or PROCESS, before something becomes useful. This means food and thoughts must be adapted or absorbed before they become functional to the being.

The last energy, the STORAGE force decides what we need and what needs to be stored for the future. This can be an idea or a vitamin. Its home is the upper part of the torso heart, lungs, chest, ear sinuses, nose and mouth. The

STORAGE force should feel strong and wide, giving a sense of "floating along" like a *swan*. Out of balance, it is still strong but now flows lethargically, almost blocked. The swan reminds us to awaken all our energies that flow internally.

A body needs all three in balance. It requires continual renewal and wisdom (snake), evolution through life (frog) and the reminder of who we are as an individual (swan). These animal images came from the ancient texts and still apply in the 21st century. Interestingly, many indigenous groups recognized corresponding personality traits long before they became Ayurvedic identifying tags. Once we recognize the animal characteristics in humans, it helps identify the imbalances of bodily energy and *then* we adjust our dietary and lifestyle habits to re-balance us. There are four keys to this health maintenance.

First, each **AGE** has a specific energy dominant strength. This is usually when we observe the ailments according to excessive energy. *Storage* energy is abundant in youth years. A baby or young child is soft, plump, *storing* information and nutrients for future needs. The illnesses of childhood are usually congestive, colds, mucus, and flu, all problems of the upper chest region. During the teens and adulthood, everything is busy being *processed* by the individual. This is a time for ulcers and skin disorders such as acne. Ailments that can be associated with fire are likely to occur during these ages. Here, there is too much *processing* energy. The last age phase is the abundance of the *movement* force. Since this force is light, fast and airy, it begins to slow down as we move out of young adulthood. I call it "the tired phase". Most ailments involve nervous disorders or blockages. The memory information is not *moving*. The joints have excess air causing arthritis. The skin is dry, hence more wrinkles than laugh-lines.

Second, each **SEASON** carries a force, or energy. Each season displays certain characteristics pertinent to a prevailing force. Once more, if that is the body's dominant force, the body becomes more sensitive during those months. It seems seasonal traits affect the human body more than other adjustments. The body suffers for four months of extra stress. The *movement* force is light, cool and dry; reminding us of a cool wind blowing, or moving, in the fall months. The *processing* force is hot, light and dry. This reminds us of summer when the growth *process* occurs. The *storage* force is cold, heavy and damp. This reminds us of the winter months when we depend upon *stored* goods.

Third, the earth's energy ebbs and flows throughout the **DAY**. Thus regardless of our personal strengths, there are times of the day when each person's traits peak even more. Our secret to great health is ensuring our diet is such that we ensure our vitality stays uniform throughout the day. Understanding the logic behind the daily cycles encourages you to plan your day around peaks and valleys of the cycle. For example, you want a fitness regime when you have more energy that is physical and a mental activity schedule when your mental processing energy is at its peak. This maximizes your body's efficiency. The daily cycle rotates in four hour periods. *Storage* energy is high between 6am to 10am and 6pm to 10pm. *Processing* energy is high between 10am to 2pm and 10pm to 2am, a time for enjoying a relaxed evening. *Movement* energy is high between 2pm to 6pm and 2am to 6am. These times are optimum for exerting physical stamina, digesting a large meal or allowing your body great dream action.

Fourth, each body has an **INNATE COMBINATION** of these energies where one will be more dominant than the other two. The body HAS to have all three but not necessarily in uniform proportions. One body may have high movement and processing with very little storage. Another may have high processing and storage with a moderate amount of movement.

Our ancient ancestors identified the importance of these to our bodily well-being. Now, in the 21st Century, we have a choice of following the *Science of Life* in detail, or incorporating the basics into daily life. Ancient Wisdoms give us a healthy mode that effectively blends into modern everyday routine. Once you discover how your energies react in your body, the next step is noting what tips your balance off, what brings you back into balance.

We connect each force to nature's elements, recognized in so many cultures. The elements help identify foods and health conditions. Notice there are opposites in each force.

MOVEMENT ENERGY FORCE - VATA, is Air and Ether. Air, like the wind, blows things as it moves and ether is a spacey passageway. It is responsible for the movement of food through our digestive system and the movement of thoughts and nerve impulses. It affects our joints and nervous system. Its prime characteristics are *changeability, unpredictability* and *variability*. **MOVEMENT** dominant people make active use of energy, spending it freely and wasting energy. This energy or force activates the physical system and allows the body to breathe and circulate blood.

PROCESSING ENERGY FORCE - PITTA, is Fire and Water. Fire consumes or processes and water puts it out. This force becomes responsible for the balance and processing. It is responsible for the digestion of our food and the *"cooking"* of our thoughts. The **PROCESSING** force is the *manager* of energy usage. Its prime characteristics are *organized* and *predictable*. It ensures effective usage of all energy. It controls metabolism and digestion. It first affects the enzymatic and endocrine systems.

STORAGE ENERGY FORCE - KAPHA, is Water and Earth. Earth is solid, stationary and full of nutrients. Water breaks it down when too much earth gathers in one place. It provides the stability of the body, surplus or shortage. The **STORAGE** force is governed by *potential* energy, combining water and earth. . Its prime characteristic is *relaxed*. It forms the body's structure and keeps it 'glued' together. These people tend to store energy, gluing it where the body needs it. It becomes the structure of bones, muscle and fat holding the body together, offering nourishment and protection (immunity). STORAGE puts all nutrients into a useable format, whether it is cellular, poundage or discharge. The STORAGE function also controls the function of mucous membranes.

Examples of each energy trait are:

A dominant **movement** person is thin, with prominent features, cool and dry skin, hyperactive, moody, vivacious, eats and sleeps at all hours, imaginative, nervous disorders, enthusiastic, infectious. impulsive energy and intuitive

A dominant **processing** person is medium build, fair, thin hair, warm, ruddy and perspiring skin, orderly, efficient, short temper, quick intelligence, ulcers, heartburn, passionate, acne, perfectionist.

A dominant **storage** person is heavyset, thick, wavy hair, slow, graceful, relaxed, slow to anger, sleeps long and, heavy, affectionate, obese, forgiving & tolerant, compassionate, high cholesterol, procrastinates, obstinate.

Initially, when there is an accumulation or excess of one force, you correct through diet and meditation. When it worsens then a visit to an Ayurvedic physician or Naturopath is required. Accumulation is not always evident to the average person. However if you know your unique blend of energy forces, you recognize imbalances quite easily. For example, stress tips our internal balance easily. Then, all you have to do is adjust your lifestyle to remove the stress-causing activity.

Five thousand years ago, human communities had the herbs and tastes that healed the previously known ailments. Today, we turn to drugs, but when we experience minor discomfort of these diseases, eating proper diet and food helps. Our in depth Ayurveda books expand the descriptions of aches, pains and food remedies. As a basic step, there are three specific flavors for each energy type. **Movement dominant** people want foods that are sweet, sour and salty. **Process dominant** people require foods that are sweet, astringent and bitter tasting. **Storage dominant** people require foods that are pungent, astringent and bitter tasting.

While we never called it Ayurveda, our Grandparents followed many remedies conforming to this ancient art. They went to Nature to find remedies for routine aches and pains. This is one example of an Ancient Wisdom that interacts with modern nature remedies.

INDEX

ENDNOTES

1   Andrews, Ted, Animal-Speak, the Spiritual & Magical Powers of Creatures Great & Small, Llewellyn Publication, St. Paul, Mi, 1995 . p133

2   Ibid P172

3   Clow, Barbara Hand, *The Pleiadian Agenda*, Bear & Company Publishing, Santa Fe, N.M., 1995

4   Ibid. Page 27.

5   http://www.lemuria.net.html. Updated 1999, accessed Dec., 2004

6   McDowell, Josh and Don Stewart, *Handbook of Today's Religions*, Nashville: Thomas Nelson Publishers, 1983

7   http://www.merceronline.com/Native/native05.htm

8   Stockbauer, Bette, http://www.bci.org/prophecy-fulfilled/ancient. htm,

9   Beversluis, Joel, *Sourcebook of the World's Religions: An Interfaith Guide to Religion and Spirituality (Sourcebook of the World's Religions)* New World Library, CA, 2000

10 www.moorlandschool.co.uk/**earth/earthorigin**.htm

11 Ibid.

12 www.Encarta.com

13 Hancock, Graham, *Underworld, the Mysterious Origins of Civilization*, Anchor Canada, 2002

14 Donnelly, Ignatius, *Atlantis: the antediluvian world*, Harper, 1882

15   Patterson, Alex, *Field Guide to Rock Art Symbols of the Greater Southwest*, Johnson Printing, Boulder, CO, 1992, P 197

16   Red Ice Creations Short Film Production, 2007 02 12 http://www.redicecreations.com/article.php?id=65

17   Von Däniken, Erich, *The Gods and their Grand Design*, G.P. Putnam's Sons, New York, 1982. P142.

18   Enslow, Sam. *Art of Prehispanic Colombia*, McFarland & Company, Inc. Jefferson, N.Y. 1990

19   Leonard, R. Cedric. The Glozel Tablets", 2001 http://www.atlantisquest.com/glozel.html. , accessed November, 2004

20   http://www.tulane.edu/~august/maps/writing1.html. Accessed October, 2004

21   Brown Peter Lancaster, *Megaliths, Myths and Men*, page 20

22   http://www.chesterfieldinlet.net/nunavut.html

23   http://anthropology.uwaterloo.ca/ArcticArchStuff/dorset.html

24   Indigenous people living on the Aleutian Islands and the shore of Mainland Alaska

25   http://www.civilization.ca/aborig/haida

26   www.haidanation.ca

27   http://www.cowichantribes.com

28   Marshall, Daniel P, *Those who Fell from the Sky*, Morriss Printing Company, Duncan, BC, P 1

29   Chaisson, Paul, *The Island of Seven Cities*, Vintage Canada, 2007

30   Ibid, p167

31   Brown, Vinson, *Peoples of the Sea Wind*, Macmillan Publishing, New York, 1977

32   Ibid., p. 162

33   http://www.merceronline.com/Native/native05.htm

34   http://www.ausbcomp.com/redman/hopi.htm

35   http://www.mohawktribe.com/

36   Snow, Alice & Susan Stans, *Healing Plants,* University Press of Florida, Gainsville, Fl, 2001

37   Ibid, P24

38   Ibid. P 93-94

39   Ibid, p62

40   http://www.icarito.cl/medio/articulo.html

41   http://www.sitchin.com/astronaut.htm,, website created November 2000, accessed January 2005. copied with permission (per article)

42   For complete article, go to www.spiritual-endeavors.org

43   https://ssl4.westserver.net/spiritual/native/cosmic-rtn.htmt

44   Kaanek, Gerardo Barrios, *Mayan Time, Prophecy and the Tolk'in.* http://www.renmag.co.za/index2.php?option=com_content&do_pdf=1&id=92 , access March 2008

45   Calleman, Carl Johan PhD, *Mayan Calendar and the Transformation of Consciousness,* Bear & Company, 2004, P xvi

46   Bonewitz, Ronald Dr., *Maya Prophecy,* Judy Piatkus (Publisher) Ltd., London, 1999. Page 89-91

47   http://www.calion.com/archeo/agust/agustine.htm

48   http://tampu.unicauca.edu.co/merlin/

49   http://www.sscnet.ucla.edu/ioa/backdirt/spring98/bear.html

50   Reichel-Dolmatoff, Gerardo. *San Agustin, A culture of Colombia.* Praeger Publishers, N.Y. 1972, p.101

51   http://www.biopolitics.gr/HTML/BIO/prizes/kogi/fpage.htm

52   Webster's New Collegiate Dictionary, Merriam, USA 1979

53   Ereira, Alan, *The Elder Brothers,* Vintage Books, 1993

54 Eriera, P 55

55 Ereira, P 196-197

56 **Ruzo, Daniel**, Markawasi: *The Story of a Fantastic Discovery.* written in Spanish 1974

57 **Definition of healing** used here is: a state of complete physical, mental, and social well-being and not merely the absence of disease or infirmity

58 For more details, go to: www.k12.hi.us/~waianaeh/waianhi/**olelo**.html

59 For more details: http://www.geocities.com/TheTropics/Shores/6794/olelono1.html

60 http://www.eco-action.org/dt/eisland.html

61 **http://arts.anu.edu.au/arcworld/nasc/abstract2.html**

62 http://www.ngaitahu.iwi.nz/

63 http://www.ngaitahu.iwi.nz/About-Ngai-Tahu/

64 I*wi* means "people" or "folk"; translating into tribe.

65 Brailsford, Barry, *Song of the Waitaha*, Wharariki Publishing Trust, New Zealand, 2003, 2nd ed. p11

66 Ibid.

67 Ibid., p15

68 Ibid, p28

69 Ibid, p39

70 Ibid, p63 ff

71 Ibid, p38

72 Ibid, p 54

73 Ibid, p42

74 Ibid, p11

[75] Ibid, P28.

[76] Ibid, p82

[77] Ibid, p39.

[78] Ibid P63

[79] Ibid, p 38

[80] Ibid, p 54

[81] Ibid, p42

[82] Ibid, p106

[83] Ibid, p95

[84] Ibid, p165

[85] Cremin, Aedeen (Editor), *The World Encyclopedia of Archaeology*, Firefly Books, 2007, P367

[86] Hancock, Graham, *Underworld, The mysterious Origins of Civilization*, Anchor Canada, 2002, p56

[87] Ibid, P57

[88] http://www.metmuseum.org/TOAH/

[89] J. Allen, In Search of the Lapita Homeland: Reconstructing the Prehistory of the Bismarck Archipelago, Journal of Pacific History, 1984

[90] World Encyclopedia of ARCHAEOLOGY, p371

[91] http://www.livescience.com/history/071029-old-cemetery.html *Ancient Headless Skeletons Found in Island Grave* , By Jeanna Bryner, **Live Science**

[92] http://www.janeresture.com/arorae/index.htm

[93] Däniken, p52

[94] Hancock, P52

[95] Ibid, p53

96   Hemley, Robin, *Invented Eden*, Farrar, Straus and Giroux, New York,, 2003, p18

97   Ibid., P26

98   Ibid., p38

99   Hancock, Graham, *Fingerprints of the Gods*, Doubleday Canada Limited, Toronto, Ontario. 1995, P 502.

100 Turk, Jon, *In the Wake of the Jomon* – Stone Age Mariners and a Voyage across the Pacific, McGraw-Hill, United States of America, 2005

101 Hancock, Graham. *Underworld, The Mysterious Origins of Civilization.* Anchor Canada. Toronto Ontario. 2002

102 Hancock, Graham. *Underworld, Underworld, the Mysterious origins of Civilization,* Anchor, Canada, P553

103 Hancock, Graham, Ibid. P52

104 http://www.wsu.edu/~dee/ANCJAPAN/ANJAPAN1.HTM, Richard Hooker, WSU. Permission granted by Richard K. Hines, Ph.D. Department of History WSU.

105 Hancock., p556

106 Ibid. p576

107 http://www.mnh.si.edu/arctic/ainu/index.html

108 http://en.wikipedia.org/wiki/Ainu

109 http://www.mnh.si.edu/arctic/html/peopling_siberia.html

110 http://www.siida.fi/english/en_menu.html

111 http://www.pbs.org/wgbh/nova/vikings/runes.html

112 G.T.Wrench, *The Source of Long Life & Health among the Hunza,* Dover Publication, New York, 2006

113 Godefroy, Christian H., *Health Secrets of The Hunzas,* http://www.positive-club.com

114 Wrench, G.T., M.D. *The Wheel of Health* London C.W. Daniel Company, 1938

115   http://nobelprize.org/nobel_prizes/medicine/laureates/1912/carrel-bio.html

116   I refer you to my first book Inner Bridges, New Age World Publishing, 2003.

117   Redfern, Gayle, *Ayurveda Demystified*, New Age World Publishing, 2003

118   Rahuyla, Walpola, *What the Buddha Taught* Grove Weidenfeld, New York, 1959

119   Ibid, p 33

120   Ibid, p21

121   NOTE: Dharmasala or McLeod Ganj is a small village in the Himalayas where the Dalai Lama and the disposed government settled

122   Landes, Johannes. *The Future Code: Find the Mystery of Your Fate*, Deciphered in the Palm Leaf Libraries of India, Norderstedt Germany, 2005.

123   Men, Hunbatz, *Secrets of Mayan Science/Religion,* Bear & Company, New Mexico, 1990, Page 58

124   Men, Hunbatz, *K'U is Sacred in Maya / K'U is Sacred in Tibet*, Mexico, 1991.

125   http://www.2013.net/multidim/mayas/nagas.htm

126   Possehl, G and Rojdi, *Harappan Civilization*, Bril Academic Pub. 1989

127   www.**harappa**.com/arrow/stone_celt_indus_signs.html

128   Baur, Susan Wise, *The History of the Ancient World*, W.W. Norton, New York, 2007, P 105 ff.

129   Keay, John, *India, a History*, Atlantic Monthly Press, New York 2000, p9

130   Ibid, p 10

131   Ibid, p13

132   Refer to my previous book, Ayurveda Demystified, 2003

133   Redfern, Gayle, M.A., *Ayurveda Demystified For Optimum Western Living*, New Age World Publishing, 2003

134   Daniken, Erich von, *Pathway to the Gods: The Stones of Kiribati*, G.P. Putnam's & Son's, 1982

135   Devereux, Paul, *Secrets of Ancient and Sacred Places*, Brockhampton Press, 2001

136   http://www.worldatlas.com

137   http://encarta.msn.com/encyclopedia

138   http://www.calvin.edu/petra/about/nabataeans.php

139   http://www.brown.edu/

140   See section below on the Zimbabwe Bird

141   http://en.wikipedia.org/wiki/Tower_of_Babel

142   Wells, Spencer, *Journey of Man, a Genetic Odyssey*, Princeton Univ., 2002

143   Merger of the two tribes, Khoi AND San

144   Sitchin, Zecharia, *The 12th Planet*, Bear & Company, Santa Fe, New Mexico, 1976

145   http://www.history.com

146   Parfitt, Tudor, *Journey of a Vanished City*, St. Martin's Press, New York, 1992, discussed in *The Times* (UK), 1999

147   Wuriga, Rabson (1999) *The Story of a Lemba Philosopher and His People* Kulanu 6(2)

148   Ibid

149   Wells, Spencer, *Journey of Man, A Genetic Odyssey*, Princeton Univ.

150   http://www.nationalgeographic.com/adventure/0508/excerpt1.html

151   http://blairgenealogy.com/dna/dna101.html

[152]   **Sykes Bryan**, *The Seven Daughters Of Eve,* Transworld Publishers Ltd (United Kingdom), 2004

[153]   Mayell, Hillary, *National Geographic*, Jan. 21 – 2003

[154]   http://www.worldfamilies.net/migration_map_wfn.gif

LaVergne, TN USA
09 March 2010
175314LV00001B/44/P